# FARE GAME

**Other Bella Books by Cade Haddock Strong**

*The Schuyler House*

## About the Author

Cade Haddock Strong loves being outdoors, especially when it involves skiing, hiking, biking, running or golf. An economist by training, she makes a valiant effort to stay up on current events. She and her wife have lived all over the US and abroad and they love to travel.

Bella Books, Inc.
P.O. Box 10543
Tallahassee, FL 32302





Printed in the United States of America on acid-free paper.

First Bella Books Edition 2019

Editor: Ann Roberts
Cover Designer: Judith Fellows

ISBN: 978-1-64247-110-6

# FARE GAME

CADE HADDOCK STRONG

2019

## Acknowledgements

During this journey of becoming a published author, my friends and family have blown me away with their support and encouragement. I cannot thank you all enough. The impromptu book discussions over cocktails and long walks have been awesome.

A special call out to Celeste, Andrew and JM for being brilliant beta readers and guiding me through the intricacies of the airline business and the law.

A big thank you to Ann Roberts. Not only for your editorial expertise, but also for being firm and pushing me. Thanks for your patience. You've taught me so much and for that I am eternally grateful. I know I still have loads to learn, but because of you, I feel as though I'm on firmer ground.

Last but not least, thank you to my wife, Lisa, for being my biggest cheerleader. Life with you is an incredible adventure.

# CHAPTER ONE

Kay Corbett, newly-minted vice president at Logan Airlines, was about to do something that might get her fired, or worse, thrown in jail. She poked her head out into the hallway. It was a glorious Saturday afternoon and Logan's corporate headquarters was a complete ghost town.

After a moment of hesitation, she tiptoed toward the much larger glass-enclosed office three doors down, thankful she had on running shoes rather than her usual weekday attire of high heels. Agility was vital.

She stood outside the door, listening. All she could hear was the persistent hum of the central air-conditioning system. The urge to bolt back to her office coursed through her, but she refused to chicken out. It wasn't her style.

The cold metal doorknob turned easily in her hand. She slipped into the office and closed the door behind her. There was no going back now. The sun was still high on the horizon and a beam of light split the spacious office in two.

Her tank top stuck to the perspiration pooling on her back. She tugged at her shirt and sat down at the sleek glass-topped desk. She'd watched her boss, Greg Brandywine, key in his password dozens of times. The idiot just cycled through his kid's names. Lyle9999. Liam9999. Lacey9999. Lane9999. He had some fascination with the number nine. Something to do with baseball. He was a freak about the game and had played right field in college.

It took her less than a minute to find what she was looking for. She pulled a thumb drive out of her pocket, slid it into the back of Greg's computer and drummed her fingers on his desk while the files saved to her device.

Her body stiffened at the sound of voices in the hallway. It sounded like two men. She looked down at the computer. The download crept toward completion. *Ninety-six percent, ninety-seven...* The second it hit one hundred, she yanked her thumb drive from the machine and logged off, praying she'd captured what she needed.

Her eyes darted around the sparsely decorated office. There was no place to hide. A small wooden conference table surrounded by six chairs sat on the far side of the room. She lurched under it and attempted to curl her nearly six-foot frame into a ball. The voices grew closer and she was certain one of them belonged to Greg. The door to the office clicked open. Kay held her breath and willed her legs not to cramp. She watched a pair of expensive leather loafers dash across the carpet. Her heart was beating so loudly, she was sure it would give her away. A set of keys jangled, and a drawer opened and closed. The shoes retreated and then the door clicked shut again.

Kay heard Greg say, "I got it."

"Good. We better get to the airport," his companion responded. Kay didn't recognize the second man's voice, and she couldn't see his face from her perch beneath the table.

She listened as the voices grew faint again and counted to twenty before she dared to unfurl herself. *Fuck, that was close. Way too close*. Her knees cracked as she stood, and she headed for the door. She reached for the knob but paused. *What had Greg taken with him?*

She crept back to the desk and hastily tugged at each of the drawers. They were all locked save for the narrow one in the center which had nothing in it except a stack of Logan embossed stationery and a few empty Tic Tac containers. She felt for the thumb drive in her front pocket and trotted back to her own office. A loud thud stopped her in her tracks. She scanned the sea of cubicles packed into the vast room. A shadow drifted over the far wall. Someone was there. She was sure of it. "Hello," she called. Silence. She slipped into her office and closed the door.

The following Tuesday morning, Greg Brandywine summoned Kay and the rest of his direct reports to his office for Logan's third quarter earnings call. They sat around his conference table, the same one Kay had sought refuge beneath a few days earlier. She eyed Greg while they waited for the webcast to begin. His crisp, blue dress shirt brought out the grey specks in his steely eyes. The gel induced sheen of his wavy dark hair practically glistened in the morning sun shining through the office window and a hint of gray sprouted near his temples. His supply of Just For Men must be running low.

Eventually, the operator came on the line to kick off the earnings call, and after the usual formalities and introductions, Howard Rome, Logan's CEO, spoke. Kay cringed as he highlighted the airline's financial results for the latest quarter. He touted "solid revenue growth across all aspects of the business" and "higher fares offsetting rising labor and fuel costs." He stressed Logan's increasingly diverse revenue base, with a growing share of money coming from non-ticket sources like checked bag fees and the airline's co-branded credit card. Logan's shareholders would eat it up like starved piranhas. The company's stock price was up more than twenty percent for the year and would likely shoot up even further in response to the rosy financial picture Howard Rome painted during this morning's call.

When the earnings call was finally over, Greg leaned back in his chair, tucked his hands behind his head and looked around at the group gathered in his office. "Pretty good results, wouldn't you say gang?"

Kay wanted nothing more than to wipe the smirk off his face, but she forced a smile. "Very impressive, Greg. Very impressive, indeed."

A few of the others at the table uttered similar responses and Kay wondered how many of them knew what was really going on. Knew Logan's finances were a massive house of cards, built on lies and artificially inflated revenue. It was true, Logan *was* charging higher fares, but they were cheating the system and totally screwing their passengers in the process. There was one thing for certain… It would all come crashing down, at least if Kay had anything to do with it. She just needed a little bit more time.

# CHAPTER TWO

"I'm twenty-nine, practically an old maid by southern standards," Riley Bauer lamented to her best friend Stephanie. It was a picture-perfect October day in Atlanta, and they were sitting at an outdoor café a few blocks from work.

"Oh, my God. Your biological clock has barely started ticking," Stephanie protested, dabbing some salad dressing off her chin with her napkin.

"I don't know Steph," Riley replied. "I figured I would have found someone by now. It's not that I mind being single. I just, you know… I really want to have kids. Family is central to people in the South and my mother is beside herself that she doesn't have any grandchildren."

"You shouldn't let your mother get to you so much."

"Have you met my mother?"

Stephanie shrugged. "Yeah, she seemed nice. And isn't your brother's wife due any day now?"

Riley groaned in frustration. "The truth is Steph, it's not just my mother. I'm beginning to think my dream of having a big family is slipping away."

"Newsflash. You don't have to be married to have kids, you know?"

"It's not that simple," Riley replied, trying to keep the irritation out of her voice. She'd tried to explain what growing up in the South was like at least a thousand times, but Stephanie still didn't get it. She'd grown up in Connecticut, and even though she now lived in Atlanta, she rolled her eyes at the mention of cotillions, collard greens and college football. "I haven't even been able to work up the courage to tell my mother I'm gay," Riley continued. "I'm certainly not about to announce I want to have a child out of wedlock." She slumped back against her chair. "Shit, she'd totally flip."

"Well, try not to fret so much about it. It'll only cause wrinkles," Stephanie said, pausing to sip her sweet tea. "Why did you break up with Brianna? It seemed like things were getting serious between you two."

Riley sighed at the mention of her ex-girlfriend. "They were. I don't know. I just sort of freaked out when she started talking about moving in together."

"Did you love her?"

Riley fiddled with the edge of her napkin. "Yeah, I did, but not in a head over heels kinda way."

"Real life isn't like a romance novel, you know?"

"Maybe not, but I'm not giving up on finding true love yet. I want to find someone who makes my heart melt when I spot her across the room. Someone who makes me laugh and comforts me when I'm sad. Someone who is honest and genuinely cares about other people. Is that too much to ask?"

"No, I guess not. It just seemed like..."

"Like what?"

"Like you had a lot of that with Brianna. It was obvious she really cared for you."

"She did, but she was way more invested in the relationship than I was, and it wouldn't have been right for me to string her along. She's a really good person. I want her to find someone who loves her as much as she loves them. She just didn't light my fire, if you know what I mean."

"Yeah, I do." Stephanie squeezed Riley's hand. "You're gorgeous, smart and funny. You'll find that special someone soon."

"Thanks, Steph." Riley unconsciously tucked her long, blond hair behind her ears. She'd always been modest, but she wasn't stupid. She knew her looks—crystal blue eyes, radiant smile and shapely athletic build—were part of the reason she'd never had a problem getting a date.

"Well, we should probably get back to the Mother Ship," Stephanie said, referring to the corporate headquarters for Logan Airlines.

"Yeah." Riley stood from the table and pushed in her chair. "I've got a big partnership meeting this afternoon and I have some stuff I need to review beforehand."

"Oh, yeah. I forgot you were working on that joint venture deal." Stephanie said as they walked back to the office. "It's with a Japanese airline, right?"

"Uh-huh. Kamadori Airlines. Actually, we're going to Tokyo next week to finalize the details."

"Wow, I'm so jealous. I never get to work on cool projects like that," Stephanie replied. "How many of you are going to Japan?"

"Seven or eight including me. Two of us from Finance, a bunch from Pricing and Network, plus at least one person from Legal. It's a pretty big group, but these agreements have a zillion moving parts."

"The whole joint venture thing is a complete black box to me. I get why we have them. They make it seamless for passengers to fly on two different airlines. They can get from Detroit to some obscure city in China without having to sew together a mess of different tickets."

"Yeah, but the deal with Kamadori will be good for the airlines too," Riley replied. "It will enable both Logan and Kamadori to make better use of their aircraft capacity and allow the airlines to harmonize fares."

Stephanie shook her head as they approached the front gate. "You're speaking Greek to me. I think I'll stick to marketing."

Just before two, Riley walked into the large conference room and slipped into a seat next to Jill, a junior member of her finance team. Jill was only two years out of college, but she was a genius with numbers and had been an incredible asset to Riley's team. So much so that Riley promoted her to manager after only a year at Logan.

"Hey, Jill," Riley said as she took a seat. "Ready for the big trip?" Riley was taking Jill to Japan. It was only fair given all the work she'd done crunching the numbers for the impending joint venture with Kamadori.

"Yeah, I'm really excited."

The conference room suddenly went quiet. Riley looked up and saw Kay Corbett, Vice President of International Pricing, saunter in. To say Kay commanded a room would be a serious understatement. Her exquisitely tailored navy power suit perfectly fit her lean frame. Toss in her high cheekbones and long, silky dark hair, and it was no surprise most men at Logan turned to mush in her presence. Riley couldn't blame them. Kay often had the same effect on her. There was something about the woman, something utterly captivating. The way she carried herself, the way her dark eyes sparkled when she smiled, the slight rasp in her voice and the fact that she was whip smart.

Riley didn't know a lot about Kay, although she'd pegged her to be somewhere in her mid-thirties, young to be a Logan VP. Based on what she's heard, Kay had been with Logan since she'd graduated from college and had worked in the pricing department the whole time.

I bet she's married, Riley thought to herself as the meeting got underway. No way a woman like her is single. Riley tried to imagine who would be worthy of Kay. A tall, dark-haired man, a successful entrepreneur…or maybe a woman? Riley didn't get a strong gaydar reading from Kay, but a girl could dream.

Riley snuck a glance at Kay while the guy from Legal droned on about some detail in the joint venture contract. Her blouse was open slightly at the neck and Riley ached to run her fingers over the smooth, tanned skin around her collarbone. When their eyes met, Kay gave her a soft smile. Riley quickly diverted her gaze.

When the meeting finally wrapped, Riley gathered up her belongings and filed out of the conference room with the rest of the attendees, but she paused when a hand gently touched her shoulder. Kay smiled at her. "Do you have a minute?"

"Um, yeah, sure," Riley stuttered.

"You did a nice job presenting some of the financial projections for the Kamadori deal, but I have a few follow-up questions." Kay gestured toward the hallway. "Why don't we go back to my office?"

Riley practically had to jog to keep up with Kay's long stride, which was somewhat of a challenge in her three-inch heels. They settled around the small conference table in Kay's office. Prior to the Kamadori deal, the two women had never worked together, and Riley decided to take her cues from Kay.

Kay played with her thin silver necklace. "I'd like to hear a little more about the assumptions you used in your revenue calculations."

Riley popped open her laptop and walked Kay through a slew of spreadsheets. They sat inches apart, their arms occasionally touching. It was near impossible for Riley to concentrate while she explained the key factors in her financial model. She knew the figures inside and out but kept losing her train of thought. Kay no doubt thought she was an idiot.

When Riley was done, Kay sat back in her chair and crossed her legs. "Thank you, Riley, that was very helpful. You've done a lot of hard work and it shows. Is this the first time you've worked on one of these deals with another airline?"

Riley cleared her throat. "I've worked on a few loyalty-type partnerships, but, yes, this is the first joint venture I've been involved with."

"Well, you're obviously a quick learner," Kay said with a wink. "These deals are quite complex, and you seem to have an exceptional grasp of the various components."

The wink threw Riley a little off-kilter. Was Kay Corbett flirting with her? No way. Riley had been working long hours over the last few months. She was sleep-deprived and it was obviously making her delusional. Kay Corbett was *way* out of her league, not just because Riley was three rungs lower on the corporate totem pole, but because Kay was...Kay. Beautiful, sexy and brilliant. "Thank you, Kay. You're very kind," Riley said as she stood to leave.

Kay walked Riley to the door of her office and gently squeezed her arm. "I'm really glad you'll be joining the team on the trip to Tokyo."

Riley looked at her feet, partly because she wasn't very good at accepting compliments and partly because the intensity of Kay's gaze made her heart flutter.

# CHAPTER THREE

Kay ran a hand over the smooth surface of the large wooden desk situated in the middle of her extra bedroom. The desk was solid walnut and it weighed a ton. It had taken four guys to heft it up the narrow staircase to the second floor of her house. It had belonged to her grandfather, Papi, and she thought of him as she sat down and tugged the chain for her desk lamp. He'd emigrated to the US from Spain as a penniless teenager, and through hard work and chutzpah, he'd built a successful tailoring business. His clients included some of New York's wealthiest women. He'd been tall for a Spaniard and strikingly handsome, which probably hadn't hurt business. Lucky for Kay, she'd inherited some of his Mediterranean good looks and she had him to thank for her flawless olive skin and big brown eyes.

Papi had been honest almost to a fault, and he'd always stood up for what he believed. He had treated everyone, from the garbage collector to the mayor, with respect, and he'd instilled his values in Kay. If he were still alive, Kay was certain he'd support what she was trying to do. *Wouldn't he?*

After logging in to her computer, she pulled a small stack of leather-bound notebooks out of one of the desk drawers. She'd stayed up way past midnight the last three evenings going through the files she'd downloaded from Greg's computer. The information was damning; there was no doubt about that, but there were no entries for the last six months. Zilch. The data just stopped in mid-May.

Even though Greg was as cocky as ever, Kay wondered if something had spooked him. She thought back to the previous spring. The earnings call for the first quarter had been exceptionally testy. The airline analysts really grilled Howard Rome about the string of healthy financial results Logan had posted quarter after quarter, even as the economy had begun to wobble and many of the smaller airlines were in the red. One of the analysts—some guy from Goldman Sachs—had questioned the "unprecedented harmony" with which Logan and some of the other big airlines had been raising fares. Implying, the frequency with which they moved in lock step was difficult to chalk up to pure coincidence. The act was too well choreographed to be improv.

Maybe Greg had begun to worry about leaving too much evidence around—evidence that Logan and a handful of other airlines were conspiring to drive up airfares. Maybe he'd decided to erase some of the evidence from his work computer, or perhaps he'd just stopped tracking the fare increases altogether in order to sever the paper trail of what he'd been doing, although Kay doubted that. Greg was way too meticulous. He kept records of everything, even stuff that could someday incriminate him.

Assuming the data for the last six months *did* exist, Kay had to get her hands on it, and the sooner the better. She slumped back in her leather desk chair and closed her eyes. "If I were Greg, where would I keep it?"

It was possible he had it saved on his home computer, but if that were the case, how the hell was she going to get her hands on it? She remembered the locked drawers in his desk. There was only one choice. She had to sneak back into his office, except this time she'd be better prepared. Surely, she could pry open the drawers with a screwdriver or an old nail file. In the meantime, she'd keep plowing through the data she had.

She scanned the files on her computer and clicked open the one she'd been reading the previous evening before her eyes had grown heavy and she'd finally dragged herself to bed. If nothing else, Greg was well organized. His files were labeled by month and year, starting with January 2012, the year he'd been promoted to Senior Vice President at Logan. Kay had worked at Logan back then, but she hadn't been senior enough to be included in executive-level meetings.

Everything had changed once she was promoted to VP late last year. It was like someone had handed her a key and invited her to join a secret society. She became exposed to the deep innerworkings of the airline, and some of what she'd seen and heard was shocking. At times, she pined for the blissful ignorance she had before the promotion.

Her first real exposure to the dark side of Logan Airlines occurred when she and Greg attended a conference in Brussels. Greg invited her to what she thought was a conference-related "meet and greet" but ended up being drinks at some seedy cocktail lounge with a small group of people. Greg referred to the group as Concordia, and Kay's mouth dropped open when he'd made introductions. The people gathered at the cocktail lounge that night were their counterparts—top level pricing executives from a handful of Logan's competitors. The gathering, even if it was just for casual drinks, had been perilous. If they'd all been spotted together, it would have raised more than a few eyebrows.

That evening at the cocktail lounge, Kay had listened intently as Greg spoke with the other members of the group. The conversation had mostly revolved around mundane things like sports and somewhat oddly, the latest men's and women's fashions, but it didn't take Kay long to realize the whole meeting was a finely choreographed dance. The hints and code words were subtle—comments like "that football club from China won by five points," a comment which on its face made no sense, but was actually a clear signal to the group gathered that night. Each carrier would raise fares to the Chinese markets they served. In other words, barefaced price fixing had taken place right before her eyes.

Kay's suspicions were confirmed the following week. Every carrier in attendance that night increased airfares to their Chinese markets by exactly five percent. The whole thing had fraud written all over it. They hiked prices knowing their competitors would do the same. It was a win-win for the airlines. More money in their pockets without the risk of passengers turning to a lower-priced competitor. All of the big powerful airlines belonged to Concordia, leaving passengers few other reliable alternatives.

Ever since the meeting in Brussels, Kay had done her best to play along, or at least pretend to play along, while she tried to figure out how to sound the alarm about what was going on. She had no choice. She loved working at Logan, but she wasn't going to stand by and let this blatant corruption continue, and she certainly didn't want to play a role in it. There was no way she'd be able to live with herself if she did.

Stealing the data from Greg's computer had been a vital first step, and although Kay had only begun to sort through it, one thing was already glaringly apparent. Greg was an arrogant fool and had kept detailed records of his wrongdoing. "Fucking moron," she mumbled as she stared at the numbers on her computer screen.

Greg knocked on Kay's office door late the next morning. He did not look happy. "Got a minute, Kay?"

"Of course, Greg. What's up?" She chewed on the pen she was holding. Maybe he was onto her? Maybe he knew she'd been in his office and had downloaded files off his computer. What if he'd reviewed footage from Logan's security cameras? She wouldn't put it past him.

He stepped inside, closed her door and leaned against it. He lowered his voice and said, "There's a Concordia call this afternoon at three. You know the drill."

Kay stopped chewing on the pen and nodded. These conference calls with their counterparts from other airlines were a relatively new thing. In the past, Concordia had only met in person like that fateful meeting in the cocktail lounge, but recently Greg had become increasingly frenzied about the need to push fares higher more often. At his insistence, the group had started holding calls on a regular basis. A few members of the group had pushed back at first, arguing it was all too risky, but Greg had brushed them off and assured them it would all be fine.

If Greg was growing more paranoid, he certainly wasn't showing it. He often made the Concordia calls on his Logan-issued cell phone, which Kay found absurdly brazen.

She gnawed on her lip before responding. "I'll meet you at the usual spot."

He glared at her. "You aren't getting cold feet, are you, Kay? You know I abhor weakness."

"No, Greg. I'll be there." She gave him the sweetest smile she could muster. "You know you can always count on me."

He opened the door. "I certainly hope so," he growled and marched out of her office.

As ordered, Kay slipped out of her office at ten of three and trudged across the vast parking lot that surrounded Logan's headquarters. A familiar nausea swept through her. Although she was doing all she could to gather evidence against Concordia, no one else knew that. At this point, she was an active and willing participant in the whole price fixing scheme. After each call, she directed her team to implement the price increases Concordia had agreed upon. If someone were to expose the fraud before she did, everyone would assume she was just as guilty as Greg, and essentially she was. This thought weighed heavily on her as she scanned the parking lot.

It wasn't hard to spot Greg's car. He drove a bright yellow Porsche. He lowered the window as she neared and spat, "Get in. We're going to be late."

She slipped into the supple leather passenger seat and set her purse on her lap. Greg peeled out of the employee lot before she'd even had a chance to buckle her seatbelt. "Today, I'm going to push for a fare increase in all of our European markets, especially during the peak summer travel season," he said as they made their way to the parking garage at the airport, which, for reasons Kay didn't understand, Greg thought was a good place to conduct the Concordia conference calls.

He whipped his car around the long spiral ramp until they reached the roof of the garage. A few cars were clustered near the entrance to the elevator, but otherwise, all the spots on this level were empty. He parked and punched a number into his cell phone. After a few rings, a loud voice echoed through the speakers of his car. "Hello."

"Who's on the line," Greg bellowed, causing Kay to practically jump out of her seat. Her purse fell to the floor and she snapped it up, praying she hadn't inadvertently turned off her phone's voice recorder. It would be such a waste. To sit through this meeting and not have evidence of it having taken place. A knot formed in her stomach and she barely uttered a word during the entire thirty-minute call.

As soon as she was safely back in her office, Kay dug her phone out of her purse and hit "play" on its recorder. When she heard Greg spell out his pricing proposal for the European markets, she collapsed in her chair. She'd captured the whole thing.

# CHAPTER FOUR

The softball slipped out of Riley's palm when she threw her first pitch. It sailed wide of the strike zone. "Ball one!" the umpire yelled.

Normally, she was cool as a cucumber on the mound, but not today. Kay Corbett was playing on the opposing team—one of the many Logan Airlines sponsored—and Riley was determined to impress her with her softball prowess. She wasn't off to a good start. She wiped her hand across the pants of her white polyester uniform and kicked the dirt with her cleat. The batter swung at her next pitch, a low ball to the outer right side of the plate and nailed a line drive straight at the pitcher's mound. The ball made a smacking sound when it landed in Riley's mitt.

"Nice play, Riley," her coach yelled from the sideline. "Major league."

Riley glanced at the visitor's dugout and was pleased to see Kay's eyes on her. She struck out the next two batters and was greeted with high fives as she trotted off the field with her teammates.

In the last inning of the game, Riley cheered when her teammate Mandy hit a triple. The game was tied at 3-3 and there were two outs. Riley was up next. She got into position at home plate and gazed toward the pitcher. The first pitch was fast and high, just how Riley liked them. She swung the bat and sent the ball deep into left field. As she rounded first base, she watched Mandy slide across home plate to score the winning run, taking out the opposing team's catcher—a petite woman—in the process.

The catcher yanked off her helmet and clutched her right leg. Riley never made it to second base. Instead, she sped toward home plate and knelt next to the catcher. It was obvious her leg was broken, and blood oozed from a nasty gash on her forehead. "Someone call an ambulance!" Riley yelled.

Riley yanked her jersey over her head and the catcher flinched when she pressed it against her head wound. As the woman writhed in pain, Riley cradled her head and whispered, "It's going to be okay. Try and stay still."

By now a crowd had gathered. "Did someone call an ambulance?" Riley asked no one in particular.

"I did," a voice replied. "They're on their way."

Riley looked up. Kay was standing next to her, a cell phone in one hand and a towel in the other. Their eyes locked, and for a split second, all the chaos in the background disappeared. It felt like they were all alone on the field.

The catcher moaned and Riley gazed down at the injured player. Kay knelt next to her and took over tending to the catcher's forehead. She removed Riley's jersey and replaced it with the towel she was holding. Together they worked to keep the woman calm and the bleeding on her forehead had almost stopped by the time the paramedics arrived.

A few of the catcher's teammates followed the ambulance to the hospital and the rest of the players from both teams wandered to the small pub across the street. The mood at the post-game happy hour was more subdued than usual.

Riley was standing near the bar with Stephanie and Mandy when she felt a hand on her arm. When she turned, she once again found herself staring into Kay's beautiful brown eyes. "Oh, um, hi, Kay."

Kay smiled. "Hi. I just wanted to come over and say that you handled the situation with Carrie, our catcher, extremely well. You just took charge and you were so calm. Thank you."

Riley felt her face go red and her ears get warm. "Thanks, Kay. You played the role of nurse pretty well yourself."

"Guess we make a pretty good team," Kay said with a laugh.

This comment made Riley blush even more. She doubted Kay had meant a team in the romantic sense, but that's what ran through Riley's head, just like it had at the Kamadori meeting earlier that week.

Kay took a sip of her beer and licked her lips, her beautiful full lips. Riley briefly fantasized about feeling those lips pressed against hers. She stared into her pint and tried to push the thought out of her mind, hoping Kay didn't notice the effect she was having on her. "I just hope Carrie is okay," she mumbled.

"Me too. Not only is she one of our best players, she's also the nicest person you'll ever meet."

Riley looked back up at those beautiful lips. "Y'all played really well."

Kay gave her a wry smile. "But we lost."

"I know," Riley said, "but we're ranked number one in the corporate league. A lot of times we win by double digits, especially when we play one of the other Logan-sponsored teams."

"Really?" Kay asked.

"Uh-huh. Last week, we played the team from Legal. It was pitiful. We put in all of our third stringers and we still beat them by fifteen runs. At least your team gave us a real run for our money."

"You're quite a pitcher. Did you play in college?"

"Um, thanks. Yeah, I did." Riley glanced back into her beer. "You're a pretty good player yourself. That one ball you dove for out in left field, that was amazing. I can't believe you caught it."

Kay seemed pleased by this comment. "I may have been showing off a bit."

"Oh?"

"Hoping you would notice."

Riley wasn't sure she'd heard Kay right. *Did she really just say that?* She got her answer when their eyes met again. Kay's eyes were full of warmth and something else…lust. The tiniest ray of hope bubbled up inside Riley. Maybe Kay Corbett liked ladies, and maybe, just maybe, she liked Riley.

# CHAPTER FIVE

As soon as the gang from Logan Airlines landed at Tokyo's Narita airport, they were whisked to their hotel downtown, just a few blocks from Kamadori's headquarters. When it was her turn, Riley approached the hotel check-in counter. She was exhausted from the long flight but mustered a smile. "Hi. Checking in. The name is Riley Bauer."

In typical Japanese fashion, the check-in process was exceptionally efficient. The clerk handed over an electronic key card. "All set, Ms. Bauer." He gave Riley a broad smile. "I've upgraded you to one of our Club Deluxe rooms with a balcony. You should have an excellent view of the city."

"Wow, great." Riley peeked down at the man's name tag. "Thank you, Aki."

The elevator zipped her up to the twentieth floor and when she waved her key card in front of the door marked 2025, it clicked open to reveal a breathtaking view of the Tokyo skyline. "Holy macaroni." She beelined for the balcony, shedding her bags as she crossed the massive room.

It was a crystal-clear afternoon and Riley shielded her eyes from the sun as she scanned the skyline. The gardens of the Imperial Palace sprawled beneath her, and in the distance, the Tokyo Tower sprouted from the sea of glass skyscrapers. It was difficult to tear herself away, but she only had forty-five minutes to unpack and grab a shower before she had to meet her coworkers back downstairs for a cocktail reception.

She was scheduled to be in Tokyo for four nights, and although she'd made a valiant effort to pack light, she'd failed miserably. She chuckled as she unzipped her bulging suitcase. "You can take a girl out of the South, but you can't take the South out of the girl," she said as she neatly organized everything in the small closet.

A representative from Kamadori appeared in the hotel lobby promptly at six p.m. and ushered the team from Logan to a small library-type room on the second floor of the hotel where there was a large table piled high with hors d'oeuvres and a makeshift bar in the corner. After proper introductions, a line quickly formed in front of the bartender. Riley opted for a glass of white wine although, given her jet lag, sparkling water probably would have been a better choice.

She spotted Kiko, her counterpart at Kamadori, and wandered over to say hello. While Kiko rattled on about the various revenue calculations associated with the Logan/Kamadori joint venture, Riley noticed Kay standing alone in the corner with her phone pressed up against her ear. It was obvious she wasn't enamored by the person on the other end. There was a lot of eye rolling.

"...agree with all of the assumptions?"

Riley returned her attention to Kiko. "I'm sorry, what were you saying." Riley tapped her watch. "Jet lag. The time change is killing me."

While Kiko continued talking, Riley struggled to stay engaged, and as much as she liked her, she was relieved when Kiko's boss called her away.

Riley jumped at the opportunity to get something to eat, hoping it would give her a much needed second wind. She piled her plate high with spicy edamame, shrimp tempura and pork potstickers and sidled up to one of the tall white tablecloth-clad tables sprinkled around the room. While she was wrestling a piece of shrimp off a skewer, Kay sauntered up next to her. "Hey Riley. Looks like that shrimp is playing hard to get," she said with a smirk.

Riley tried not to laugh as she swallowed. "Dainty has never been my strong suit."

"I love that you're so self-deprecating."

Riley blushed. Kay looked at her intently and she felt her legs go weak. She gripped onto the table to steady herself. She flashed back to what Kay had said at the softball game, about how she'd been showing off in hopes Riley would notice. She and Kay had spent countless hours in meetings together, but since the softball game, the dynamic between them had shifted. Kay's body language was different—more relaxed, more inviting. Riley wiped her mouth with a napkin and gave Kay a shy smile. "I saw you on the phone earlier. Is everything okay?"

Kay tensed. "Yes. Everything's fine. A small crisis at the office."

Riley looked at her watch. "It's five a.m. in Atlanta. You must have some seriously dedicated people on your team."

Kay let out a nervous laugh. "Ah, yes. Very dedicated."

Riley decided to shift gears. "Everyone seemed to get along pretty well tonight, don't you think?"

Kay took a sip of her wine before answering. "Yeah, I've been through a few of these joint venture deals, and knock on wood, this one's gone extraordinarily well, at least so far. Obviously, it's a win-win for both airlines. The only thing we really went to battle on was how to bucket fares."

"Bucket fares?" Riley asked.

"Oh, sorry, pricing jargon. Sometimes I forget you're from the finance side. We put fares in virtual buckets, which we can open and close as needed. That way we can control how many fares we sell at each level. Flights would sell out way too fast if we made every seat available at a discount. We've got to protect or set aside some seats on every flight to make sure we have some left over for the high-paying business travelers who book at the last minute. The trick is not to have too many left over and go out with empty seats. It's a delicate balance."

Riley's financial brain began to churn. "How do you determine how many cheap seats to sell?"

"It's complicated," Kay said, "but basically it comes down to simple economics, good old supply and demand."

"You mean kind of like how at Thanksgiving it's always impossible to find a cheap ticket because everyone and their mother wants to fly then?"

"That's the gist of it. Lots of algorithms are involved, need I say more?"

Riley started to respond but Kay held up her hand. "Enough shop talk. Did you manage to get any sleep on the flight?"

"Some, but I'm beat, and I'm definitely looking forward to getting a good night's sleep."

"Yeah, same here," Kay said and grabbed an edamame off Riley's plate. "Oh, shit, this stuff is spicy."

Riley laughed. "I know. It made my eyes water."

"How's your room?" Kay asked. "I hope it's okay."

"Oh gosh, it's more than okay. It's amazing. I must have drawn the lucky straw. They upgraded me to a deluxe suite. My room has this massive balcony with an incredible view of the city."

"Wow, lucky you. To have a view like that. I find city skylines so captivating, especially at nighttime."

A pang of guilt shot through Riley. After all, Kay was a superior. She probably should've gotten the upgrade. *Note to self. Resist urge to broadcast your upgrade*. She was about to mumble some sort of apology, but Jill walked up before she got the chance.

"I'm exhausted, think I'm going to call it a night."

"I should probably head up too," Riley said.

Kay gently touched her arm. "It was really nice talking to you. Sleep tight."

When Riley got up to her room, she slapped her hand on her forehead. She was such an idiot. She'd totally missed the hint. Kay had wanted to see her view.

* * *

The next two days were jam-packed. Meetings all day, cocktails and marathon dinners each night. Mercifully, Thursday's agenda was a little lighter. Riley's morning was free until she, along with the rest of the Logan team, was scheduled to tour Kamadori's airport facilities in the afternoon. She decided to use her limited free time to sneak in some much-needed exercise. She power walked the 5K loop around the Imperial Palace, and even though the temperature was still fairly cool, she worked up a pretty good sweat. As she neared the hotel, she slowed her pace.

"Hey, Riley!" a voice called.

Riley glanced over her shoulder. Kay was a few paces behind her and had apparently just finished a run. Her cheeks were flushed, and her muscles glistened with sweat. She looked *Sports Illustrated*-amazing in her cropped tank top and skimpy running shorts; however, Riley was struck by how thin she was, almost too thin. It wasn't as noticeable when she wore one of her power suits, but now, scantily clad, it was clear Kay needed to log some serious time at an all-you-can-eat buffet.

Kay smiled broadly. "What are you doing up so early on our morning off?"

"Just trying to stay fit."

While she took a long pull on her water bottle, Kay gave her a not-so-subtle up and down. "I'd say you're doing pretty well in that department."

"Um, thanks."

"Wanna grab a bite to eat? I stumbled upon this cute café just around the corner from the hotel."

Riley was a little surprised at the invitation. "Yeah, sure."

Breakfast in hand, Riley and Kay settled at a table outside in the sun.

"So, do you think the meetings with Kamadori went well?" Riley started.

"Um, yeah. I'd say I'm generally pleased with the way things went."

"Well, that's good to hear."

Kay shifted gears. "So, is this your first time to Japan?"

"No, second," Riley said, hesitating as she decided how much to reveal about herself. "I came to Tokyo last year with my now ex-girlfriend."

Kay's eyebrows arched ever so slightly. "Ex-girlfriend, huh?"

Riley nodded.

"I hope it wasn't a bad breakup?"

"Nah. I kind of freaked when things started to get serious. It's a long story. She's a good person, but, well, you know…"

Kay gave her a knowing smile. "She just wasn't *the one*?"

"That, and she was lukewarm about having kids. Having a family is pretty much paramount to me."

"I'm with you on that. I adore kids."

"Oh, do you have children?"

"Nope, but I hope to someday."

Unconsciously, Riley looked down at Kay's bare ring finger. "You're not married," she blurted and immediately covered her mouth with her hand to prevent any additional crass comments from escaping.

If Kay was offended, she didn't show it. "No, I'm not. I'm divorced."

"I'm sorry." Riley had a million questions but figured it was safer to keep her mouth shut. She was a bit surprised they were having such a personal and frank conversation. It made her feel somewhat uneasy. She was doing her damnedest to view Kay strictly as a coworker, not someone she lusted after, but the tall, thick stone wall she'd tried to build between them was threatening to crumble down.

"No need to be sorry. It's okay. We got married right out of college. I was young and stupid. Unfortunately, I didn't realize, or more likely hadn't accepted, that I was gay until after we were married."

A smile crept across Riley's face. "Oh."

The two women ate in silence until Kay eventually asked, "So, how long have you been with Logan?"

Riley was still reeling from the fact that Kay was into women. "A little over four years," she stammered. "I worked for an aviation consulting firm when I first got out of college and Logan was one of our biggest clients. Long story short, Gabe

Suarez, the VP of Finance, pulled me aside one day and asked if I'd consider coming in-house. I jumped at the chance."

"Well, Gabe must have been seriously impressed with your work if he just came out and offered you a job at Logan."

Riley glanced down at her hands. "Yeah, I guess so."

"Gabe's a really good guy," Kay said.

Riley nodded enthusiastically. "Yeah, he's great. He's really taken me under his wing. I feel extremely fortunate to work for him."

The expression on Kay's face changed slightly. "You're lucky to work for someone you respect."

Riley detected a sadness in Kay's eyes that hadn't been there moments earlier. Without meaning to, it appeared her comments about Gabe had touched a nerve. Kay reported to Greg Brandywine, and as far as Riley knew, he was the cat's meow at Logan. Was Kay implying otherwise? Riley may have been reading too much into it, but she didn't think so. Kay seemed less relaxed; her posture was more rigid than it had been just moments before. Riley sipped her coffee before asking, "How about you? How'd you end up at Logan?"

The sparkle in Kay's eyes quickly returned. "My dad was a pilot for Logan. Retired last year." Kay chuckled. "Aviation runs in my blood. It was basically a forgone conclusion I'd come to work for the airline after college."

"That's so cool that your dad's a pilot."

"Yeah, he taught me to fly when I was a kid."

"Wow, that's awesome," Riley said. "Whenever I fly in the cockpit jumpseat, I close my eyes during the landing. Guess I wouldn't make a very good pilot, huh?"

Kay laughed. "Yeah, not so much. They typically recommend you keep your eyes open during the landing."

"I have no issues when I'm seated back in the cabin, but it just freaks me out to actually watch the plane hit the runway."

"Well, we usually try not to *hit* the runway," Kay said with a wry smile. "The goal is to gently touch down."

Riley scraped the bottom of her yogurt container with her spoon. "Maybe I could go up with you one day. You can show me how it's done."

"I think we can arrange that."

After the tour at the airport, the group from Logan disbanded. Most folks had flights back to the US that evening and a few were headed to London for another business meeting. Riley wasn't flying out until the next day, so she grabbed dinner at a ramen place before heading back to the hotel. As soon as she stepped on the elevator, her phone vibrated. Her flight back to Atlanta the next day had just been cancelled.

She had Logan reservations on speed dial and was already working her way through the airline's brain-numbing automated phone system by the time she got back to her room. When a human finally came on the line, Riley explained her situation and waited patiently as the agent pulled up her reservations and looked for alternative flights back to the US.

A *tap, tap tap* echoed over the phone line as the agent's fingers skittered over her keyboard.

"I'm afraid things are pretty booked up," the agent finally said in a heavy southern drawl. "It looks like I can get you on a flight out tomorrow afternoon but hold on…" More typing. "Unfortunately, you'll have to connect in New York. If you want to take the nonstop, you'll have to wait and fly out the following day."

Riley didn't have any big plans for the weekend, and it would be nice to have a day to play tourist in Tokyo. "I'll wait and take the nonstop."

When she hung up with the airline, she called down to the front desk to make sure she could keep her palatial room for one more night. She wondered how long Kay would be in Tokyo. Maybe she'd get to show her the beautiful view from her room after all.

# CHAPTER SIX

Riley woke up early the next morning, grateful she had the whole day in Tokyo to herself. After another power walk around the Imperial Palace, she showered and made her way to the Ginza Shopping District. Her ex, Brianna, hated to shop which meant Riley hadn't even stepped foot in the famous shopping district the last time she was in Tokyo. She wandered into a few stores but mostly gazed in the extravagantly decorated shop windows. The district's main street was closed off to cars and people streamed down its wide boulevard. In Riley's opinion, the people watching was far more interesting than anything the shops had to offer. She admired all the fashionable outfits, some of which were downright weird, and giggled when she spotted a woman towing her cat down the street on a skateboard.

A little after dark, she made her way back to the hotel. Her heart jumped when she saw Kay stepping off the elevator into the lobby. She was dressed in black jeans and a white T-shirt. Her long, dark hair hung loosely over her broad but boney shoulders. Kay didn't often wear her hair down, and Riley loved the way it framed her face and set off her rich brown eyes. If possible, it made her look even more beautiful.

"Riley, what are you doing here?" Kay asked as she approached. "I thought you were flying back to Atlanta today."

"I was supposed to, but my flight got cancelled. I'm not flying back until tomorrow. What about you, why are you still here?"

"I decided to spend an extra day in Tokyo—that was my original plan—before I head off to London to join the rest of the pricing gang for another meeting." Kay ran a hand through her hair and cocked her head to the side. "Do you have plans for dinner? I was just heading out to find a place to eat."

Riley smiled at the invitation. "Um, sure, that would be great." She glanced down at her jeans and sneakers. "Do you mind if I run up to my room super quick to freshen up? I've been out all day."

Kay shook her head. "Not at all." She waved her hand toward the far corner of the lobby. "I'll wait for you in the hotel bar."

Riley zipped up to her room, stripped out of her clothes, touched up her makeup and ran a comb through her long blond hair. She pulled on her favorite mini skirt and reached for the small shopping bag on the bed. She'd made one purchase in Ginza—a blue V-neck shirt with small flowers stitched on it. It was a splurge for her but now she was happy she'd bought it. It was perfect for her impromptu dinner date with Kay. Okay, maybe date wasn't the right word, but Kay had seemed almost shy when she'd asked if Riley had dinner plans.

When she wandered into the hotel bar, she spotted Kay sitting at the far end, a martini glass perched in front of her. "Is this stool taken?" Riley asked in jest.

Kay had just plucked an olive off her cocktail pick, but she winked at Riley and gestured for her to sit. The bartender appeared out of nowhere. "May I get you something to drink?"

"Yes, please." Riley nodded toward Kay. "I'll have what she's having."

"One dirty martini coming up," the bartender replied.

Riley scanned the room. The place had a pretty good vibe for a hotel bar. There was a decent crowd, but it wasn't too packed and upbeat jazz piped through the speakers overhead.

The bartender set a martini glass in front of Riley, added three plump olives and theatrically strained the contents of his shaker into it until the cloudy liquid reached right to the rim. Once he was gone, she slowly lifted it and looked toward Kay. "Cheers."

"Here's to an unexpected night together in Tokyo," Kay said as they gently clinked glasses.

"Ah, that tastes good," Riley said after she'd taken a few small sips. "It's been a while since I had a good martini."

"I've been watching him," Kay said, waving toward the bartender. "He's quite a mixologist and his martinis are shaken, not stirred." She tossed back the last few drops of her drink and set the empty glass on the bar. "So, what did you do with yourself today?"

"I just wandered around the Ginza shopping district, and actually," Riley tugged at her shirt, "I got this there."

"Wow, that's beautiful," Kay replied. "I love the delicate flowers that are sewn into it, and the color really brings out the blue in your eyes."

"Thanks," Riley said, blushing slightly. "What about you? What did you do today?"

"I went for a run, of course…"

"Of course." Riley was learning that Kay was a bit fanatic about her running regime.

"After that, I did a little work and then went to the National Garden. I tried to read but I think I did more people watching than anything."

"The people watching in Ginza was out of this world." Riley said as she twirled the olives around in her drink. "What are you reading, or maybe I should say, what were you trying to read?"

"Promise not to judge me?"

"Promise."

"A steamy romance novel. Kindles are a wonderous thing. No one can tell what you're reading."

"No reason to be ashamed of that," Riley replied. "Nothing beats a good romance novel. Gosh, life can be so hectic and intense. Sometimes it's nice to escape."

Kay gave her a soft smile. "I knew there was a reason I liked you."

The bartender wandered back over. "Care for another round?"

"Yes, please," they replied in unison.

"Do you want to just stay here and have dinner?" Kay asked once the bartender headed off to make their drinks.

"Works for me. Let's ask the bartender for menus when he comes back."

They ordered an array of appetizers and a bottle of red wine and settled into the bar for the night. At first, conversation centered around work, but eventually it turned more personal.

Kay spoke about growing up outside New York City. "My dad was based out of JFK," she explained. "Being a pilot meant he was gone a lot, but it also meant he was home for long stretches at a time. During those periods, he was a super engaged father. His schedule kept him from coaching any of my sports teams, but when he was around, he came to every single one of my games."

"What about your mom?"

"My mom's a pediatrician. She still works, although she's cut back on her hours significantly. My dad has flight benefits with Logan for life, so my parents travel a ton. Paris is their favorite place to visit. On top of that, they're trying to run a marathon in every state before their bodies give out."

"That's impressive. Now I know where you got the I-must-exercise-until-I-collapse gene."

"Ha ha. Believe it or not, I'm the laziest person in my family."

"No way."

"It's true. All my brothers play soccer, tennis, golf, you name it, and my parents have been avid runners for as long as I remember."

"So, is that how you got into running?" Riley asked. "Because of your parents?"

"No, not really. As a kid, I was always active, but I hated running just for the sake of running. I'd happily run around the soccer field for hours but good luck getting me to do a 5K with my parents. No, running is something I took up on my own after college. I think I felt a little lost without sports after I finished school. I played sports all through college. Running not only helps keep me in shape, it's also a really great way to clear my mind."

"I've heard you're into marathons."

Kay nodded. "Yeah, I've done a few, mostly at the urging of my parents, but I'm not breaking any world records."

"I think you're being modest."

Kay shrugged her shoulders. "What about you? Where did you grow up?"

"Georgia born and raised. My parents live in Buckhead. They're crazy conservative. I haven't even told them I'm gay."

"Oh, wow, really?"

"Yeah, I know. It sucks. I'm too darn chicken." Riley could tell Kay was a bit taken back by this news, but she didn't want to get into the myriad of reasons why she was still closeted to her parents, at least not right now. Instead, she moved on. "Anyway, my dad's a lawyer and my mom stayed at home with us kids, although now that we're all grown up, she does a ton a volunteer work and plays a lot of tennis and golf."

"Siblings?" Kay asked.

"Yeah, I've got two older brothers. What about you? You mentioned brothers…"

"Uh-huh," Kay said, "Five of them, all older. My mom said she wasn't giving up until she got a girl."

"That's awesome. Things must have been insane at your house. Ours was pretty out of hand with only three of us. Tell me some stories about growing up," Riley begged.

Kay obliged and made Riley laugh so hard she almost spat out her wine.

After dabbing the red liquid off her upper lip, Riley said, "That certainly wasn't ladylike. My mother would be horrified."

Kay waved her off. "It's my fault for making you laugh."

"More wine ladies?" the bartender asked.

"I'd love another glass, but we should probably call it a night," Kay said.

Riley nodded. "Just the bill, please."

After they settled up, they made their way across the lobby to the elevators. Kay raised an eyebrow when Riley stabbed the button for the top floor. "Oh, yeah, I forgot you got the big upgrade."

Riley's mind flashed to Kay's earlier comment about being captivated by skylines at night. "You want to come up and see?"

"Sure, I'd love to."

Kay's eyes grew wide when she stepped in Riley's room. "Holy cow, I can't believe how massive this room is."

"You ain't seen nothing yet. Follow me." Riley made her way across the room but stopped midway. "Wow, what's this?" she asked, pointing to a large metal ice bucket sitting in the middle of her coffee table, the telltale neck of a champagne bottle sticking out. A small white card next to the bucket indicated it was compliments of the hotel's general manager. "No idea what I did to deserve this. Want a glass?"

"Sure. I'd hate for it to go to waste."

"Will you do the honors? Opening champagne terrifies me. I'm afraid I'll take someone's eye out with the cork."

Kay unwrapped the foil around the top of the bottle and carefully wiggled the cork off with a towel, muffling the pop. She handed Riley a flute of the hissing liquid.

"Cheers again," Riley said. "Thank you for a wonderful evening, Kay."

"The pleasure was all mine. Now, where's that view you promised?"

She slid back the glass door to her balcony and motioned for Kay to step outside.

"Shit, you weren't kidding. This view is absolutely stunning."

They stood side by side, sipping their champagne in silence. It was a clear evening and sparkling lights stretched as far as the eye could see.

"I think I could stand here all night," Kay said quietly, not taking her eyes off the skyline.

Riley set her glass on the table and rested her elbows on the railing. "Yeah, me too."

Kay linked an arm through one of Riley's. "Be careful. It's a long way down." They were standing inches apart and when their eyes met, Riley's throat went dry. Her gaze drifted toward Kay's lips and she leaned forward but hesitated, pausing to seek out Kay's eyes again. They told her what she needed to know. They both wanted the same thing. She cupped Kay's cheek with her hand and closed the gap between them, eliciting a whimper from Kay when their lips met. The kiss was soft and lingering.

Riley pulled back slightly and whispered, "I've been dying to kiss you all night."

The breeze had blown some of Riley's hair out from behind her ear and Kay tucked it back in place. "Me too," she replied.

Suddenly, Riley felt shy. She looked down at her feet. "You have?"

"Uh-huh."

Kay tugged them together and Riley sought out her warm lips again. This time the kiss was deeper, more passionate, and somewhere, in the back of her mind, Riley was aware she was kissing Kay Corbett, the drop-dead gorgeous VP who she'd lusted after for months. Kissing Kay was far better than she could have imagined. Minutes passed before they finally broke apart, and when they did, Riley's limbs felt numb. She'd never in her life been kissed like that. The fire between them was undeniable. Kay literally took her breath away, something Riley thought only happened in movies.

"You all right?" Kay whispered.

Riley nodded but remained completely still. Kay reached for her hand and led her inside. They kissed for a long time before Kay stepped back and slid Riley's new blue shirt over her head. Riley didn't protest. She felt incredibly aroused. Kay slowly undressed her, stopping often to place soft kisses on her skin. Her body tingled as warm hands smoothed her bare breasts.

Kay paused to peel off her own shirt and release her bra, revealing her full breasts. Riley's fingers trembled as they traced Kay's collarbone and drifted over her chest. They fell together on the bed, their bodies touching for the first time. Riley succumbed to Kay's touch and let herself go completely.

The sky was still dark, with only a hint of orange peeking over the horizon, when Riley woke up the next morning. She eyed the tall, trim body sleeping soundly next to her and smiled. She pressed her breasts against Kay's bare back and placed a few soft kisses behind her ear.

Without opening her eyes, Kay turned in her arms and smiled. "Morning."

Riley brought their foreheads to touch. "Morning."

"What time is it?"

"Too early for a run," she replied and snuggled into the crook of Kay's arm. She closed her eyes and fell back to sleep. When she opened them again a few hours later, the bed beside her was empty. The sun was beaming in the hotel room window and she used her hand to shield her eyes. "Kay?" she called out. There was no response.

She swung her feet onto the floor, padded to the bathroom and flicked on the light. There, tucked neatly beneath her toothbrush, was a note scrawled on hotel stationery.

> *Riley,*
> *I have to catch my flight to London. You were sleeping so soundly, I didn't dare wake you. I had a wonderful evening. I'll see you back in Atlanta.*
> *Kay*

As she brushed her teeth, she felt a mix of excitement and anxiety. Everything about the night with Kay had been amazing. Still, she had no idea how they'd ended up in bed together. She'd wanted Kay, there was no doubt about that, but she was not exactly in the habit of one-night stands, especially where a coworker was involved, and not just any coworker—Kay-fucking-Corbett.

She spat out her toothpaste and stared at her reflection in the mirror. A million questions coursed through her head. Was last night a one-time thing? How did Kay feel about it? Was something more even possible between them? Would Kay brush it all off as nothing more than a quick roll in the hay?

# CHAPTER SEVEN

Kay settled into her business class seat for the long flight from Tokyo to London and felt a quiver in her stomach as she thought back to the night before. Riley was an incredible woman. Beautiful, funny, smart and sexy as hell, and although she couldn't put her finger on it, there was something about her, something really special. Kay couldn't believe they had ended up in bed together.

She'd been attracted to Riley since the first day they'd met, a day that was still vivid in her mind. They'd had the kick off meeting for the Kamadori project, and the moment Riley had walked into the conference room, she'd taken Kay's breath away.

Unfortunately, this wasn't a simple case of mutual attraction. Riley was a coworker, a coworker who happened to be junior to her. They didn't work in the same department, and Kay wasn't her supervisor, so there was nothing in Logan's HR guidelines that said they couldn't date each other, but still, it wasn't an ideal situation. On top of that, Kay's life, with everything that was going on with Concordia, was complicated enough. Was it really a good time to be starting something new? Was it fair to bring someone into her life when it was full of so much chaos? *Maybe I should have thought of that before I jumped into bed with her*. She pinched the bridge of her nose. *Why did things always have to be so damn complicated?*

"Anything to drink before we take off, Ms. Corbett?" a flight attendant asked, pulling Kay from her thoughts.

"Just some water please." She rested her head back against the seat and closed her eyes. Images of Riley filled her mind. It had been a very long time since someone affected her the way she did. Kay did not want to walk away. She wanted to go full steam ahead. She wanted something with Riley. *Why should the mess with Concordia prevent me from following my heart?* There were a million reasons why it wasn't a good idea, but love didn't always happen at a convenient time.

The plane backed away from the gate a few minutes later. Once they were airborne, she nibbled on her breakfast and dug her nose into work before her eyes grew heavy, likely from the lack of sleep the night before. She closed her eyes and thought of Riley as she drifted off to sleep.

With the time change, it was mid-afternoon on Saturday when Kay's flight touched down in London. She hopped the Heathrow Express train into the city, switching to the Tube when she got to central London and surfacing a few blocks from her hotel near Hyde Park. She checked her watch. There was just enough time for a quick run before she was due to meet her friend Jessica for dinner.

A few miles around the park did wonders to shake off her jet lag, and by seven thirty she'd showered and was on her way to the restaurant. She waved when she spotted her friend sitting in a small booth at the back of the old wood-paneled restaurant.

Jessica stood and pulled her into a hug. "Kay. It's so damn good to see you."

"It's been way too long," Kay replied as she slid into the worn red leather seat on the opposite side of the booth. "I haven't been coming to London as often as I used to."

"We need to fix that." Jessica pointed to her half-empty pint. "Want a beer?"

"Nah, just a water for—"

"Nonsense," Jessica said, motioning toward the waiter.

Kay relented and ordered a Guinness.

"Since when are you a teetotaler?"

Kay shrugged. "Just jet lagged."

"Bullshit."

"Okay, fine." A smile crept across Kay's face. "I didn't get a lot of sleep last night."

Jessica gave her a knowing look. "You sly dog. Who was she?"

"Promise not to judge me?"

"Promise."

"A coworker, a younger coworker."

"Oh."

"Yeah, 'oh' is right."

"A one-night stand with a coworker? And here I thought you were an upstanding citizen."

"Bite me," she countered. She took a sip of her Guinness while she decided just how much to tell Jessica. They'd known each other since college and Jessica had always been a voice of reason. "The thing is, I really like her."

"Like you want something more with her? That kind of like her?"

Kay nodded. "Yeah, but I'm conflicted."

Jessica's eyes grew wide. "Oh, my God. Are you her boss?"

"Shit, no. Come on Jess, I'm not *that* bad. We work in different departments and we just happened to be put on the same project. That's why we were both in Tokyo."

The waiter appeared and they ordered some cheese and bread to share. "And I assume you aren't seeing anyone else right now?" Jessica asked once he was gone.

"No, there hasn't really been anyone since Tabatha. That relationship left me a little jaded."

"I know, and that's understandable."

"I've had a few flings here and there, but nothing serious." She leaned back against the padded wall of the booth and let out a sigh. "Truth is, Jess, I've been so focused on work over the last few years, climbing the corporate ladder and all that, I just haven't had time for—"

"A personal life?"

Her shoulders sagged. "Yeah, one of those."

"What's her name?"

"Riley. Riley Bauer."

Jessica let out a deep laugh.

"What's so funny?"

Jessica rested her elbows on the table and looked Kay in the eye. "The way you said her name. Your eyes sparkled and you got all dreamy."

"Did not."

"Did so."

Kay felt her face get hot. "I think I could fall for her."

Jessica sat up straight again, the expression on her face softening. "Just be careful."

"I will." Kay drained her beer and set it back down on the table.

"How are things at work? I mean when you aren't screwing your coworkers."

"Ha ha, very funny. For the record, this is the first coworker I've ever slept with. But, to answer your question, things at work have been stressful, really stressful."

"Are we talking long hours and pressure to perform since your big promotion or something more than that?"

"Something more than that."

"What's wrong? I thought you loved Logan."

"I do, or at least I did. It's just, now that I'm a VP, I'm privy to a lot more and let's just say there's some seriously fucked-up shit going on. I fear it may extend to the C-suite."

"Oooh, like what? Sounds juicy."

"It's nothing I can talk about right now. Let's just say I've seen some stuff that makes me uncomfortable."

"Come on," Jessica pushed. "I've known you forever. You can tell me."

"I really wish I could, Jess, but I can't. I shouldn't have said anything. I'm sorry. It's just been on my mind." Kay shifted gears. "So how about you? How are things working out at Zephyr? Are you liking the new job? You've been there what, almost a year now?"

Jessica's demeanor changed. She clenched her jaw and her posture stiffened. "Things at Zephyr are going well, thanks for asking. I've been able to get up to speed more quickly than I expected, but marketing is marketing, ya know? Doesn't really matter what industry you're in."

"Yeah, I guess you're right."

"They hired me to try and expand the airline's branded credit card. You cannot believe how much the airlines make off those things."

"You mean those credit cards that give you a free checked bag or whatever?"

"Uh-huh."

"I can't believe you and I both ended up in the airline industry."

"I know, crazy, huh?" Jessica flagged down the waiter and started to order them both another round, but Kay held up her hand. "I'm good. I'll stick to water." Jessica looked annoyed and went ahead and ordered a pint for herself. Something about the way she was acting made Kay uneasy. "Are you sure the new job is going okay?" Kay asked. "You seem a little upset."

"I'm not upset," Jessica barked. She took a long sip of her new pint.

Kay decided it might be best to get away from the topic of work. "Are you seeing anyone?"

Jessica gave her a wicked smile. "Yeah, as a matter of fact I am."

"And?"

"He's older, and married."

"Oh, Jess. That's not good. You know it can only end badly."

"Why don't you let me worry about that?" Jessica glanced at her phone. "Hey, listen I gotta go. I'm sorry." She stood abruptly, threw back the rest of her pint, and tossed some money on the table. She squeezed Kay's shoulder. "Catch you around."

Kay watched her walk out of the restaurant. *What the hell just happened?* Had she said something to set Jessica off? Had it really bothered her that Kay wouldn't tell her more about the saga at Logan? It wasn't like Jessica to get upset over something like that.

# CHAPTER EIGHT

With the thirteen-hour time change between Tokyo and Atlanta, Riley landed at Hartsfield-Jackson International around five p.m. on Saturday, nearly the exact same time she'd left Tokyo. Air travel is a remarkable thing, she mused. Once she was through immigration, she went in search of her suitcase. Her penchant for over packing meant she always had to check her bag. When she reached the baggage carousel, it was still idle. Riley let out a low growl.

While she waited for her bag, she shot Stephanie a text. *Back from Tokyo. Can you do brunch at Murphy's tomorrow? Need to talk.*

Finally, a yellow warning light flashed, and the carousel groaned to life. A sole bag popped out from behind a flapping rubber curtain and began the slow journey around the belt. Minutes later, more bags spilled out. A response came in from Stephanie while Riley wheeled her bag toward the long-term parking lot. *Sure. Brunch works for me. BTW, grabbing drinks with Mandy and Wilma tonight. Care to join?*

As much as she wanted to see her friends, Riley was emotionally drained. She'd thought about Kay for approximately the entire twelve-hour flight home. She was exhausted. Right now, all she wanted to do was put on her pajamas, binge on Netflix and go to bed.

At nine the next morning, Riley wandered into Murphy's, a small restaurant/bakery in the Virginia Highland neighborhood of Atlanta, and found Stephanie standing near the hostess stand. There wasn't yet a wait for a table because they'd arrived before the rush of the after-church crowd.

"So, how was last night?" Riley asked once they were seated. "Sorry I wasn't up for meeting you guys."

"It was fun," Stephanie replied. "We went to that wine bar you like in Inman Park, and if you ask me, I swear there's something going on with Mandy and Wilma."

"Huh, I didn't know Wilma was into women."

"Yeah, me either, but hey, stranger things have happened."

"Ha, that's for sure." *Just wait until you hear about my trip to Tokyo.*

Riley fidgeted as they looked over the menu, unsure how Stephanie was going to react to the news about Kay. Heck, even Riley felt emotionally conflicted about it, which was why she was dying to tell Stephanie what had happened.

"So, what's up with you?" Stephanie asked as soon as they'd placed their order. "You look like shit."

"Ah, thanks a lot," Riley said with a smile. Even though she'd been exhausted, she'd tossed and turned all night, and her makeup did little to conceal the big dark circles under her eyes.

"Did something happen in Tokyo?"

"What do you mean?" she asked, but it was no use. Stephanie knew her too well. She took a sip of water. "Okay, yeah, something happened. I'm kind of freaking out."

A look of concern crossed Stephanie's face and she gestured for Riley to continue.

Riley shifted in her seat and asked, "Do you know who Kay Corbett is?"

"Of course." Stephanie gave Riley a look that said "duh". "She's the totally hot VP in pricing. I think everyone at Logan knows who she is. God, half the men in my department drool when she walks by."

"Okay, well she was on the Tokyo trip too…"

"Yeah, it makes sense she'd be there."

"Well, while we were in Tokyo, I…kind of slept with her."

Stephanie's jaw dropped and her eyes grew wide. "What do you mean, kind of slept with her? You either slept with her or you didn't."

"Keep your voice down," Riley said through clenched teeth, her eyes darting around the restaurant. "Okay, fine. We slept *slept* together, the last night I was in Tokyo."

Stephanie let out a soft whistle.

"I honestly don't know how it happened. Gosh, let's see. She and I were the only two left in Tokyo, everyone else had left, and we ended up having dinner together, sort of by chance, and well, one thing just kind of led to another…"

"Well, how was it?" Stephanie asked.

"How was what?"

"The sex, dumbass."

Riley played with the buttons on her linen blouse. "Oh," she said, and a smile crept across her face. "It was a-mazing."

"So, was this a one-time thing or do you think, you know, you two will see each other again?"

Riley shrugged. "I don't know. I'm definitely into her, but I have no idea how she feels."

"Did you spend the night together, I mean, after you—"

"Yeah, she spent the night in my room. I want to think it was more than just sex, but God, I don't know. She got up super early to catch a flight to London, and we haven't talked since then."

"Well, it should be interesting when you run into her at the office."

"Yeah, right, I know." Riley ran a hand through her hair. "She won't be back in the office until Wednesday. We've got a meeting together that day, a debrief of the Kamadori trip."

Stephanie cackled. "Yeah, I bet she'll want a *full* debrief from you."

* * *

When Wednesday morning rolled around, Riley was a complete and utter ball of nerves. On the way to work, her mind had been so in the clouds, she'd almost missed her exit. She absentmindedly straightened her already perfectly organized desk and logged in to her computer. As usual, her calendar was full of meetings, meetings and more meetings. Her gaze navigated to the meeting at two o'clock—the debrief for the Kamadori project—and her palms began to sweat. It had been radio silence from Kay since their night together. Riley had picked up her phone more than once over the last few days to text her, but she'd never gotten up the nerve to actually send her a message.

The more she thought about seeing Kay that afternoon, the more nervous she got. She closed her eyes and took a few calming breaths in an effort to ward off a panic attack. When she felt mildly calmer, she opened her eyes and weeded through her email inbox. She sighed. It was no use. All she could think about was Kay. She shot Stephanie a text. *Coffee?*

A response came back immediately. *Meet you downstairs in 5.*

Moments later, the sound of a phone ringing pierced the silence in Riley's office. She jolted upright and almost fell out of her chair. It was the phone on her desk, and it almost never rang. She checked the caller ID. It read Katherine Corbett. Riley scrambled for the handset. "Hello," she said softly.

"Hi Riley, it's Kay."

"Oh, hi." Riley said, her voice an octave above normal. "Are you back in the office?" Riley smacked her hand on her forehead. *Real smooth, Bauer. You just read her name on the caller ID.*

"Yeah, I got back from London last night, and anyway, I was wondering… Can you swing by my office around noon? I was hoping we could chat before the meeting at two."

"Um, yeah, sure. I can do that."

"Okay, great. I'll see you then."

She slowly hung up the phone and immediately began to dissect their twenty second conversation. Kay was all business.

She was probably just hoping to clear the air and put what happened in Tokyo behind them. "That's cool by me," Riley muttered as she walked out of her office and headed downstairs even though nothing could be further from the truth. She spotted Stephanie waiting in line at the Starbucks on the ground floor of Logan headquarters.

Stephanie gave her a quick one-armed hug. "Shit, girl. You okay? You look like you've just seen a ghost."

Riley's shoulders slumped. "I just talked to Kay."

"Oh, *right*." Stephanie gave her a knowing grin. "She's back in the office today."

"Uh-huh. She wants me to—"

"Morning ladies, the usual?" the barista asked.

Stephanie nodded and looked over at Riley. "Coffee's on me today. Why don't you go find us a table?"

Riley found one near the windows and twirled her hair while she waited. "So, what did Kay say?" Stephanie prodded as soon as she sat down.

"Not much. She wants me to stop by her office before lunch."

"Did she say why?"

"Nope. She probably just wants to say it was all a big mistake. And that's totally fine with me…"

"You are so full of shit," Stephanie replied.

"No, really, it's all good."

Stephanie took a few small sips of her coffee. "Your eyes don't jive with what your mouth is saying."

Riley's last meeting before lunch was running long. She glanced at her watch. 12:07. *Crap*. She stared at the guy leading the meeting and willed him to stop yapping. When he finally shut up, Riley was out of her chair before he'd even adjourned. She bolted from the conference room, bypassed the elevator and scaled the two flights of stairs up to Kay's office.

Her office door was open, and Greg Brandywine was sprawled out in one of the chairs opposite her desk. He was gesticulating wildly, and Kay sat there with her arms crossed and just stared at him. It was hard to tell if the look on her face was one of disgust or amusement.

While she waited her turn, Riley leaned up against a nearby wall. Her perch offered an unobstructed view of Kay and she took full advantage of it. The top two buttons of Kay's white silk blouse were open, exposing a span of smooth, tanned skin just below her collarbone, skin that Riley had grazed with her lips in Tokyo. Thinking of their night together caused Riley's groin to pulse and she shifted her stance and stared at the floor. When she looked up again, Kay's eyes were on her.

"Come on in, Riley." Kay turned to Greg. "Can you give us a minute?"

Greg stood and glared at Riley as he passed to leave. "I was finished anyway."

Riley was impressed. Kay had guts. To just boot her boss out of her office like that. Riley took a seat in the chair Greg had just vacated and as soon as she heard the door click shut behind her, her heart started beating wildly. She looked into Kay's rich brown eyes and felt like she was going to melt.

Kay gave her a broad smile. "Hi. It's good to see you."

"It's good to see you too," Riley croaked.

"So, I… I wanted to talk about what happened in Tokyo…"

"Okay," Riley replied, happy Kay wasn't one to beat around the bush.

"I'm not sorry it happened. I'm extremely attracted to you, Riley, and I'd like to get to know you better." Kay paused briefly before asking, "Will you have dinner with me tomorrow night?"

Riley's mouth fell open and she quickly snapped it shut. This was not at all the response she was expecting. She swallowed hard and tried to get her emotions in check. "Um, sure. That'd be nice."

"Okay, great." Kay leaned back and seemed to visibly relax.

Did she actually think I'd say no? Riley wondered. Crazy woman.

"You live in Kirkwood, right?" Kay asked.

"Yep."

"How about if I pick you up around seven?"

"Sounds good. I'll text you my address."

"Okay, perfect," Kay said before shifting gears. "See you in the debrief at two?"

Riley nodded again. Right now, the Kamadori debrief was about the furthest thing from her mind.

"All right, see you then."

Riley stood to leave. "Bye, Kay. See you in a bit."

When she opened the door, she was surprised to see Greg was still lurking nearby. He looked up from whatever he was reading and said, "She must have had something *really* important to discuss with you." The tone of his voice gave Riley goosebumps.

Riley forced a smile. *If you only knew.*

# CHAPTER NINE

Greg was standing by the floor-to-ceiling windows on the far side of his office, staring out at downtown Atlanta. Kay rapped her knuckles against the office door. "You wanted to see me?"

He snapped his head in her direction and waved her in. Just the sight of him was enough to make her stomach churn. The trip to Tokyo and London had been a welcome break from the shit show back at Logan's headquarters, and now that she was back, she had to steel herself to confront it all again.

She lowered herself into one of the chairs across from his desk and looked over at him. Kay smiled to herself. He'd touched up the grey near his temples while she'd been out of town.

Greg shoved his hands in his pockets and paced around the office like a caged animal. He looked tired. The bags under his eyes were a blemish on his otherwise handsome face. "Zephyr Airlines is getting cold feet," he said, referring to one of the airlines in Concordia, the one her friend Jessica worked for. "I need you to call them."

"And say what exactly?" Kay bit back, exposing a crack in her faux-calm demeanor.

"Kindly remind them how much we all benefit from our... *arrangement.*"

Kay sprang out of her chair. "I'm not comfortable doing that, Greg."

"I don't really give a shit if you're comfortable with it or not." He rested his hands on his hips and scowled at her. "We cannot have one of the members stray from the flock. You'll do as I say or else—"

"Or else what?"

"Don't push me."

"Why don't you call them yourself?"

"I'm not an idiot, Kay. I know some of the other Concordia members view me as a bully."

She couldn't contain a laugh. That was the understatement of the year. She knew most of the other airlines in Concordia were petrified of Greg. In fact, she was amazed Zephyr even had the guts to push back. There could only be one explanation. Concordia was getting reckless, increasing fares too much, too often. Zephyr knew it. Maybe they sensed the guillotine was about to come crashing down. That, or maybe... Had Jessica picked up on something when they'd had beers in London? She glowered at Greg. "And you think they'll listen to me?"

"Yes. You're a woman and—"

"What the hell does that have to do with anything?"

"I just think they might be more willing to listen to you."

She was trapped. She couldn't risk upsetting Greg, not if she was going to have any shot at exposing Concordia. She had to remain privy to their every move, and that would become harder if Greg picked up the scent of fear. She needed him to believe, without a doubt, that she was all in. But calling Zephyr... She wasn't sure her conscience would allow it. Doing so would only suck her deeper into this whole mess, and not only that, she actually respected Zephyr for having the guts to stand up to Greg.

Greg walked back toward his desk and looked at his watch. "It's almost seven p.m. in London. Why don't we try Nicholas right now?" he asked, referring to their counterpart at Zephyr. "He should be home from the office."

Kay sank back into her chair. She tried to reason with Greg, tell him that they shouldn't make these sorts of calls from the confines of Logan Headquarters, but he was unmoved. He pulled Nicholas's number up on his cell phone, hit the green call button and shoved it in her direction. Reluctantly, she pressed the phone to her ear, praying Nicholas wouldn't pick up. The fluorescent overhead lights in Greg's office suddenly felt much brighter and she pinched her eyes shut to escape their glare. Just when she thought it was about to go to voice mail, Nicholas's deep voice echoed in her ear.

"Nicholas, its Kay Corbett. I'm here with Greg."

Kay could almost hear him grimace on the other end. "To what do I owe this honor?"

"Rumor has it you've fallen out of love with Concordia. That you've got some apprehension."

"Damn right I do. I want out."

"I think that would be terribly misguided, Nicholas."

"I don't give a shit what you think, or Greg for that matter. It's gotten completely out of control. This whole thing is going to blow up in our faces."

"What makes you think that?"

"Come on, Kay. You know as well as I do, it's only a matter of time—"

"You do realize, Nicholas, straying from Concordia will hurt no one more than Zephyr. We'll bury you."

"Are you threatening me Kay?"

"We're all in this together. You're a fool if you think you can just walk away."

"I'm no fool, Kay. I see the writing on the wall, that's all."

"If you leave, trust me, you'll come crawling back."

There was a long pause before Nicholas responded. "I don't know, Kay."

Kay glanced over at Greg and nodded. The tone of Nicholas's voice had changed. Using well practiced Concordia code language, she did her best to reassure him the recent flurry of fare increases was nothing to be concerned about. It didn't take much to change his mind and Kay was disappointed he acquiesced so easily. She ended the call and flung Greg's phone back across the desk. "Happy?"

"Well done, Kay. I knew you had it in you."

*Asshole*. She felt like she might get sick. She'd crossed a line, a serious line. Up until now, she'd considered herself a soldier in the Concordian army, but she'd just moved up the ranks. Worse, she'd successfully pulled Nicholas back to the dark side. He was no angel and had been a leading voice in Concordia since its inception, but that didn't excuse what she'd done. She just hoped it was worth it. She hoped she'd finally secured Greg's trust, that he would no longer doubt her. It would make it so much easier to take him down.

She checked her watch as she walked back to her office. It was two o'clock on the dot. She was going to be late for the Kamadori debrief. After a quick pass by her office to grab a few documents, she rushed toward the elevators, tripping over a trashcan someone had carelessly left in the hallway, and nearly dropping all the files she was carrying in the process. "God fucking damn it."

"Sorry I'm late," she huffed when she traipsed into the meeting. She sank into the last empty seat at the table and batted a few errant hairs away from her face. The room was silent as she shuffled through her papers to find the meeting agenda. When she looked up, nine sets of eyes were on her. "Well, what are you waiting for," she barked. "Let's get started."

An update from Finance was first on the agenda. Riley cleared her throat and clicked to the first slide in her presentation. All eyes turned toward the large screen at the front of the room. About halfway through Riley's update, Kay interrupted with a slew of questions.

Riley clicked back a few slides. "I, um, covered some of that here…"

Kay felt her face get red. Obviously she hadn't been paying very close attention. "Well, perhaps…never mind, carry on…" She'd almost remarked that maybe Riley hadn't been very clear, but she doubted that was the case. Riley was probably the smartest person in the room, and she was excellent at describing complex financial models in laypersons terms. Kay sat back and tried to focus, but it was a lost cause. She was so goddamn angry about the whole fiasco with Zephyr.

As Riley walked through the rest of her slides, she occasionally glanced at her. Each time, Kay diverted her eyes. She felt dirty and ashamed by what she'd just done. If Riley looked into her eyes, she might see it. She might see the turmoil boiling inside of her.

When the meeting was over, Riley caught her by the conference room door. "Is everything okay, Kay?"

"Of course. Why do you ask?"

"You just seem, I don't know, upset."

"I'm just under a lot of stress." Kay looked down at her feet and then met Riley's gaze. "I'm sorry I jumped on you during the presentation. It's just, I had to deal with…an issue before the meeting and I'm frustrated. I shouldn't have taken it out on you."

# CHAPTER TEN

Riley cursed when her curling iron grazed her jawbone. "Ow, shit!" She dropped the hot wand on the counter and inspected the small singe mark on her skin. Satisfied that it didn't look life-threatening, she went back to fixing her hair. In less than thirty minutes, Kay would be at her front door and she was nowhere near ready. After almost burning herself a second time, she gave up and ran a brush through her hair, perplexed as to why she was suddenly incapable of curling it, something she had done practically every day of her life since she was ten.

Her hands were clammy; that must be it. She hadn't seen or heard from Kay since the Kamadori debrief the day before. She assumed their dinner date was still on, but what if Kay had changed her mind? Surely, she would have called or texted to cancel, wouldn't she? To just not show up would be downright rude… Maybe that was how Kay rolled. She'd been a downright bitch during the Kamadori meeting. Maybe she wasn't that sweet, kind person Riley had spent time with in Tokyo.

Riley tried to push those thoughts out of head. She glanced at her watch. Twenty minutes. She darted over to her closet.

What the hell was she going to wear? Sundress? Too casual. Cocktail dress? Too formal. She groaned as she scanned her wardrobe. Everything she owned was girly and southern. Aside from her work clothes, nothing in her closet felt even remotely sophisticated. Finally, she settled on a flowery skirt and a light pink sleeveless silk top. It would have to do. She was out of time. She grabbed a navy cardigan off the back of a chair in the corner of her room and draped it over her shoulders. It was late October, and although the days were still fairly warm, it was starting to get cooler in the evenings.

Her doorbell rang while she was rummaging around for a small purse to carry. It was seven o'clock on the dot. She took a deep breath, bounded down the stairs and opened the front door. There on her front porch, stood Kay, looking as stunning as ever in black jeans, black cowboy boots and black cotton blazer that looked like it was custom made to fit the curves of her body. Her intense dark eyes settled on Riley. "Hey," she said, leaning in to give Riley a peck on the cheek.

Riley almost had to pinch herself. This beautiful woman was here to take her to dinner. "Hi," she said. Her earlier anxiety all but evaporated. Kay's smile put her in a giddy trance.

"Are you ready?" Kay asked.

"Um, yeah, almost." Riley held open the door. "Do you want to come in for a sec?"

Kay stepped inside and said, "Wow, this place is really cute."

"Thanks." She stuffed her phone and wallet into her purse and searched around for her keys. "I'm just renting but I love these old Craftsman houses."

"Yeah, me too. My house in Virginia Highland is a Craftsman. It was a dump when I bought it and I spent over a year gut renovating it."

"I bet it's gorgeous. I'd love to see it sometime." Riley felt her cheeks get warm. *Be a little more forward, why don't you?*

Kay skipped down Riley's front steps and opened the passenger door to her Jeep, motioning for Riley to climb in.

"I hope you like Italian?" Kay asked as she backed down the driveway. "I made reservations at Sotto-Sotto in Inman Park. I was actually surprised they had a table."

"Oh, I love that place. I mean, I've only been there once but I remember the food being delicious."

The drive to the restaurant took less than fifteen minutes, and Kay, who was normally cool as a cucumber, seemed really nervous. It was kind of cute.

The hostess led them through the bar to the back of the narrow restaurant and seated them at a cozy table tucked against the wall. The lighting was dim, and two candles flickered on the table.

"Yum, everything sounds so good." Riley said. She peeked over her menu. "What are you thinking?"

"Hmm, I think I'm going to start with a salad and then go with the mushroom risotto for my entree. What about you?"

"I'm definitely going to start with the Buffalo mozzarella, and then, gosh, I can't decide, either the tuna or the salmon."

"Ooh, tough choice." Kay slowly licked her lips. Something about the way she did it was incredibly sexy, and Riley wanted to lean over and kiss her, but the waiter walked up before she got the chance. He rambled off the specials before asking, "Can I get you anything to drink?"

Kay glanced at Riley. "Wine good for you?"

"Twist my arm."

Kay pointed at a page in the wine list and looked up at the waiter. "We'll have a bottle of the Nebbiolo."

"Excellent choice," the waiter replied before rushing off. When he returned, he held the bottle up for Kay to examine, and once she nodded her approval, he effortlessly extracted its cork and poured her a splash to taste. She swirled the glass expertly, took a sip and signaled for the waiter to pour them each a glass.

Once he was gone, Kay picked up her glass and smiled. "To Tokyo."

They clinked glasses. "To Tokyo," Riley echoed, surprised at how comfortable she felt being there with Kay. She'd worried things might be awkward between them, given that they basically jumped in bed together, and since she was an expert at finding things to worry about, she'd wondered if things would be different between them now that they were back home in Atlanta. In Tokyo, something between them had just clicked, and she wondered if that would still be the case. When she looked across the table and into Kay's sparkling eyes, her anxiety faded. Kay seemed completely at ease, so different than the persona she held at the office.

"A penny for your thoughts," Kay said.

"My grandfather always used to say that." Riley smiled. "I was actually thinking about how good it feels to be here with you."

Kay's face lit up. "Oh really, cuz I was just thinking the same thing."

That sat there smiling goofily at each other until the waiter walked up with their appetizers.

After she took a few bites of her mozzarella, Riley asked, "Have you been to a lot of places in Asia, I mean besides Tokyo? Given your dad was a pilot for Logan, I bet you've traveled all over the place."

Kay nodded. "Yeah, I'm lucky, I've been all over the world, seen so many amazing places." She paused and sipped her wine. "It's funny though, I feel like I haven't taken the time to explore my own country. Sure, I've been to Singapore and Santiago, but I've never been to Seattle, if you can believe it. My dad always jokes that our family drinks jet fuel in the morning, but my dream is to take a big long road trip around the US."

Riley laughed. "Really?"

"Yeah, really."

"Is that something you've always wanted to do?"

"Yep, ever since high school. I read this book called *Blue Highways*—it was assigned as summer reading—about this guy who was a little down on his luck, and for lack of a better idea, decided to drive his dilapidated van around the US. The book was interesting because he avoided the major interstates and instead stuck to the old, secondary roads. He made the trip in the 70's—way before Google maps or GPS—and apparently, the secondary roads were depicted in blue in the old road atlases, hence the name of the book."

"Wow, that actually sounds pretty cool."

"Yeah, and the best part is that, because he avoided the major highways, he drove through all these small quirky towns—the towns you blow past at seventy miles per hour today on the highway—and he met all these interesting people."

"In some ways, I'm in the same boat as you," Riley said. "There's so much of the US I haven't seen. Sure, I've been to most of the major cities in the US, but I haven't really explored some of the more rural areas and small towns." She swirled the wine in her glass. "Do you still have the book?"

Kay shook her head. "No, but I'd love to reread it someday."

The waiter swung by to top off their wine glasses and deliver their entrees.

"So, what sorts of vacations did your family take when you were a kid?" Kay asked as they dug into their meals.

"We *always* went to the beach. Beach and golf, those are the only two words my family knows when it comes to vacations."

"It doesn't sound like you enjoyed the trips."

"Ah, they were fine. Just no variety. It just sort of got old after a while, although I know I shouldn't complain. I'm lucky my family could afford to go on nice vacations."

If Kay thought she sounded like a spoiled brat, she didn't show it. Instead she asked, "I assume you've traveled a lot since joining Logan?"

Riley grinned. "Definitely, that's one of the best things about working for the airline, the flight benefits. Growing up, I didn't even know there was a big wide world outside of Georgia and Florida."

Conversation flowed easily over dinner and Riley was disappointed when the waiter came to clear their dinner plates. She didn't want the night to end, and even though she wasn't even remotely hungry, she quickly agreed to share a cheese plate with Kay for dessert.

"Any coffee for you?" the waiter asked after he jotted down their dessert order.

"None for me," Riley said.

Kay shook her head. "I can't do caffeine this late at night. I'd never fall asleep."

Riley glanced at her watch, surprised to see that they'd been at the restaurant for nearly three hours. She couldn't put her finger on it. There was a subtle intimacy between her and Kay and she felt so incredibly drawn to her. In fact, she didn't think she'd ever felt so utterly captivated by another human being.

A tingle shot through her body as she watched Kay's elegant fingers slip a piece of cheese into her mouth. Almost unconsciously, she reached over and grazed those long fingers with her own and was rewarded with a soft smile, and suddenly there they were again, staring goofily at one another.

The waiter clearly realized he was interrupting a moment. He cleared his throat, slid the check on the table and scooted away. Riley snapped out of her Kay-induced daze and looked around the restaurant. All of the other tables were empty, save for one occupied by an older amorous couple in the opposite corner.

The valet pulled up with Kay's Jeep just as soon as they stepped out of the restaurant.

"You all buckled in?" Kay asked before she pulled away from the curb.

Riley thought it was cute of her to ask. "Yep."

Kay shifted the car in gear, made a quick U-turn and headed off in the direction of Kirkwood. It was late but Riley felt wide awake when they pulled into her driveway. After she put the Jeep in park, Kay smiled and said, "I had a wonderful time tonight. Thank you."

A nearby streetlight cast a soft glow over Kay's face and Riley was desperate to kiss her. "I did too," she croaked. "And thank you for dinner."

Kay shifted in the driver's seat and ran her fingers over Riley's cheek before leaning in to bring their lips together. The kiss was brief, almost chaste and it left Riley aching for more. She slid a hand into Kay's hair and pulled her into another, deeper kiss.

When they finally broke apart, Riley's body was humming. She closed her eyes and tilted her head back against the seat. "Wow, kissing you is even better than I remember."

Kay chuckled. "Oh, really? Well I might say the same."

"Do you want to—"

"Come inside?"

Riley nodded.

"As much as I'd love to," Kay said, "I promised myself I'd behave tonight. I enjoyed spending time with you and getting to know you better and I want the evening to be about that." She reached for one of Riley's hands. "I want our relationship to be based on more than sex. Don't get me wrong, I like sex, a lot, it's just..."

Riley smoothed her thumb over Kay's hand. "No need to explain. I want nothing more than to take you to bed, but I respect what you're saying. I like you, Kay, and I want to explore that too, a relationship that's not merely about sex." Riley smiled. "I just lack your resolve."

"Well, don't give me too much credit." Kay held her thumb and pointer finger up in the light. "My resolve is this close to cracking."

Riley gave her a quick peck on the lips and opened the passenger door. "Goodnight, Kay," she said when her feet hit the ground.

"Hey," Kay called out before Riley shut the car door.

Riley looked back into the car. "Yeah?"

"Can I cook you dinner on Saturday night?"

"I'd like that."

# CHAPTER ELEVEN

At three p.m. on Saturday, Kay decided to give up and go home. She'd come into the office that morning, under the guise of catching up on work in hopes of sneaking back into Greg's office so she could go through his desk drawers. Unfortunately, an incredibly cheap fare had been erroneously filed the night before—forty-nine dollars round trip to London. Twitter had blown up about it and more than a thousand people snatched up the fare before Logan was able to pull it down. Now, a group from the transatlantic pricing team, the team whose cubicles occupied the area right outside Greg's office, were at work trying to fix the mess.

Kay kept hoping they'd finish and go home, but she couldn't wait any longer. Riley was due at her house for dinner in three hours and fifty-three minutes, not that she was counting, and she still needed to swing by the grocery store. It just meant she'd have to come in to the office again the following day.

Even though she was frustrated she hadn't been able to get into Greg's office, her mood shifted as soon as she stepped outside. She caught herself whistling as she walked out to her car in the Logan parking lot. It was a beautiful day and a beautiful woman was coming to dinner. Earlier she'd had some nagging doubts about pursuing something with Riley. She'd briefly considered cancelling their plans for tonight, but she couldn't bring herself to do it. She was too damn excited. Her heart won over her mind.

The grocery store near her house was a zoo, and she cursed under her breath when someone rammed their cart into her heel while she was sorting through a mound of tomatoes. She turned around to give them a piece of her mind but aborted her rant when her cell phone jingled. She glanced at the caller ID. It was Ethan, her best friend since high school. She hesitated before answering. A little girl in a pink tutu was having a complete meltdown in the produce department and Kay was not sure she'd be able to carry on a conversation over the racket. Still, she decided to try. She hadn't talked to Ethan since he and his husband Derek returned from their honeymoon. "Hey, Ethan."

Ethan's deep laugh filled her ear. "Did you decide to adopt a child while I was out of the country?" he asked.

"Hah, good one, Ethan. No, I'm in the grocery store and there's this little girl, never mind, how was your trip?"

"Fucking fantastic but let me call you later when you're home. I'll walk you through the photos Derek posted online. What are you doing at the grocery store, anyway? I thought you only ate takeout."

"Remind me again why we're friends… For your information, I have a date. I'm cooking her dinner."

"Ooh, pulling out all the stops. Does she know you can't cook worth shit?"

"Just because I don't cook doesn't mean I can't."

"Who is she? Last I checked, you were a swinging single."

"She works at Logan," Kay said as she maneuvered her cart toward the meat department and away from the tutu meltdown.

"Uh-oh, a coworker?"

"You're the lawyer, but last time I checked, it wasn't a crime to have relations with a coworker. Plus, we're in totally different departments. She works in Finance."

"Fair enough."

"Anyway, when I was in Tokyo last week, we sorta happened to fall into bed together."

"I see. Mixing business with pleasure, are we?"

"I've had a crush on her forever. It's not like I fell into bed with any old coworker."

"Okay, okay. Speaking of which, how are things going at good old Logan these days."

Ethan was the only person Kay'd told about Concordia. "Not so great. I can't get into it now, not in public, but the whole"—Kay paused to pull a number from the ticket machine at the meat counter.

"The whole price fixing thing," Ethan finished for her.

Kay knocked over a display of Hamburger Helper. "Shhh. Jesus, Eth." She tucked her phone between her ear and her shoulder and picked up the boxes she'd sent scattering across the floor. "It's getting out of hand. I'm in deep and I'm scared shitless."

"Oh, sweetheart. I'm here for you."

"I've got to go. I'll call you over the weekend."

Kay ended the call just as her number came up on the LED display above the meat counter. Ethan was right about one thing, she was a miserable cook although she could grill a mean steak. She ordered two ribeyes and set them next to the salad fixings in her cart.

After a quick pass through the wine and cheese section, she paid and hurried back out to her car, but stopped dead in her tracks when she spotted a car that looked suspiciously like Greg's, pulling out of a nearby parking spot. The tinted windows prevented her from seeing the driver, but how many canary yellow Porsches could there be in Atlanta? Greg lived on the opposite side of town, but she wasn't taking any chances. She snatched the bags out of her cart and ducked behind a parked car until the coast was clear. Greg was the last person she wanted to see right now.

# CHAPTER TWELVE

A Taylor Swift song blared through the car speakers and Riley tapped to the beat as she made her way home Saturday afternoon. That morning she'd decided she hated every single thing in her closet and had promptly set off for the mall, determined to find something suitable to wear to dinner at Kay's. She'd splurged on a new pair of jeans, which, in her opinion, were way better than the seven pair she already had, and a billowy orange top that the saleswoman said beautifully set off her rich blue eyes. She was such a pushover.

It was almost five o'clock by the time she got home. That didn't leave her much time. She was due at Kay's at seven. She cut the tags off her new outfit and laid it out on the bed. After she'd showered and dressed, there was just enough time to put a few curls in her hair. On her way out the door, she grabbed the bottle of wine she'd bought earlier that day—being the good southerner she was, she'd no sooner run down main street naked than show up at someone's doorstep emptyhanded.

The clock on Riley's dashboard read 6:59 when she pulled into Kay's driveway and the front door opened before she was even out of the car.

"My alarm dings when someone pulls in the driveway," Kay explained.

Riley climbed the front steps. "You mean you weren't standing at the window eagerly awaiting my arrival?"

"Busted," Kay said with a laugh and gave her a peck on the cheek. "Come on in."

Riley handed her the bottle of wine and stepped into the foyer where she could see straight through to the back of the house. "Oh, wow, Kay. This place is amazing." Like most of the other Craftsmen in the Virginia Highland neighborhood, the house was probably built in the 1920's; however, its interior was extremely contemporary.

"Thanks, and thanks for the wine. Let me show you around."

They wandered into the living room, its walls covered with what looked like African and Asian art, through a formal dining room and finally into the kitchen near the back of the house. "Okay, I have serious kitchen envy," Riley said as she ran her hand over the polished concrete countertops and cooed at the six burner Wolf stove. "You must be quite the cook."

"Ah, not so much. I'm sorry to report this kitchen is woefully underutilized."

"That is a crime, you know that?"

"Yeah, I know. I keep saying I'll learn to cook… Here, let me show you my favorite room." Kay took Riley's hand and led her into a small sunroom off the kitchen. The room's furnishings were overshadowed by a wall of floor-to-ceiling shelves full of books. "Oh. I see why you love this room. It's so cozy, and in my opinion, you can never have too many books."

"Yeah, I spend almost all of my time in here, and you should see it in the morning. The sun just beams in."

They continued their tour, passing a small den and a powder room before heading upstairs where there were two small bedrooms, one with two twin beds and the other dominated by a massive wooden desk, a Jack and Jill bathroom between them, and a master suite. When they entered the master bedroom, Riley oohed and aahhed. It was much more spacious than the other bedrooms, and it had a nook outlined with more bookshelves. A large, colorful area rug covered much of the hardwood floors and two skylights floated over the bed. "Well, that's the grand tour," Kay said as they made their way back downstairs. "Now how about we get you a glass of wine? Would you prefer red or white?"

"Whatever you have open is fine."

"I've got plenty of both. We're having steak for dinner, but it's unseasonably warm for this time of year. What do you say we start with white and move to red for dinner?"

"That sounds perfect."

Kay opened a bottle of Sauvignon Blanc and poured them each a glass. "Why don't we sit out on the back patio? It's supposed to get chilly once the sun goes down, but it's still pretty nice out there."

"We might as well sit outside while we still can. Old Man Winter will be here soon enough."

"Winters here are nothing. At least not compared to those they get up in New York."

"I know, I'm a total softy. I go into full hermit mode when it drops below freezing."

Kay scooped up their wineglasses and nodded toward a small tray of cheese and crackers on the kitchen island. "Can you grab that?"

Riley obliged and followed her outside.

The backyard was beautifully landscaped. A low stone wall encircled the flagstone patio, separating it from a small grassy area, and a tall wooden fence ran the perimeter of the property.

Two lounge chairs and a small table were neatly arranged in front of a gas fire pit. "I know it's a little warm, but do you mind if I turn on the fire?" Kay asked. "I love watching the flames and it doesn't give off that much heat."

Riley settled into one of the chairs. "I don't mind at all. That would be nice." The sun was low in the sky and she could already feel a small nip in the air.

Kay pressed a button to start the fire and sat down next to her. "They say it could drop into the forties overnight and they're calling for rain all day tomorrow."

"Well, all the more reason to sit out and enjoy the nice weather tonight."

Kay propped her feet up on the fire pit. "I couldn't agree more." Just then the watch on her arm buzzed. She glanced down at it and grimaced. "Shit, that's a call from Greg. I need to take it. I'm sorry. I'll be right back."

Riley watched her retreat into the house. That poor woman. Greg never left her alone.

Kay looked shaken when she returned to the fire. She took a long sip of wine and then apologized again for having to take the call.

"I heard about that crazy low sale fare that was filed by mistake. Is that what Greg was calling about?"

"Nah, he has a bee up his ass about, another matter," Kay replied.

"I figured he'd be furious about the fare mistake."

"He wasn't happy about it, but let's just say he's got bigger fish to fry. That, and luckily, the transatlantic pricing team was pretty quick to get the erroneous fare out of the system."

Riley thought dealing with the aftermath of a forty-nine-dollar fare to London would be of umpteen importance, but what did she know. "Did you rip into the person who made the mistake?"

Kay shook her head. "That's not my style. The person who made the mistake feels bad enough about it. We all make mistakes and me causing a huge stink about it wasn't going to fix the problem. Let's just say, I feel confident that the person won't make the same mistake again. The problem is, these types of errors are made so much worse in the world of Twitter."

"Twitter?"

"Yeah, Twitter can be both a blessing and a curse in our business. Back in the old days, when a fare was filed by mistake, we might sell a dozen or so tickets before we caught the error. Nowadays, as soon as even one person stumbles on the fare, it goes viral on Twitter and other social media outlets and thousands of people snap up tickets before we have a chance to react."

"But I bet that also means Logan is made aware of the error sooner than they might be?"

"True," Kay said. "In that case, Twitter can be a blessing."

Riley shrugged. "I'm clueless about the world of pricing, but aren't there safeguards built into the pricing software to catch an abnormally low fare before it's filed and available for sale?"

Kay chuckled. "Yes, our system has lots of protections built in and it generally does a good job, but airline pricing is insanely complicated. The forty-nine-dollar fare that was filed yesterday was actually legit, it just wasn't supposed to be widely available. It was intended for one corporate client, but the restrictions were entered incorrectly, and just like that, it was available to anyone and everyone."

"I read somewhere once that, if you look around a plane, it's likely every single person on that flight paid a different fare."

"I'd say that's probably true. Like I said, airline pricing is incredibly complex."

Neither of them spoke for several long moments. The last sliver of light vanished from the sky as they sipped their wine and stared into the fire. Riley was again struck by how comfortable she felt in Kay's presence. There was nothing awkward about the silence and it was refreshing to sit with someone and not feel compelled to speak. She reached over and curled her hand around Kay's.

"I suppose I should go ahead and fire up the grill," Kay said eventually.

"Well, you did promise me dinner," Riley said with a smile, "although I've got to admit, you're going to have a hard time dragging me away from this fire."

Kay stood and walked over toward the grill. "If the temperature doesn't drop too quickly, we can eat out here."

"I'd like that. What can I do to help with dinner?"

"Nothing. We're having steak and salad, pretty simple. Just sit and enjoy the fire."

After dinner, Riley insisted on helping with the dishes. "You cooked, it's the least I can do."

"More wine?" Kay asked when they were done.

"Yes, please. I'd love some more of that red we had with dinner. It was delicious."

"It is good, isn't it? I'm embarrassed to admit I only bought it because I thought the label was cool."

Riley laughed. "I like you more every minute. All my wine buying decisions are based solely on whether I like the label or not."

"Why don't you make yourself comfortable in the sunroom and I'll bring you out a glass?"

"Okay, thanks." She wandered into the adjoining room and scanned the photographs that dotted the bookshelves. There was one of Kay with a group Riley assumed was her family at a ski area, and then another one of Kay at the controls of a small aircraft. She chuckled when her eyes moved to a teenage Kay posing with her soccer team. Kay was holding a big trophy and her baggy uniform stood out next to the short shorts and snug tops worn by her teammates.

"What's so funny?" Kay asked when she entered the room.

Riley turned to face her. "Just looking at some of your photos. I love that you were such a little tomboy."

Kay handed her a glass of wine. "Yeah, big time. Still am."

"What was the trophy for?" Riley asked.

Kay gave her a blank look and Riley pointed toward the bookshelf. "In the photo with your soccer team."

"Oh, we won the state championship," Kay said. "I think that picture was taken my senior year of high school."

"You don't remember what year you won the championship?"

"It's just, well, we won the championship all four years I was on the team."

Riley rolled her eyes playfully. "Of course you did. What position did you play?"

"Forward."

"Let me guess. You were the team's leading scorer."

Kay blushed slightly. "Only my junior and senior year."

"Why am I not surprised?"

Kay took a sip of her wine and eyed Riley over the rim of her glass. "Did you play?"

"Yeah, but I wasn't that great. I made varsity but I spent most of my time warming the bench. I liked it though. Being part of a team, I mean."

"Yeah, that was my favorite part about it too. The camaraderie and all that. I actually miss playing on a team like that," Kay replied. "We should kick the ball around sometime."

Riley nodded enthusiastically. "Yeah, that would be fun. It's been ages since I touched a soccer ball. As you know, I play on one of the Logan softball teams but I've always preferred soccer as a sport."

"I'm with you. Softball is okay, but I was always a lot more passionate about soccer."

Riley glanced back at the photos on the bookshelf. "What about this one?" she asked, pointing to one of Kay in a dress. "It must have been a special occasion."

"Ha, yeah. It was my oldest brother's wedding. I was still in high school. In fact, that may have been the first time I ever wore a dress, or at least the first time I wore one without shorts underneath. I refused to wear a dress until I was like sixteen."

Riley giggled. "Now that I think about it, I don't think I've ever seen you wear a dress. You rock the high heels, though," she said, "and your power suits are as sexy as hell."

Kay gently nudged Riley with her hip. "Oh, they are, huh?"

"Yeah, when you strut around the office in one of those—"

"I do not strut."

Riley burst out laughing. "Uh, yeah, you kind of do. Don't get me wrong. It's hot, really hot."

Kay set her wineglass down on the bookshelf and snaked her arms around Riley's waist, pulling them together. Riley let out a whimper when their lips touched. The kiss was tender but incredibly sensual and it left her feeling completely dazed. How was it that one kiss from Kay could throw her so off balance?

"You okay?" Kay asked.

"Yeah, it's just, kissing you… It's like nothing I've ever experienced."

"I hope in a good way?"

Riley nodded and gave her a soft smile. "Yeah, in a really good way." She tugged Kay's shirt gently and pulled her into another, deeper kiss. When they broke apart, Riley's body was on fire. She brushed tentative fingers over Kay's breast.

Kay arched back against the bookcase.

"Kay?" Riley asked, her voice cracking slightly.

"Yeah?"

"Will you take me to bed?"

A smile crossed Kay's face. "What happened to getting to know each other better first?"

"Hmm, yeah that. Around you I have no willpower. Zilch."

Without another word, Kay grabbed Riley's hand and led her upstairs to the bedroom. The room was dark, absent the moonlight shining through the skylights over the bed. Kay wrapped her arms around Riley's waist and left a trail of soft kisses along her neck. A moan escaped Riley's mouth as Kay nibbled the soft spot behind her ear, and when their lips finally came together, the throbbing in her groin was on full blast.

Without breaking the kiss, Riley drew Kay down to the bed and attacked her mouth with renewed vigor. When their lips finally broke apart, Riley rolled over and straddled Kay's waist. She reached up and pulled her own shirt off before turning her attention to the buttons on Kay's blouse. She ran her fingers over Kay's taut stomach before reaching back to unlatch her bra. Her hands slid over Kay's silky bare breasts, her arousal flaring as she felt nipples harden in response to her touch.

Riley leaned forward to graze Kay's breasts with her own, and as they moved together, she delighted at the sensation of her nipples brushing over Kay's. Her hand made its way inside the waistband of Kay's jeans. "Off," she muttered. Kay complied, shifting beneath her to wriggle out of her pants and Riley followed suit, rolling over to kick her pants to the floor.

Once they were naked, their bodies came together again. Riley arched her back as Kay circled her breasts first with her fingers and then with her tongue. Kay's lips gradually moved down her body, gliding over her stomach and to the inside of her thighs before finding the warm wet mound between her legs.

"Yes, Kay, yes," Riley cried out as Kay's tongue teased her swollen clit. She closed her eyes and grabbed the sheets, letting the orgasm build slowly. Her chest tightened, and she suddenly felt weightless. When it crashed through her, its intensity caused her to buck up against Kay before she collapsed on the bed. "Jesus, Kay. I don't think I've ever come that hard in my life."

Kay crawled back up next to her. "I aim to please."

Riley rolled on top of Kay and kissed her playfully. “Now it’s time to see how wet you are.”

# CHAPTER THIRTEEN

A few hours later, Riley woke to the pitter-patter of a soft rain hitting the skylight above the bed. She smiled at the feel of Kay's naked body nestled against her. She reluctantly extricated herself from the long, strong arm curled around her waist, and padded to the bathroom.

"You okay?" Kay asked when Riley slipped back into bed.

"Yes. Shh. Go back to sleep."

It was light outside the next time Riley opened her eyes. It was still raining, but there was no longer a warm body next to her in bed. She heard water running in the bathroom and called out, "Kay?"

A fully dressed Kay wandered out of the bathroom, dabbing her face with a towel. "Morning, baby."

Riley rolled over onto her stomach and propped herself up on her elbows. "Good morning."

"I was just about to walk down to the bakery to get us some breakfast."

"What time is it?" Riley asked.

"Almost nine."

"Wow, I can't believe I slept so late. Give me a sec to get dressed and I'll join you."

"Great, I'll go down and make some coffee while you get ready," Kay replied and started toward the bedroom door, pausing midway. "Do you want to borrow a T-shirt or anything?"

"A T-shirt would be great, thanks."

"I'd offer you some jeans too, but I think they'd be too long."

Riley nodded. Kay had to be a good three or four inches taller than her. "You're probably right. No problem, I can wear the jeans I had on last night." She looked around on the floor. "Assuming I can find them," she said with a wry smile.

On her way to the dresser, Kay reached down to grab Riley's jeans off the floor and tossed them in her direction. She pulled out a long sleeve T-shirt and held it up. "Will this work?"

"Yep," Riley said as she rolled out of bed.

Kay ogled Riley's naked body, running her gaze from Riley's blue eyes down to her brightly painted toes. She set the shirt on the bed and trailed a finger down Riley's arm as she strode toward the door.

"Oh, and Kay?" Riley asked.

"Yeah?"

"Do you have a toothbrush I could borrow?"

"Oh, of course," Kay walked back toward the bathroom, rummaged around in the linen closet and set an unopened toothbrush on the edge of the vanity. "There's toothpaste in the drawer next to the sink. Feel free to help yourself to whatever else you need."

"Thanks, see you downstairs in a minute."

The coffee was finished brewing by the time Riley made her way downstairs. Kay handed her a steaming mug of coffee and said, "It looks like the rain is finally letting up, but I'll bring an umbrella just in case."

Riley leaned on the kitchen island and blew on her coffee to cool it down. "So, what sort of stuff does this bakery have?"

"The usual, muffins and bagels, but I go there because they make the best breakfast burritos in Atlanta."

"Yum, I'm totally getting one of those."

"The only problem is, they're almost too big. I turn into a sloth after I eat one."

"So, not your go-to meal before a run?"

"Yeah, not so much."

"How many days a week do you run?"

"I try to run four or five days a week if I can," Kay replied, "although, even if I don't run, I try to get some sort of exercise every day."

"Wow, that's pretty impressive. No wonder you have a body to die for," Riley said and gave her a wink. "I try to stay in shape but I'm not as devoted as you are. Maybe hanging out with you will be good for my health."

"Might just be. In the meantime, hurry up and finish your coffee. I'm starving."

Riley took a few more sips from her mug and set it on the counter. "Ready when you are."

The sun made a brief appearance while they walked to the bakery, but it was drizzling again when they stepped outside after breakfast. Kay popped open her umbrella. "Come here," she said, curling an arm over Riley's shoulder. "I don't want you to get wet."

About halfway home, the sky opened up. Kay and Riley huddled together under the umbrella and started to run, but it was no use, they were both drenched by the time they got to the front door. "Shower?" Kay asked as they stood dripping in her foyer.

"Yeah, that would feel good." Riley shivered. "I'm freezing. I can't believe how much the temperature dropped overnight."

"Here, let me help you out of the wet clothes."

"Oh, aren't you the sly one," Riley said with a laugh. "I know you're just trying to get me naked."

Kay held up her arms. "Guilty as charged."

They both stripped out of their wet clothes and ran upstairs to her oversized shower.

"Ooh, this feels wonderful," Riley said as soon as she stepped under the spray of hot water.

Kay grabbed the bottle of bath gel, squeezed a large blob of the blue liquid into her hands and began to knead Riley's shoulders. It didn't take long for her hands to drift downward to caress Riley's bare chest. "I can think of a great way to spend a cold rainy day," Kay said.

Riley leaned back against her, giving Kay full access to her erect nipples. "Oh, really. What did you have in mind? Watching football?"

"Not exactly," Kay replied. She rested her chin on Riley's shoulder and whispered, "I was thinking of something a little more interactive."

The familiar ache between Riley's legs made a return appearance. She turned in Kay's arms and playfully kissed her lips. "What is it that you had in mind?"

Kay turned off the water, handed Riley a towel and led her back into the bedroom. They gently made love before falling back to sleep to the sound of the rain on the roof.

# CHAPTER FOURTEEN

It was almost noon when Kay woke up again. She looked over at the naked body sprawled across her bed and her stomach stirred with emotion. She was whipped, there was no doubt about it. She wanted nothing more than to spend the rest of the afternoon in bed with Riley, but reality reared its ugly head and signaled an end to their idyllic morning. Kay had no choice. She had to go to the office. She stared up at the ceiling and watched the rain splash on the skylights over the bed. With each passing day, she became more deeply involved with Concordia. She had to put a stop to it, and soon, lest it consume her and bring Logan to its knees.

As if sensing her angst, Riley stirred and snuggled up against her. Kay cursed Concordia. It was like she was being tested. What kind of idiot would leave a beautiful woman in a warm bed to venture out into a cold gray day? Her ethics won out and she gently shook Riley awake. "Hey, baby. I'm sorry, but I have to get up."

Riley rubbed her eyes and mumbled, "Um, what?"

"I have to go to the office."

Riley slowly sat up and leaned against one of the overstuffed pillows. "But it's Sunday…and didn't you work all day yesterday?" She stifled a yawn. "Come on, stay in bed with me."

"I wish I could," Kay replied, "but I can't. I have something important to take care of and it can't wait."

Riley pouted and began to protest.

"Riley, please. We need to get up, now." The words came out more harshly than she intended, and the expression on Riley's face change from post sex blissful to like *whoa, what?*

She patted Riley on the arm. "Listen, I'm sorry. I just…I'm under a lot of pressure to get something done."

The smile returned to Riley's face. "Fine, but if you're going to the office, I am too. I've got a ton of stuff I need to catch up on, and if I can't spend the afternoon in bed with you, I might as well go to work."

A wave of panic swept through Kay, but it abated as she considered the situation. There was no need for Riley's presence at the office to impact her plans. Their offices were on different floors and at opposite ends of the large glass building that was Logan Headquarters.

They drove separate cars to the office since Riley was expected at her parents' house for Sunday dinner at five p.m. sharp. They parked next to each other in the nearly empty employee lot. "Text me if you get hungry or thirsty," Kay said as they rode up in the elevator. "Maybe we can grab coffee later at the deli across the street."

The elevator jerked to a stop at Riley's floor. She gave Kay a soft kiss on the lips and stepped off. "Will do," she said as the doors slid shut.

As she strode across the seventh floor to her office, Kay let out a sigh of relief. There was not a soul in sight and all of the offices that lined the perimeter of the room were dark. She flipped the switch on her small desk lamp. She preferred the soft light it offered to the stark fluorescent lights overhead.

She checked her watch. It was one o'clock on the dot. As much as she wanted to sneak into Greg's office right away just to get it over with, she thought it would be wiser to wait a bit.

In truth, she didn't know exactly how sophisticated Logan's security was, and it was possible cameras captured her every move, at least when she was outside of people's personal offices. She was banking on the assumption that Logan didn't monitor inside individual offices. That would be creepy, and she didn't think the top brass at Logan was that paranoid. She certainly hoped not.

At any rate, working for a while before she wandered toward Greg's office seemed like the safer bet. Like the last time, when she'd downloaded the files off his computer, she'd concocted a story about looking for a report she'd left on his desk in case she was caught entering or leaving his office.

Exactly an hour later, she stood, pulled a small screwdriver from her purse, and stuffed it in her pocket. The office furniture at Logan could very well have come from IKEA, and she was pretty confident she could jimmy open the locks on Greg's desk without much effort. As she started for the door, her phone pinged to announce an incoming text, but she didn't stop to check the screen. If she did, she worried she might lose her nerve.

The door to Greg's office was unlocked, and this time, she left it open when she stepped inside, hoping it would make her presence in his office look less suspicious if she were caught. She marched toward his desk but froze before she got there. It was like her courage evaporated in thin air. She was about to flee when a photo above Greg's desk caught her eye. It depicted him accepting some aviation industry award. The snide look on his face was enough to push her forward. She couldn't give up now.

Three large file folder-size drawers flanked the right side of his desk. Screwdriver in hand, she tried each drawer. The first one was unlocked, same with the second and the third, and all three drawers were completely empty minus a few stray paperclips. She stared at them in disbelief. She thought back to the last time she'd snuck into his office and she was certain they'd been locked. Hadn't they? She slowly slid each one shut, returned the screwdriver to her pocket and hurried across the carpet, pausing at the office door to make sure the coast was clear. It wasn't. Riley had just rounded the corner and was approaching Kay's office door.

"Over here," Kay called out, hoping she came across much more calmly than she felt.

Riley peered in her direction and held up a paper plate weighed down by two massive slices of pizza. "I brought you something to eat."

Kay forced a smile and tried to push aside the panic. How much had Riley seen? "I didn't find it," she muttered.

"Didn't find what?"

Kay gestured in the general direction of Greg's office. "The report I was looking for." At least that part was true. She hadn't found what she'd been looking for. She hadn't found anything at all.

Riley looked confused. "Um, sorry to hear that," she said and nodded toward the plate in her hand. "Are you hungry? A few of my coworkers are in the office today and they ordered in pizza. I sent you a text, but you didn't respond so I figured I'd just bring you up some. I don't dare have any because my mother would murder me if I spoiled my dinner. She always makes roasted chicken for Sunday..."

Kay struggled to focus. She took the plate from Riley and simply said, "Thanks."

Riley gently touched her arm. "Kay, are you okay? You seem a little bit out of it."

"Yeah, I'm fine. I just have a lot on my mind."

# CHAPTER FIFTEEN

The tires of Riley's car crunched on the gravel as she made her way up her parents' long, winding driveway. She cursed when she eyed the clock on her dashboard. 5:21. Her mother would not be pleased. She'd left the office at three, thinking she had plenty of time to run home, shower, change into something her mother would deem appropriate, and drive to Buckhead, but traffic on I-75 had been even more horrible than usual.

As she'd crawled along the highway, she couldn't shake the feeling something bizarre was going on with Kay. When Riley had brought the pizza up to her, she'd acted so weird. Like she'd gotten caught with her hand in the cookie jar, which Riley deduced, meant her visit to Greg's office hadn't been wholly justified.

Even though they'd become intimate, Riley still didn't know Kay all that well. Most of the time, she was charming and funny and sweet, but once or twice, Riley had seen a flash of something—fear or frustration—cross her face. If there was something upsetting Kay, she was determined to figure out what it was. And she hoped it would explain Kay's odd behavior at the office that afternoon.

Riley cursed again when her parents' house came into view. As expected, her brother Bobby's black SUV was parked in the apron near the garage. It was the white Mercedes sedan next to it that was the problem. Apparently, Riley's Auntie Jo and her husband had also been invited to dinner. *Fucking fabulous*. As if her mother wasn't bad enough, Auntie Jo was always trying to set her up with so-and-so's son or neighbor. Too bad Riley was too chickenshit to tell them she wasn't into men. *If only they had gaydar…*

She parked next to Bobby's car and checked her makeup in the rearview mirror. Her mood improved drastically when she climbed out of the car and spotted the car seat in the back of Bobby's SUV. She couldn't wait to see his brand new baby girl, Carly. His wife had gone into labor the day before Riley left for Tokyo, and she'd only seen Carly once at the hospital right after she was born. If she played her cards right, hopefully, she could spend most of the evening playing with the baby and ignoring everyone else.

Bobby greeted her at the door, Carly gurgling in his arms. "Oh, she's so beautiful," Riley cooed. She gave her brother a kiss hello, set her purse on the table near the front door and shrugged off her cotton jacket. "Can I hold her?"

Bobby handed her the baby, and she cuddled Carly into the crook of her arm. She was so small. Her little hands were curled into balls and she had the most amazing long thick eyelashes that fluttered when she blinked. Riley couldn't take her eyes off her. "Oh, Bobby, you and Lynn are so fortunate. She's perfect. You better watch out, I might take her home with me."

"You're welcome to babysit," Bobby replied.

"Oh, I'd love to. Anytime," she said, although she doubted he and Lynn would ever ask. Even though they only lived forty-five minutes apart, they rarely saw one another outside of family events. She looked up at him. "Where's Mom?"

Bobby gestured toward the kitchen and wandered into the neighboring room, leaving Riley standing in the foyer with the baby. The telltale sounds of a football game came from the study, and her brother was probably eager to get back to it. She and Bobby were barely two years apart, but they'd never been close. There was no real reason; they were just different and had generally ignored each other since childhood.

She was much closer to her big brother Beau, but he lived in Singapore and he and his long-term girlfriend, Shelia, only made it home once or twice a year, usually when work brought one of them to the US. Beau was the only person in Riley's family who knew she was gay. She'd never bothered to tell Bobby. She didn't think he'd care all that much one way or another, but they didn't talk about anything personal. When Bobby's wife Lynn was pregnant with Carly, Riley was pretty sure she was the last member of the Bauer family to learn the first grandchild was on the way. It was like telling her had been an afterthought.

When she stepped into the kitchen, her mother looked up from whatever she was cooking. "Hi, honey."

Riley gingerly shifted the baby from her right arm to her left and reached down to snatch a piece of cheese from a platter on the counter. "Hey, Mom."

Her mother smiled. "Look at you, you're such a natural with Carly."

She grimaced slightly. Her mother's comment was a dig. Riley sure would make a good mother if only… "She's such a good baby," Riley replied as she walked around the counter to give her mother a kiss. "How come you didn't tell me Auntie Jo was coming for dinner?"

"Oh, I'm sure I did…"

She let it slide. The last thing she wanted was to get in a fight with her mother. She eyed the various bowls and ingredients arrayed on the kitchen island. "What are you making?"

"Those cucumber salmon boat hors' d'oeuvres your father loves."

"Need a hand?"

"Sure, sweetie, thank you." Her mother pointed toward the baby bassinet/rocker contraption set up near the kitchen table. "You can set Carly in there. She loves that thing."

Riley carefully set the baby down, strapped her in and grabbed an apron from a nearby hook.

It took her mother all of three minutes to bring up *the topic.* "I played tennis with Mrs. Windsor earlier this week… Her nephew Arthur recently moved to Atlanta."

Riley cringed and remained laser focused on the piece of salmon she was trying to roll into a perfect cylinder. "Mmm hmm."

"He's single…"

*Wonderful.*

"And apparently, he's quite handsome. He's just accepted a job with Winkler-Peabody," her mother said, referring to one of the big law firms in downtown Atlanta.

With a forced a smile she said, "Mom, thanks, really, but I'm not interested." *Why do we have to have this conversation every time I'm home?*

"Come on, Riley, it can't hurt to just meet him. You never know…"

"Mom," Riley said, trying her best to suppress her frustration. "Please, can we just drop it?"

Mercifully, Bobby's wife Lynn emerged from the study to check on the baby. Further discussion about the wonderful Arthur Windsor would have to wait until later.

During cocktails, the baby was the center of attention until Lynn took her up to bed before dinner. As soon as the baby was gone, Auntie Jo pounced. "Your mother tells me you aren't seeing anyone…"

Riley grabbed a salmon boat off the platter on the coffee table and chewed it deliberately before responding. "I'm doing just fine, Auntie. No need to worry about me." She gestured toward the coffee table. "These salmon cucumber things are delicious, aren't they?" Her effort to change the subject was futile. Once on a mission, her aunt was not easily deterred. "My Charlie," she said, referring to her youngest son, Riley's cousin, "just got engaged. That means you'll be the only Bauer who's not…"

While her aunt droned on, Riley did her best to zone out, nodding occasionally, until she swore the word "sex" came out of her aunt's heavily lipsticked mouth. All she caught was, "very important to your health." As far as Riley knew, Auntie Jo had fairly conservative views about sex outside of marriage, and therefore, likely assumed Riley was missing out on this important aspect of life. She stared at her aunt. "I'm sorry, what did you, just—"

"Time for dinner gang," her father's voice boomed. "Roasted chicken and all the fixin's."

Auntie Jo never had to be asked twice to come to the dinner table. She excused herself and waddled off toward the dining room. It was just as well. Riley *really* didn't want to hear Auntie Jo's thoughts on sex. It made her think about Auntie Jo and unkie, eww… She ducked into the powder room and tried to purge the image from her brain. After she'd used the toilet, she stared at herself in the mirror while she washed her hands. She looked tired. Probably because she and Kay hadn't gotten a lot of sleep the night before. She let out a chuckle that sounded more like a grunt. If Auntie Jo thought sex was important to your well-being, Riley had been a downright health nut in the last twenty-four hours. If her aunt and mother only knew…

When she emerged from the bathroom, she wedged herself into a seat between her dad and her brother, mindful to sit as far from Auntie Jo as possible. Bobby hoisted the carafe of wine that sat in front of them. "Want some wine, Rye?" he slurred. *Great.* Bobby was already buzzed, and they hadn't even had dinner.

"Just a splash. I need to drive home," Riley said, pausing before she added, "I assume Lynn is the designated driver tonight?"

A flash of anger crossed his face. "What exactly are you implying?"

"I'm not implying anything, Bobby. It was just a question."

He tossed back half his glass. "As a matter of fact, she is."

"Gravy?" her father interjected.

"Sure, thanks, Dad." She drizzled the rich brown liquid over the mountain of peas, mashed potatoes and chicken on her plate and passed the pitcher to her still somewhat irritated brother.

"How's work kiddo?" her father asked.

"Um, work's fine Dad. Never a dull moment."

# CHAPTER SIXTEEN

After spending most of the afternoon at the office, Kay had a splitting headache. On her way home, she stopped to pick something up for dinner, but she practically had to force the food down her throat. She knew she wasn't getting enough to eat lately. Her once perfectly-tailored suits now hung off her frame, but after a few bites, she gave up and stuffed the containers in the fridge.

She tried to busy herself with chores around the house, but it was no use. She couldn't stop thinking about the events at the office that afternoon: the empty drawers in Greg's desk and Riley's ill-timed arrival on the seventh floor. Had Riley seen her rummaging around Greg's desk? It had been practically impossible to read her reaction. She'd handed Kay the pizza and fled almost immediately, although who could blame her? Kay hadn't exactly acted happy to see her.

While she folded laundry, she cocked her head from side to side to try and release some of the tension in her neck and shoulders. When she was done, she went downstairs in search of her phone and began to compose a text to Riley but decided to call her instead. Maybe if they talked on the phone, she'd be able to garner a hint as to what Riley had or hadn't witnessed at the office earlier that day. Riley's phone rang a few times but went to voice mail. She was probably still in Buckhead. Kay stabbed the button to end the call without leaving a message and tossed her phone on the couch in her sunroom, only to snatch it up seconds later when it beeped to indicate an incoming text. It was her brother Doug. *You watching the game? I'm already pulling my hair out.*

Kay's entire family was rabid Jets fans and tonight they were playing the New England Patriots, the team she and her brothers loathed with every bone in their bodies. She hastily responded and reached for her remote to find the game. *Almost forgot. Turning it on now.*

Doug responded immediately with an emoji-laden text. *Almost forgot? I may have to disown you as my sister.* But, moments later another text came in from him. *Everything okay?*

She smiled. Her brother knew something had to be seriously amiss if she'd forgotten about *the* big game. She responded to reassure him she was okay, even though she really wasn't, grabbed a beer from the fridge and sank into the couch. At half time, she tried Riley again. Still no answer. Her anxiety level inched up a notch. She hammered out a quick text. *Tried to call. Hope dinner with your parents was good.* She paused and then added *Miss you* before hitting send.

The football game was a complete blowout. The Patriots were up by twenty points by the end of the third quarter. Kay clicked off the TV, turned out all the lights on the first floor and trudged upstairs to her room. There still was no word from Riley.

The sheets on her bed were twisted in a knot when she woke at six the next morning. She'd slept horribly. Her finger hovered over the snooze button on her alarm as she contemplated skipping her morning run, but a text came in from Riley before she had the chance. *Morning. Sorry I missed your calls. Dinner with my parents was okay. See you at the office.*

Kay stared at the words on her screen, frustrated that the message didn't offer her any real clues about Riley's sentiments. She tossed the phone on her nightstand and swung her feet to the floor. Ten minutes later she was out the door and jogging toward the park.

Later that morning, Kay made her way up to the executive conference room on the tenth floor of the Logan Headquarters. They were scheduled to give Logan's senior leadership a status update on the joint venture with Kamadori. The deal with the Japanese carrier was all but finalized and now it was time to figure out how to implement the various facets of the agreement. Kay stepped off the elevator and strode purposefully toward the conference room, but her confidence vaporized as soon as she stepped inside. A stern-faced Riley was standing in the far corner talking to Greg Brandywine. Her legs trembled slightly as she took her seat near the head of the large oval table.

Moments later, Howard Rome, Logan's CEO entered the room and gruffly called the meeting to order. She caught Riley's eye as she took her seat. Riley gave her a soft smile, but it did nothing to calm Kay's nerves. When it was her turn to speak, she stumbled through her portion of the presentation. Greg approached her after the meeting and asked, "You all right, Kay? You seemed a little off today."

Kay stood tall and looked him in the eye. "Yeah, I'm fine, Greg." She almost mumbled something about being a bit under the weather but held off. She had never been one to make excuses. Greg shrugged and walked away without saying another word, which was just as well. She was eager to catch Riley before she left the meeting. She rounded the table, but Mark Peters, the assistant general counsel, cornered her before she reached Riley. Mark was a brilliant lawyer, but he was also an arrogant prick. By the time he finished droning on, Riley was gone. Kay pulled out her phone and sent her a text. *Are you free for lunch?*

A response came back immediately. *Sure. Meet you downstairs in a few?*

In an attempt to get her emotions under control, Kay took a few deep breaths during the elevator ride to the first floor. It was futile. Her heart was excited to have lunch with Riley, but her brain was in freak out mode. When she stepped into the lobby, Riley greeted her with a smile. That was a good sign.

"Do you have enough time for Fitzgerald's?" Riley asked, referring to the small café a short walk from Logan's headquarters.

Kay checked her watch. "Yeah, that sounds perfect."

"I tried to catch you after the Kamadori meeting," Riley said as they began walking, "but good old Mark Peters was talking your ear off."

The tension in her shoulders eased ever so slightly. "God, I know. The guy is such a bore."

"I've heard he's a bit of a womanizer too and he's clearly a card-carrying member of the Kay Corbett Fan Club."

"He's enamored with anything that has tits. He's been trying to get in my pants for years. Poor guy doesn't realize I bat for the other team."

"I considered running interference, but you're a tough cookie and I figured you could handle yourself."

"He's such a worm, but yeah, nothing I can't handle. If he ever crossed the line, I'd put him in his place so damn fast..."

Riley chuckled. "I bet he'd have an aneurism if he knew we were sleeping together."

Kay laughed out loud. "Ha, you're probably right."

By the time they got to the restaurant, Kay had almost forgotten her worries about Riley, but they came roaring back as soon as they were seated in the restaurant. Nothing Riley did or said seemed out of the ordinary, but still, Kay couldn't shake her paranoia. What had Riley seen the previous day at the office and what were she and Greg talking about that morning before the Kamadori meeting? Over the course of lunch, Kay almost came right out and asked her, but she couldn't get up the nerve. What if she didn't like the answer?

That night when she got home from work, Kay was a complete wreck. Greg had avoided her all afternoon, and Riley had left for a two-day business trip to Boston. On top of that, she still hadn't finished weeding through the data she'd pulled from

Greg's computer two weeks earlier. She grabbed her phone and called Ethan.

As soon as he picked up the phone, she started to cry. Big tough Kay Corbett was starting to crumble. Ethan patiently listened as she told him about sneaking into Greg's office for the second time, only to find nothing and the possibility Riley had caught her in the act. She described walking into the meeting that morning and seeing Riley and Greg talking quietly in the corner. She ended by saying, "And Riley and I had lunch before she left for the airport."

When she finally came up for air, he asked, "Did you ask her if she'd seen you in Greg's office?"

She ran her hand through her hair and sighed into the phone. "No. I was too afraid to hear the answer. What if she did?"

"You really like her, huh?"

"Yeah, Ethan, I do." She sat down on one of the stools in her kitchen and rested her elbows on the island. "And now, what if she thinks I'm a thief and a liar?"

He didn't respond right away. "You need to talk to her," he said finally. "There's no way your relationship with her can move forward if you don't. Even if she didn't see anything, you'll drive yourself crazy wondering if she did."

"So, what am I supposed to say? Hey Riley, did you happen to catch me snooping around my boss's office on Sunday afternoon?"

"Yes, something like that." He shifted into lawyer mode and laid it out for her. "Let's consider the scenarios," he said. "Scenario one. She didn't see you."

"Okay, fine, but if she and I have this conversation, I'll be admitting I snuck into Greg's office. I'll have to give her a damn good reason for why I did."

"That's okay. I think it's time you spell the whole thing out for her."

"You mean tell her about Concordia?"

"Yes."

"I don't know, Ethan. I trust her, but is it really fair to suck her into this mess? I mean, I'm not exactly playing in the kiddie pool here. There are *a lot* of risks."

"You need to tell someone else at Logan. You need an ally, and think about it, she works in Finance. Maybe she has access to documents that'll help support your case."

Kay stood and paced around her kitchen. "I hear you, and I don't disagree. I need an ally, but I also don't want to be selfish. If I tell her, I can't un-tell her. She'll be forced to take on the burden of knowing about Concordia."

"True, but what she does with that information is her decision. She may decide she wants to help, or she may decide she wants nothing to do—"

"With me," Kay said with a laugh.

"I bet she'll want to help."

"I hope so."

"Think about it. If the situation was reversed, wouldn't you want her to tell you, and wouldn't you be eager to help in any way you could?"

"I guess. Maybe you're right."

"I am right."

"What if she flips when I tell her about the price fixing and explain my involvement?"

"If you two keep seeing each other, there's no way you'll be able to keep this whole thing hidden from her. Think about it. You're completely consumed by it. You can't just push it aside when you're with her. Better to find out now how she'll react to the news."

"I suppose," Kay said and sighed deeply.

"But we also need to consider the other scenarios." He cleared his throat. "Scenario two. She saw you but hasn't told anyone."

"In which case, it would also be better to come clean and explain myself."

"Exactly, because otherwise, the foundation of any relationship you build with her will be built on distrust. But, let's also consider the third scenario… She saw you and ratted you out to Greg."

Kay slumped against the counter. "Then I'm just royally fucked."

"Maybe, maybe not. At least you'll have a heads up that shit is about to hit the fan and you can bring what information you have to HR. You know, get ahead of this thing."

"You make it sound so easy."

"Just promise me you'll talk to her."

"I will."

As soon as she got off the phone with Ethan, Kay sent Riley a text—*Can you come to my place for dinner when you get back Wednesday night?*—and paced her house while she impatiently waited for a response. When her phone finally chimed, she snatched it up.

*I'd love to but you've already cooked me dinner once. Why don't you come to my place instead?*

*You can cook me dinner another time, I have something I want to show you.*

It was only eight o'clock, but Kay was exhausted. She wandered upstairs, brushed her teeth and climbed into bed. Her once orderly life was becoming more chaotic and complicated by the minute. For someone who generally tried to steer clear of drama, she was doing a pretty good job of creating a lot of it. Granted, not all if it had been her doing, but much of it was. She was the one who'd decided to try and bring down Concordia, she was the one who'd welcomed Riley into her life, and she was now poised to ask Riley to join her at the edge of a cliff.

Why was it she'd willingly stepped in quicksand? She stared at the ceiling, knowing sleep was a long way off.

# CHAPTER SEVENTEEN

As soon as she landed in Atlanta on Wednesday evening, Riley drove straight to Kay's house. The second Kay opened the door, she knew something was terribly wrong. It wasn't just that she had dark circles under her eyes. There was a coffee stain on the arm of her hoodie, baggy sweatpants hung low on her hips, and although her long, dark hair was pulled back in a ponytail, it had not seen a brush recently.

"What's wrong?" Riley asked.

"A lot. Come inside and I'll try to explain."

Riley shrugged off her coat and hung it on the hook near the door. "Did you go to the office today?"

She shook her head. "No, I called in sick…for only the second time in ten years."

"Do you think you are coming down with the flu or something? We can postpone din—"

"No, I'm not sick, at least not in the traditional sense." A weak smile crossed Kay's face. "I certainly wouldn't have invited you over if I thought I had the flu." She pointed toward the kitchen. "Can I get you anything to drink?"

"Just some water."

They walked back toward the kitchen and Kay sluggishly pulled two glasses out of the cupboard next to the sink and filled them each with tap water. It was like watching a video in slow motion. "Ice?"

Riley shook her head and accepted one of the glasses. "Are you going to tell me what's going on?" she asked, not even trying to keep the concern out of her voice.

"Follow me," Kay said.

Riley's anxiety mounted as they climbed the stairs to the study on the second floor. When Kay had given her a tour of the house a few days earlier, the study had been immaculate, not even a paper clip out of place. Today, the room looked like it belonged to a mad scientist. Papers were strewn everywhere, a pizza box and a dirty plate sat on the small couch in the corner, crinkled soda cans littered the coffee table and two laptops sat open on the desk.

The needle on Riley's concern-o-meter inched into the red zone. It was like someone had kidnapped the dashing confident Kay Corbett and replaced her with a deranged, glassy-eyed look-alike. Riley briefly wondered if Kay was on drugs. She seemed to be getting thinner by the day and she'd occasionally been jumpy and bitchy, a bit on edge. It didn't fit, though. Kay was way too obsessed with health and fitness to be messed up on drugs. *Wasn't she?*

Kay cleared off a nearby chair, pulled it up to the large wooden desk and motioned for Riley to sit. Kay squinted like she was in pain. After a long silence, she said, "Last Sunday, when we were at the office..."

"Uh-huh."

"You came up to my floor, and I was—"

"Just coming out of Greg's office."

Kay crossed her arms. "I was in there for a good reason."

"Okay. I believe you."

"Then…" Kay scratched her head. "What were you and Greg talking about before the Kamadori meeting?"

"God, I don't even remember," Riley said. "Nothing important." She sat back in her chair and stared at Kay. "Why does it matter?"

Kay sat up straight and stared back at her. "I'm about to tell you something really fucked up. Promise me you'll hear me out…and give me your word you won't tell another soul."

"Fuck, you're freaking me out, Kay, but yes, you have my word."

Kay opened her mouth to say something and then snapped it shut.

"What is it Kay? Talk to me."

Kay's eyes hardened. "There is some really, *really* bad stuff going on at Logan. Like people might go to jail kind of bad stuff."

The hair on the back of Riley's neck stood up. "I don't understand," she sputtered. "What are you talking about?"

"It started years ago, but I didn't realize it was going on until I got promoted to VP."

"Realize what was going on?"

"A massive price fixing scheme involving Logan and a number of other airlines…"

Riley couldn't believe what she was hearing. She crossed and then uncrossed her legs. "I don't, I… What do you mean?"

"Logan, or Greg Brandywine, to be specific, is communicating with other airlines to set airfares. That's why, lately, the airline has been able to get away with so many fare increases, across the board."

"You're fucking kidding me."

"I wish I was." A sad smile crossed Kay's face. "Greg's in deep, really deep. He's the de facto leader of a little group he derisively calls *Concordia*. Concordia is a Latin word that roughly means *agreement* or *harmony* in English."

"Okay," Riley said with a nervous laugh. "Latin was never my strong suit, but I'll take your word for it."

"Anyway," Kay continued. "Concordia is comprised of pricing representatives from Logan and a handful of other airlines. The group sometimes convenes in person, but lately they've been communicating by phone, on a regular basis, and even though it's totally fucking illegal, they discuss pricing."

"Are you trying to tell me that Logan and the other airlines have been *colluding* to set prices?"

Kay shifted in her seat. "That's *exactly* what I'm saying."

"Holy shit, that's huge."

Kay took a sip of her water. "Yeah, fucking huge."

"How do they do it? I mean, how do they get away with it?"

"It's complicated and simple at the same time. Most of their scheming surrounds *surcharges*—you know what those are, right?"

Riley tilted her head to the side and shrugged. "Yeah, of course, at least in theory." Working in Finance, she was well aware of surcharges. They added a lot to Logan's bottom line, but she didn't really understand how they worked.

"Let me try to explain," Kay said. "Surcharges are an incredibly handy tool in the wild and wacky world of airline pricing. They're generally a fixed amount—say $100—that gets added on to the published airline fare, and more often than not, they're applied across all citypairs in a given market. For example, you'll probably see the same surcharge applied to all citypairs—Atlanta-Paris, Atlanta-Amsterdam, Atlanta-Frankfurt etc., in the transatlantic market. Airlines like surcharges because they are a quick and easy way to effectively increase or decrease airfares across an entire market all at once. Kay took another sip of her water and looked over at Riley. "Are you with me so far?"

Riley was enthralled. "I think so…You're saying, Logan might have a *published* fare of $500 to travel roundtrip from New York to London, but then they tack on a surcharge, $100 in your example, so the passenger pays $600, plus tax, right?"

"Yeah, that's the gist of it. As I've said, airline pricing is incredibly complex. In reality, Logan doesn't have just one published fare between London and New York, there could be hundreds, maybe even thousands. The fare a passenger sees depends on a million factors such as when they book and when they want to travel, but that's what makes the surcharge scheme even more genius. The airlines in Concordia just have to change one number—the amount of the surcharge—and boom, all fares in a particular market go up or down. That's a heck of a lot easier than changing every single published fare in the market."

Riley was on the edge of her seat, and although Kay had started talking faster and faster, she hung on her every word. "Shit, that is genius. Fucked up, but genius," she said. "Is Greg the one who dreamed this all up?"

"Yes and no," Kay replied. "He *inherited* the price fixing from his predecessor, but he's since perfected it. He's the one who suggested they use surcharges as their lever. I know because he brags about it, although I must admit, it was very clever on his part. It also happens to be a sneaky way to conceal what the airlines in Concordia are doing."

"How do you mean?"

"Well, using your example, Logan can hold their London-New York published fare steady at $500 while simultaneously driving up the overall fare—the fare the passenger actually pays—simply by increasing the surcharge from say $100 to $125."

Riley got the idea. "So the airlines don't have to be perfectly aligned in their published fares—Logan may charge $500 and Zephyr $510 for travel between New York and London, but behind the scenes—"

"They're increasing surcharges in lockstep," Kay said. "And, not only that, surcharges are buried in the price of an airline ticket. That makes them more inconspicuous."

Riley shook her head. She was utterly dumbfounded. "Doesn't it occur to them that someday, someone will catch on to what they are doing? I mean, we're talking an Enron-like scandal. Did people learn nothing from that?"

"Who knows? They're all so damn arrogant. In Greg's case, he thinks he's smarter than everyone else."

Riley couldn't get her questions out fast enough. "So, how did you find out about this secret little group?"

Kay had regained her composure, and aside from her coffee-stained hoody and wild hair, she almost seemed herself again. "Well, once I became a VP, Greg started including me in Concordia meetings and conference calls and I—"

Riley's eyes went wide. "Wait, what? He invites you to the meetings?"

"Yeah, at first, I couldn't believe he looped me in to what was going on, but eventually I realized he really didn't have a choice. I mean, I am the VP of International Pricing. If I was in the dark about Concordia, I'd most certainly push back if he constantly told me when and by how much to increase fares in the markets I oversee." Kay grunted and shrugged. "I've also come to understand Greg's so corrupt, he's completely lost touch with how crazy illegal it all is."

Riley's head was spinning. Kay's story was insane. She squirmed in her chair. "How did you react when Greg first invited you to one of these meetings? You must have freaked."

Kay laughed. "To put it mildly. I was completely flabbergasted. The price fixing is so incredibly blatant."

"So, how does Concordia operate? Is there some sort of secret handshake?"

"The group agrees on a surcharge increase, and then bingo. Practically overnight every single one of the airlines in the group implements it."

"How do they know for certain everyone in the group will follow along?"

"Well, funny you should ask," Kay answered. "I asked Greg that same question once and he, in his typical condescending tone, explained to me that the members of Concordia made a vow early on to never ever deviate from the agreed upon plan. It was as simple as that. The whole thing is stunning both in its precision and its scope." Kay turned toward the computers on her desk. "Here, let me show you."

Riley inched her chair closer and peered over Kay's shoulder at the laptops, both of which displayed spreadsheets with rows and rows of numbers.

"This is surcharge data from Logan and the other airlines in Concordia. I've been tracking them." Kay clicked on one of the spreadsheets. "And I've made all these graphs."

"Oh, wow, where did you get all this data? I mean, I know you'd have access to fares Logan filed, but what about the other airlines."

Kay leaned back against her chair and looked at Riley for a long while before she responded. "I downloaded the data off of Greg's computer a few weeks ago."

Riley was stunned. "You mean you—"

"Yes."

"That's—"

"I know."

Riley took a minute to process what Kay was saying. She'd always been a strict rule follower, and Kay had just admitted to… She looked Kay in the eye. "That took some serious guts. If I'd been in your shoes, I probably would have done the same thing."

Kay visibly relaxed. "Really?"

"Yeah, really. It may sound weird under the circumstances, but I'm proud of you."

"Thanks, I think." Kay stood up and paced. "God, I was so worried about how you'd react. Under normal circumstances, I don't go snooping in people's offices."

"The circumstances are anything but normal," Riley said with a laugh. "Have you told anyone else?"

"No one, well, no one else at Logan. My best friend Ethan knows, but that's it."

Riley's head began to pound. She pinched the bridge of her nose. "You've got to tell someone Kay, like HR or Legal or something. You have to blow the whistle on this whole Concordia thing."

"That's exactly what I intend to do, just not yet."

"Aren't you worried you'll get caught up in this mess? I mean, right now you're an acting participant and you could be found guilty if—"

"I'm well aware of the risks," Kay snapped. She let out a long sigh. "Sorry, it's all just so stressful."

"I can imagine."

"Greg would fire me in an instant if I pushed back on anything Concordia had done."

"And if you get fired, Concordia will keep marching on…"

Kay sat back down. "Exactly, but at the same time, I have to be patient. I need solid evidence before I can accuse a Senior VP, and a bunch of other senior leaders of a major airline of price fixing."

Riley slapped a hand on her thigh. "Have you considered… What if this whole price fixing thing is just the tip of the iceberg, a small piece of a much larger scheme?"

"Say more."

"Like, what if Logan is manipulating their finances—using the higher fares to cover up problems in other parts of the airline?"

"You mean like using the money from the surcharges to prop up the airline's balance sheet?"

"Uh-huh," Riley said.

"That thought had crossed my mind, but I don't have any hard evidence to back it up. Still, I think it's a very real possibility. The fraud might bleed into other parts of the airline." Kay tapped a finger on her desk. "Now that I think about it… On Logan's last earning call, Howard Rome went out of his way to tout the airline's increasingly diverse revenue base."

"You're right. I remember him mentioning that Logan was getting a larger and larger percent of its revenue from non-ticket items like bag fees and those stupid Logan branded credit cards. He knows that's what Wall Street wants to hear these days. But what if revenue from checked bags and all that other stuff really *isn't* growing? What if they're just using the higher fares—which are only achievable because they're fixing prices—to make it look like they are."

"You mean like moving money around?"

"That's exactly what I mean."

"If that's the case, it would mean…"

Riley spread her arms wide. "Yeah, that this thing could be a whole lot bigger. They could be outright defrauding investors." She looked Kay in the eye. "I want to help you."

Kay was desperate for an ally but she needed to make sure Riley understood the risks. "This is not something you can enter into lightly. We could lose—"

"Our jobs," Riley said. "I know."

"That, and a whole lot more. People, powerful people could come after us, threaten us. Not to be overdramatic, but people have lost their lives for sticking out their neck and blowing the whistle." Kay pointed toward her computer. "I could show you dozens of horror stories."

"I've seen some of the stories. We studied them in business school." She paused briefly and said, "I'm willing to take the risk."

"You need to be sure, really sure. Take some time to think about it. When I first started down this road, I thought long and hard about what it could mean for me, for my life. I briefly considered leaving Logan but given my history and my father's history with the airline, I didn't want to turn my back on it and all the good people who work there. Instead, I decided to stay put and do what I could to expose the truth. If I had kids and a family to support, the decision would have been a lot harder."

"I don't need any more time to think about it. I'm in."

# CHAPTER EIGHTEEN

First thing the next morning, Riley cleared her calendar of all but the most essential meetings and locked herself in her office. Her new mission in life was to figure out what other illegal and immoral crap was going on at Logan. The night before, she and Kay had decided she should start with the low hanging fruit—the financial reports Logan and every other publicly traded company filed with the Securities and Exchange Commission (SEC) each quarter. Riley had an MBA, and she knew her way around corporate financial filings better than most people. In fact, she sometimes read them for *fun*.

She navigated to the investor relations page on Logan's website and downloaded the airline's financial reports for the last twelve quarters. Some of the reports were as long as a hundred pages so she only printed out those for the previous four quarters and saved the rest to a thumb drive so she could review them later.

Next, she scrolled through the hundreds of folders situated on the shared drive she and her colleagues in Finance used to store all of their internal documents. It was somewhat mind numbing. She opened Excel spreadsheet after Excel spreadsheet and stared at an endless stream of graphs and charts. Everything seemed pretty innocuous. Financial projections under every possible scenario: high oil prices, low oil prices, soaring global GDP, plunging domestic GDP, expanding Logan's capacity, reducing it, closing one of their hubs, opening a new one, you name it.

Riley was about to get up and go in search of coffee when she spotted a folder named CNCRDIA. Was it possible? She clicked on it. There were dozens of Excel files in the folder, each corresponding to a different quarter. 3Q2018.xlsx, 2Q2018.xlsx etc. The files went back at least five years. Riley tried to open one, but it was password protected. Same for the next one, and the next. "Shit," she muttered and continued down the line, clicking on file after file. "Bingo," she said when the one labeled 1Q2016 finally opened without prompting her for a password. Before she looked at it, she went back and looked for the SEC filing for the corresponding quarter. When she found it, she pulled it up on the computer screen next to the Excel file from the CNCRDIA folder. Her heart began to race as she compared the numbers in the two files, most of them matched, but not all them…

A soft knock on her office door startled her. She quickly saved the Excel file to her flash drive and got up to open the door. It was her boss, Gabe Suarez. He gave her a questioning look. "Hi Riley. Your door was locked."

She turned on her southern charm. "Oh, uh, gosh, was it?" Gabe didn't really seem phased. If her past reviews were any indication, Riley was an exemplary employee, and from her perspective, she and Gabe had an excellent working relationship.

"Do you have a minute?" he asked.

Riley nodded and said, "Sure. Come on in." She walked back toward her desk and that was when it hit her like a ton of bricks. Gabe, a man she respected deeply, might be a key player in the whole Concordia mess. He was the VP of Finance after all. If any financial funny business was happening at Logan, he had to know about it, right? She tried to push the thought out of her mind. Gabe was her mentor. Although it was unlikely, she held on to the hope he wasn't involved. Suddenly, her legs felt like they might give out. She grabbed onto her desk and practically fell into her chair.

"Riley, are you okay?" he asked, concerned.

She tried to keep her voice even. "Yeah, I'm fine. Just a leg cramp from sitting too long." She glanced up at him, praying the panic coursing through her was not manifested in her expression. Somehow she managed a smile, but it didn't last long. The 1Q2016 Excel spreadsheet was still up on her computer screen, and even she, who was so well practiced at the phony southern smile, could not hide the shock from her face.

She scrambled for her mouse and clicked the file shut. It was hard to tell if Gabe had seen it, but given the way her computer screen was positioned on her desk, there was a good chance he had not. She took a deep breath in and a deep breath out. If Gabe was corrupt, he had absolutely zero reason to suspect she knew what was going on at Logan. "What is it you wanted to ask me," she asked as calmly as she could muster.

Gabe gave her an odd look but didn't comment on her strange behavior. Instead he said, "Oh, I had a question about one of the projections in the Kamadori agreement. Would you mind opening the file with the final numbers?"

As soon as Gabe left her office, Riley snatched up her phone and shot Kay a text. *I think I found a smoking gun. Call me.*

While she waited to hear from Kay, Riley frantically downloaded as many files as she could from the Finance department's shared drive, praying she could find more Excel files in the CNCRDIA folder that were not password protected. She cursed the fact that she had meetings all afternoon and a softball game that night. At this point, she was obsessed, and she wanted to keep digging. She needed to find out just how broad and deep the fraud at Logan really was.

"I've got an idea," Kay said when she'd finally called and heard what Riley had discovered on the shared drive. "Why don't we go to New York this weekend and sort through everything we have so far. The pieces of the puzzle are starting to come together."

That evening, Riley printed out as many of the quarterly reports as she could, stuffed them in her bag and rushed off to her softball game. Playing softball did nothing to keep her mind off the potential landmine she'd uncovered at work that day, and the coach pulled her out of the game in the third inning after she walked the fifth batter in a row.

# CHAPTER NINETEEN

The following afternoon, Kay and Riley boarded their flight to New York and settled into their first-class seats, one of the many perks of being a VP for an airline. After a flight attendant appeared with two glasses of bubbling Champagne, Kay raised hers and said, "Here's to a productive weekend in the Big Apple." She took a sip and then reached over to capture one of Riley's hands in her own. "I know it will be a working weekend, but I'm still really looking forward to it."

Riley held her gaze. "Me too Kay. I'm—"

"Hey, Riley. How'd you score a seat in First?" a male voice asked.

Riley looked up and slowly pulled her hand from Kay's. "Oh, hi, Wayne," she said, cringing slightly.

A sinister grin crossed his face as he glanced at Kay sitting in the neighboring seat. "You two, uh, headed away together for the weekend?"

Riley didn't answer his question. Instead, she nodded toward Kay. "Have you two met?"

"Not formally." Wayne eagerly stuck out his hand. "Wayne Jones."

Kay put on a practiced smile and shook his hand. "Kay Corbett."

Wayne was holding up the boarding process and the flight attendant prodded him along to find his seat.

"Who was that?" Kay asked once he was out of earshot.

"A guy I work with in Finance. He's a complete tool."

Kay laughed. "Yeah, I got that sense."

The rest of the flight was uneventful, and even though there was a fair amount of turbulence, the plane touched down at LaGuardia (LGA) right on time, no small miracle for an airport that was notoriously congested—the smallest operational hiccup or weather event often had a major domino effect, causing flights to get delayed for hours.

Once they deplaned, they followed the signs for ground transportation, and thankfully, there was no sign of Wayne. Given he was seated in coach, he probably wasn't even off the plane by the time they were in a taxi. It was six p.m. on a Friday and traffic into Manhattan was heavy.

After they checked into the Hyatt across the street from the New York Public Library and Bryant Park, they quickly freshened up and headed out for dinner. The plan was to spend all day Saturday cooped up in the room, combing through all the intelligence they'd gathered, but tonight, drinks and dinner were on tap.

The concierge at the hotel directed them toward a small neighborhood wine bar a few blocks from the hotel.

"I totally love this place," Riley said as they claimed two stools at the horseshoe-shaped bar. A fire was roaring in the small stone fireplace off to the right. "It's so cozy."

A bartender materialized seconds later. "May I get you two lovely ladies something to drink?" she asked in a husky voice.

"Do you have a wine list?" Kay asked.

"Sure do." The bartender slid two thin leather books in front of Kay. "Wine menu and dinner menu."

"You good with red?" Kay asked Riley.

"Yep."

After she scanned the wine list, Kay looked up at the bartender. "A bottle of the Treetop Cab, please."

The bartender gave her a wink. "Excellent choice. I'll be right back with the wine."

While they waited, Riley flipped open the dinner menu and studied it intently. Kay smiled as she watched her. The expression on her face changed as she read the entrée descriptions—from furrowed brow to wide eyes and pursed lips. Her long blond hair glowed under the lantern-like pendant lights over the bar. *God, she's beautiful.*

It was hard to believe it had only been two weeks since Tokyo. So much had happened since then… Almost overnight, the frenzy of the Concordia nightmare had thrust the two of them so close together. It felt like they were a team, and it was incredibly comforting. Kay had had a crush on Riley since day one, but her feelings were quickly growing much deeper. In the past, that might have scared her, but not this time. She felt elated. That in itself was telling. There was no other place in the world she'd rather be right now.

"Here we go," the bartender said, interrupting her thoughts. "One bottle of the Treetop Cab."

Kay shook her head to get it out of dreamy Riley mode and inspected the bottle. Once she nodded her approval, the bartender whipped a corkscrew out of her back pocket and made quick work of extracting the cork. "Have you two decided on anything to eat?" she asked and gave Kay a splash of wine to taste before pouring them each a glass.

"Oh, gosh. I haven't even looked at the menu," Kay responded.

"No rush. Enjoy your wine. I'll check back with you in a bit." The bartender gave Kay a smile and sauntered down to the other end of the bar.

Riley nudged Kay with her shoulder. "I think she likes you."

"Whatever," Kay said with a wave of her hand. "I hope you know I'm not interested."

Riley smiled. "Don't worry, I'm not the jealous type, but you're a beautiful woman. I bet women flirt with you all the time."

Kay blushed. “Sometimes,” she said, “but, more often than not, it’s men I have to deal with and it’s more irritating than anything. They can’t seem to get it through their thick skulls that I’m not even remotely interested.”

After dinner, they strolled down Fifth Avenue and walked past Rockefeller Plaza. “I can’t believe people are ice skating,” Riley said. “It’s not even Thanksgiving yet. I don’t know, it just feels like skating is something you do in the dead of winter.”

“At least they haven’t put the big Christmas tree up yet,” Kay pointed out.

“Heh, yeah, I guess you’re right, but I’m sure that will happen any day now.”

“Have you ever gone ice skating?”

Riley laughed. “Heck, no. I’m from Georgia, remember?” She looked down at the people circling the rink. “It looks hard. I’m sure I’d fall on my ass right away. Why? Do you want to try?”

“Nah, I don’t do figure skates and I’m pretty sure that’s the only kind they rent here. I’m a hockey skate kind of girl.”

Riley shrugged. “To be honest, I didn’t even know there was a difference.”

“Figure skates have a jagged toe,” Kay explained. “That way you can do twirls and stuff.”

“Like in the Olympics?”

“Uh-huh. But hockey skates aren’t like that. They’re smooth up front.”

“Because hockey players don’t do triple lutzes?”

Kay laughed. “Not usually, except maybe during the playoffs.”

“Let me guess, you were about as likely to be caught wearing figure skates as you were to be wearing a dress?”

Kay put her arm around Riley’s waist and pulled her close. “Yep, pretty much.” It had just started to drizzle. “What do you say we head back to the hotel?”

“How does a bath sound?” Riley asked when they got back to their room.

Kay gave her a thumbs up. “It sounds fantastic.”

Riley wriggled out of her coat and marched into the bathroom to fill the large jacuzzi tub. She shook some bubble bath into the rising water and bubbles begin to sprout. In a matter of seconds, her clothes were pooled on the floor. "Oh my God, this is heaven," she said as she sank into the warm water.

Kay dipped a toe into the water and yanked it out. "Shit, that water is hot."

"No, it's perfect."

Kay lowered one body part at a time into the tub, and when she was finally submerged, Riley floated over next to her and nestled her head against Kay's shoulder.

The warm water gradually soothed Kay's tense muscles. She closed her eyes and savored the feel of Riley's naked body cuddled against hers. They sat in silence for a long while and Kay nearly dozed off.

When the water began to cool, Riley asked, "You ready to get out?"

"I suppose. Want me to grab us each a robe? I saw two hanging in the bedroom closet."

"Thanks, babe." Riley shifted to allow Kay to climb out of the tub.

As Kay toweled off, she saw Riley's eyes roam her body. She smiled. "What are you looking at?"

"Your totally amazing body," Riley said as she climbed out of the tub and grabbed a towel. "You know, I don't think we'll be needing those robes after all." She gently pushed Kay up against the wall, placing one hand on her bare hip and the other behind her head. Their lips came together forcefully, and they stumbled toward the bed.

Kay stepped back slightly, pulled down the covers and playfully pushed Riley down onto the crisp white sheets. As she crawled on the bed, she brushed her lips over the hollow of Riley's stomach, her firm breasts, her collarbone before finding her soft warm lips. The kiss was long and lingering and full of passion. For a brief moment, Kay thought of nothing but the beautiful naked woman beneath her. She ran her hands over Riley's erect breasts, squeezing them gently before sucking hard on one and then the other. Riley squirmed beneath her and spread her legs in response, inviting Kay to dip a hand between them. Kay teased her hard clit before drifting her fingers slowly through the moist folds. Their eyes locked as Kay rhythmically caressed her.

Riley's back arched. "I want you inside me," she croaked.

Kay complied. Slipping two and eventually all four fingers deep into Riley. She climbed up on her knees and hovered over Riley, giving her the leverage to push harder and deeper. "Come for me, baby," she whispered when she felt Riley tighten around her. She pumped until Riley's body jerked beneath her.

"Oh, God, yes." Riley cried out before sinking into the mattress.

Kay slowly extracted her fingers and brought them to her nose, breathing deeply to inhale the scent. "I love fucking you."

Riley threw one leg over Kay's torso and sat up to straddle her. She stared down into Kay's eyes. "I love the way you fuck me." She thrusted her hips back and forth, rubbing herself against Kay. "Now it's my turn. I want to taste you."

A jolt coursed through Kay at the first swipe of Riley's tongue. As the sensation between her legs intensified, she clawed Riley's shoulders. She hung on the edge for as long as she could, but eventually it was too much. She gasped and cried out as the orgasm crashed through her.

Riley snaked up her body and nestled up next to her. Their ragged breathing was the only sound in the room.

# CHAPTER TWENTY

A few laps around the reservoir in Central Park did wonders to get their blood pumping the next morning, and after a quick bite to eat, Kay and Riley got straight to business. By noon, they'd been at it for more than two hours. Three laptops were humming on the small desk in the corner of their hotel room and reams of paper were neatly organized on the bed. "Are you ready to walk me through the financial records?" Kay asked.

"Yeah, I think so," Riley replied. She set down the report she'd been reading, pulled her laptop toward her and looked up at Kay. "Okay, as I mentioned the other day, I stumbled across a folder called 'CNCRDIA' on the shared drive."

Kay nodded. "Morons. You think they would have named it something a little less obvious."

"I know. This brings 'hidden in plain sight' to a whole new level. Anyway, most of the files saved in the CNCRDIA are password protected."

"Not surprising."

"No, but apparently someone got sloppy because I was able to open two of the Excel files. They both contain quarterly financial data." Riley stood up and strode over to the bed, and after scanning the piles she'd laid out, snatched one up and waved it in front of Kay. "This is what Logan filed with the SEC for the first quarter of 2016, but take a look at this…" She sat back down and turned her laptop so Kay could see it. "This spreadsheet also includes the financials for the first quarter of 2016."

Kay donned her reading glasses and pulled a chair up next to Riley. "Okay, let me guess. They don't match."

"No, they don't." Riley used her mouse to highlight the figure for baggage fees on the spreadsheet and pointed to the same line item on her printout. "The figure in the SEC filing is a good bit higher."

"What's your theory?"

Riley leaned back in her chair. "Well, as you know, airlines have made a fortune from charging customers to check bags. The thing is," Riley reached over and grabbed a stack of printouts off the desk, "Logan's revenue from bag fees, as compared to other airlines, started to decline a few years ago and this probably made investors nervous. Bag fees are a major revenue generator, and as we discussed the other night, they help airlines diversify their revenue stream."

"So the airline isn't dependent on airline ticket revenue for all their income."

"Exactly." Riley flipped her printout to a different page. "At the same time, Logan was showing an increase in ticket revenue—the amount passengers are paying in airfare—quarter after quarter."

"Which makes sense," Kay said. "Because Logan was fixing prices and raising airfares across the board."

"Right, but it also made the decrease in bag fees even more curious. Ticket revenue was going up, but bag fees weren't keeping pace. Common sense would dictate that ticket revenue and bag fees should rise in unison, or at the very least, not move in opposite directions."

"So, let me guess, you were right. Logan started to fudge the numbers."

"Yep. They began shifting money from one column to another—from ticket revenue to bag fees—which I'm sure you know, is *not* exactly in line with standard accounting procedures."

Kay tapped her index finger on her lips as she mulled the information. "But, why? Why would they take the risk and move money around? I mean investors are usually just happy to see the bottom line increasing, right?"

"Usually, but it's more complicated than that. I think Logan started to mess with the numbers because the growth in ticket revenue has skyrocketed—"

Kay snickered. "Because they're cheating the system."

"Right," Riley replied, "and this dramatic rise was likely to draw a lot of scrutiny from investors, and maybe even government regulators, especially because the economics of the market haven't exactly been conducive to constant price hikes. Shifting the money around enabled them to conceal the spike in ticket revenue and it also helped to ease investors' anxiety about the lower bag fee revenues."

A lightbulb went off in Kay's head. "So, effectively, they were killing two birds with one stone."

"Yep, and check this out." Riley clicked open another file. "They are doing the same thing with the Logan-branded credit card. They're covering up falling revenues there too."

"Shit, those credit cards are a complete cash cow for Logan. That's why they make flight attendants hawk them to passengers on every flight."

"Uh-huh, and investors would flip if they knew the income from the credit cards was slipping."

Kay ran a hand through her long brown hair. "Fuck, this thing just seems to get bigger and bigger."

"I know. It's downright terrifying how massive the fraud is." Riley closed her laptop. "And the whole scheme is highly dependent on one thing…"

"Airfares need to keep going up," Kay said, "and the best way to make sure that continues to happen is—"

"For Concordia to keep doing what they've been doing, fixing prices."

Kay laughed.

"What so funny?"

"In some perverted way, I almost feel bad for Greg. He's gotten himself in so deep and the whole thing has just snowballed. God, he's got to be under such tremendous pressure. Now I know why he keeps pushing Concordia to take more and more risks."

"Speaking of Greg, did you finish sorting through the data you got off his computer?"

"Yeah, finally, but like I told you the other night, I still haven't been able to find anything recent. It all stops abruptly as of about six months ago."

"Any idea why?" Riley asked.

"My only guess is that he's started to panic, started to worry that someone—investors or the SEC—is going to figure out what's going on. Although that hasn't stopped him from acting like a cocky asshole."

"Any idea where he's keeping the most recent data?"

Kay shook her head. "I don't know, but if I had to guess, I'd say his house."

"You know what I don't get?"

"What?"

"I work in Finance. How did I not know any of this shit was going on?"

Kay pursed her lips while she decided how to respond. "For a few reasons," she said finally, and took one of Riley's hands in her own. "First, and don't take this the wrong way, you're a General Manager, not super high up the totem pole yet. People above you have been doing a masterful job of covering it all up. I mean, think about it. They've fooled a lot of people on Wall Street. And, second, your specialty is analyzing agreements we enter into with other airlines. You don't work on the financial reporting side of things."

"Maybe you're right. I just find it hard to believe that this is all going on right under my nose."

"Don't beat yourself up about it. My guess is most people at Logan have no idea the airline is scheming investors *and* passengers."

Riley slumped in her chair. "It's just so depressing." She looked up at Kay. "So, where do we go from here?"

Kay nibbled on her bottom lip. "I don't know." She was quiet for a minute. She had another question on her mind. She looked Riley straight in the eye. "Can I ask you something?"

Riley twirled a pen in her fingers. "Of course."

"Have you thought about the fact that Gabe Suarez is probably caught up in all of this?"

"Yes," she said quietly. "I know it's possible."

"I'd say it's highly probable, Riley. He's the VP of Finance and the corruption has to reach to the top. There's no other way—"

"My brain knows that, but my heart isn't ready to accept it quite yet. He's been such a mentor to me."

Just then, another thought occurred to Kay. She felt the blood drain from her face. *Maybe some of the other airlines in Concordia were tweaking their finances too. What if Zephyr was one of them. That could mean…her friend Jessica in London might be up to her eyeballs in this mess. Hadn't she mentioned working on something related to Zephyr's co-branded credit card?* The thought made her shiver.

# CHAPTER TWENTY-ONE

Riley's coworker gave her the evil eye for at least the third time, but who could blame him? She'd been obsessively tapping her pen on the table for practically the entire thirty-minute meeting. She couldn't help it; she was nervous. The next meeting on her calendar was her monthly one-on-one with Gabe. They'd met loads of times over the years, but this time was different. Now, Riley had this nagging doubt about him. Was Gabe the hardworking and honest man she'd always thought he was, or was he a corrupt bastard like Greg Brandywine? The thought made her wince. She tucked the pen in her bag, clasped her clammy hands in her lap and tried to focus on the PowerPoint presentation her colleague was giving.

Ten minutes later she was standing outside Gabe's door, waiting for him to finish talking to some guy Riley had never seen before. He had fire-red hair and looked like he belonged on a rugby field. When Gabe finally waved her in, he said, "Morning, Riley. How was your weekend?"

The hairs on Riley's arms stood up. Normally this would be an innocuous question, but not today. Not after Riley had spent the entire weekend reading sham financial documents. Gabe didn't look any different to her. He hadn't grown fangs or anything. She held on to the glimmer of hope that by some miracle, his hands were clean. "Hi, Gabe. My weekend was, uh, good, I went to New York and—"

"I heard," he replied.

She was caught off guard. "Oh?"

Gabe pointed in the general direction of the cubicles clustered outside his office. "Wayne said he saw you on the flight to New York."

*Fucking Wayne*. "Oh, um, yeah."

Gabe leaned back in his chair and tucked his hands behind his head. "I didn't realize you and Kay Corbett were *seeing* each other."

Riley bit down hard on her lower lip. Her mind raced. Something about Gabe's demeanor and his tone made her squirm in her chair... Was this just small talk? They didn't typically discuss her personal life, although she was pretty sure he knew she was gay—or was he insinuating something? She tried to read his expression. He didn't look angry or uneasy. Was he worried about her consorting with the VP of Pricing? Did he have reason to worry she'd been able to connect the dots? She tried to smile. "Um, we've been spending time together, yes."

"I see," he said and then abruptly shifted gears. "Are you ready to go over the numbers we discussed last week?"

Riley nodded. "I sent you an email this morning. If you open the attachment, I can show you what I've come up with so far."

As they walked through her spreadsheet, Riley edged toward full freak out mode. What ifs swirled through her mind. *What if* Gabe *was* involved? *What if* he had discovered she'd been poking around in the CNCRDIA folder on the shared drive? *What if* he got notifications when the files were opened? *I'm an idiot, I should have been more careful.* She nodded in response to something Gabe was saying, but she wasn't really paying attention. When the meeting was over, she practically bolted from his office. She pulled out her phone and hammered off a message to Kay. *Meet me outside in five. It's important.*

She dropped her laptop on her desk, yanked her coat off the door and darted down the stairs.

Kay stepped off the elevator a few minutes later. "What's going on?"

Riley pointed toward the front door. "Not here. Let's walk the perimeter," she said, referring to the gravel walking path that circled the Logan campus.

As soon as they got outside, Riley started talking a mile a minute. "I just met with Gabe. I think you're right; he's involved. He asked me about you, about us. It was weird. He was acting weird. Kay, I'm flipping out. I think this whole thing is about to explode."

Kay linked her arm through Riley's. "Breathe baby, breathe. I don't blame you for being paranoid. This whole thing is a bigger shit show every day, but we've got to do our best to stay calm."

"I can't. What if Gabe knows? What if he knows I downloaded the files—"

"Shhh, calm down. I'm sure he doesn't know, and remember, you accessed them on a *shared* drive. A drive everyone in your department has access to."

Riley yanked her arm free and glared at Kay. "I can't calm down. We need to do something. We need to tell someone, now!"

Kay gently touched Riley's arm, but her voice was stern. "Not yet. You need to trust me. I've been entangled in the whole Concordia mess for a lot longer than you have."

Riley jammed her hands in her pockets and stomped ahead.

"Please, baby," Kay pleaded. "Please trust me."

Riley plopped down on one of the benches along the path. "I do trust you, with my whole heart, but what are we waiting for?"

Kay sat down next to her and reached for her hand. "I just don't want to pull the trigger before we're ready. The accusations we're making… We need to be damn sure we can back them up."

Riley shook her head. "Think about it, Kay. You've recorded Concordia meetings, taken copious notes, compiled months of pricing data, created fancy Excel charts. And now, on top of all that, we've uncovered the financial irregularities."

Kay leaned back against the bench and closed her eyes. After a long moment, she opened them and said, "Maybe you're right, but it's just such a big step."

Riley wrapped her hands around Kay's. "I'm just scared. Scared that this thing is going to blow up and take you down with it."

"I'm scared too. I just don't know what to do." Kay looked down at her watch. "Shit, I have to go. As luck would have it, I have to meet Greg for a Concordia call in ten minutes."

"Are you taking the call from the parking garage at the airport?"

"Yeah. Same drill as always."

"Well, be careful."

"I will."

Greg grunted a hello when Kay climbed in his Porsche. "Did you bring the reports I asked for?" he asked as he threw the car into reverse and peeled out of the Logan parking lot.

Kay looked at him and nodded. He looked like shit and his upper lip had this weird twitch. She'd never seen him like this. He'd even been sneaking outside for an occasional cigarette, a habit he'd kicked years before. Maybe he was about to crack. Kay went out on a limb. "Maybe we should hit the pause button on all this?" she asked.

"Don't be ridiculous, Kay."

"I'm serious. How can you sleep at night?"

Greg gave her a sad smile. "There's nothing to worry about unless…"

"Unless what?" she asked.

"Someone opens their big mouth." Greg gripped the steering wheel tightly with both hands and wound the car up to the top level of the parking garage.

Kay watched the planes take off on a nearby runway as Greg dialed into the Concordia conference call. Right now, she'd kill to be on a plane heading as far away from Greg as possible.

Greg put his phone on speaker. "Hey, gang. "How's everyone doing today?"

A few responses echoed over the phone line.

"Good old Kay thinks we should hit the pause button on the price increases? She's worried someone is going to figure out what we're up to. Anyone else on the call agree with her?"

No one uttered a word. Greg's question was greeted with complete silence.

# CHAPTER TWENTY-TWO

Kay felt especially out of sorts that night. The Concordia call that afternoon had only gotten worse as it went on. Greg goaded her repeatedly for being a coward, and each time the other participants had snickered. Riley was working late, trying to finish a report that was due the next day. Kay mindlessly puttered around her house while she waited for her to get home from the office.

*Maybe Riley was right. Maybe it was time to take what they had and go to HR?* She was about to call Ethan to get his two cents on the matter when she heard a knock at the door. She wandered out toward her front foyer. "Rye, is that you?" She stuffed her phone in her pocket and opened the door. "Did you forget your—"

"Hi, Kay."

Kay took a step backward. Her friend Jessica from London was standing on her front stoop and she looked pissed, really pissed. "Um, hi," she stammered. "What are you doing here? I didn't know you were in town. I…"

Jessica pushed her way into the house. "Surprise," she said, her expression devoid of emotion. "I'm in town."

Kay backed away from the door, nearly tripping over a pair of running shoes she'd carelessly left on the floor.

"It was a last-minute trip," Jessica said. She didn't elaborate. She glared at Kay. "You aren't about to do something stupid, are you?"

"What are you talking about?"

"Come on Kay, you're a bright woman. I think you can figure it out."

Kay took a deep breath and tried not to flinch under Jessica's stare. "Maybe you should spell it out for me."

Jessica rolled her eyes. "I'm talking about Concordia. Ring a bell?"

"Concordia?"

"Oh, spare me the act, Kay."

Kay dropped the guise. Apparently, her suspicions about Jessica had been right. "How the hell do you know about Concordia?"

"I work for Zephyr. Did you forget?"

"No, of course not. I just didn't know… I thought you worked in marketing. I didn't realize you knew about…"

"I do work in marketing."

"But, then…"

Jessica stepped into Kay's space. "You remember when Nicholas threatened to pull Zephyr out of Concordia?"

Kay didn't say anything.

"And you called him and begged him to reconsider?"

She remembered the day as clearly as if it had been yesterday. Greg Brandywine had put her up to the task and she'd only called Nicholas in an effort to gain Greg's trust, prove to him she was all-in as far as Concordia was concerned. "I, um…"

"Imagine that. I've rendered the wonderful Kay Corbett speechless. Someone get me an award." Jessica laughed at her own joke. "Well, guess what? Nicholas and I have been having an affair for months. I was at his house the night you called. I heard it all." A wicked grin crossed her face. "Better yet, I recorded it."

Kay gasped audibly.

"I thought that might get your attention. It's going to be pretty hard to deny your role in the group with evidence like that, huh?"

"Are you threatening me?"

Jessica lurched toward her. "Damn right I am," she yelled. "You go babbling about Concordia, I'll sink you. Drag your fucking name through the mud."

"I'm shivering in my shoes."

"You always were a little too arrogant for your own good. People will be waiting in line to get a piece of you. I'd watch your back if I were—"

"What the hell is going on in here?" Riley asked as she stepped into the house.

Both Kay and Jessica turned to her.

Jessica cackled. "Oh, let me guess. You're Riley. The young little cupcake Kay fucked in Tokyo." Jessica looked Riley up and down. "Pretty, very pretty. Kay always knew how to pick 'em."

Kay put her hand on Jessica's chest. "I think you should leave *right now*."

"Or what, Kay?

"Or I'm going to kick your ass," Kay said. Jessica was bigger than she was, but Kay was in much better shape. From the looks of it, Jessica hadn't seen the inside of a gym in a very long time.

Riley walked over next to Kay. "We're both going to kick your ass."

Jessica grabbed her purse off the floor and stormed out of the house. She stopped and looked over her shoulder. "You're in way too deep, Kay. There's no way out. Trust me, I know."

Kay was too stunned to move. She watched Jessica march down her driveway and climb into the backseat of a big black Mercedes sedan.

"What the fuck was that all about?" Riley asked after she'd closed the door behind them.

Kay explained who Jessica was and gave her a quick synopsis of what had happened.

"She just showed up here?"

Kay nodded.

"Jesus Christ, are you okay?" Riley grabbed her hand. "Shit, Kay. You're shaking."

"I'm fine." But she wasn't fine at all, she just didn't want to admit how much Jessica's visit had shaken her. "She's more bark than bite. I bet Greg put her up to it."

"I can't believe she heard you on the phone with Nicholas?"

"I know. That's a game changer."

"We've got to tell someone. We've got to blow the whistle before someone else does. Otherwise…"

"Otherwise, I might go down with the ship. They'll think I'm just as guilty as everyone else."

"Exactly," Riley said.

Kay let out a long sigh. "But blowing the whistle is a *very* big step."

Riley rubbed her back. "A step we've been working toward."

"I know, Rye, but it is not a step to take lightly. All hell could break loose. Greg, and everyone else who's caught up in the mess, won't stand by idly. They'll come after us. There's no telling what they'll do to keep the truth from getting out."

"You're scaring me, Kay."

Kay wrapped her arms around Riley. "You should be scared. We should both be scared."

Riley stepped back. "This is getting out of control."

Kay stifled a laugh. "Getting out of control? It's been out of control for a very long time."

Riley took her hand and pulled her down on the couch. "We don't have a choice. We have to tell someone. And remember, this isn't just about us. We've got to remember what drove us to swim in the shark-infested waters."

An image of Greg's smirking face popped into Kay's head. "To stop the fraud. To get the cheating fucking bastards."

"That, but also to bring it all to light. To let people know, people like our passengers who are paying higher fares because of Concordia, and people like Logan's investors who are being fed a pile of bullshit about the airline's financials."

Kay leaned back against a plush cushion and put her feet up on the coffee table. "In my heart I know blowing the whistle is the right thing to do. It's just… I don't know. We'd be taking such a huge risk. That, and I think about people like my dad who worked for Logan for his entire career. The airline is everything to him and when he finds out about all this, it's going to kill him. He may never forgive me."

"I've never met your dad," Riley said, "but from what you've told me, he's a good honest person. I find it hard to believe he won't support what we're doing. It will be a blow to him, for sure, but he's got to see we don't have a choice."

"But we do have a choice."

"Do we? You're trying to tell me you'll be okay stuffing all the evidence we have into a box and just forgetting about it. You're willing to continue being a key player in Concordia?"

"No, I'm not saying that."

"I can't believe, after all we've been through, that you're getting cold feet. I mean, why the hell have we been wasting our time gathering all this evidence if we aren't going to do anything with it?"

"I'm not getting cold feet. This is a big deal."

"No shit, it's a big deal," Riley sat on the edge of the couch, "but if we don't speak up, someone else will."

"I know, we've been through that."

"Well it's settled then," Riley said. "We need to go to HR. First thing Monday. We'll take the next few days to get our ducks in a row."

Kay was quiet for a long time as she thought it through. "Under one condition."

"What's that?"

"I'm going alone."

"To hell you are."

"It's not open to debate. I don't want you dragged into this mess."

"It's a little late for that, don't you think? I helped uncover—"

"Riley, I'm in deep. My hands are dirty. Yours aren't. I'd like to keep it that way."

# CHAPTER TWENTY-THREE

The head of HR at Logan was a woman named Heather Corn. Kay considered her a friend. They'd served on a few committees together and they were often the only two women in the room. Heather had a reputation for being a straight shooter, and Kay hoped she'd be willing to listen to what she had to say. On the Monday before Thanksgiving, she showed up outside Heather's office unannounced. After convincing the HR admin that it was an emergency, she was escorted into Heather's office.

Heather was pleasant at first, but her southern charm faded fast. Just as she and Riley had rehearsed over the weekend, Kay began with a summary of the corruption she'd witnessed, but before she could finish, Heather interrupted. "These allegations are *very* serious, Kay."

"I understand that. I wouldn't be here if I wasn't absolutely sure." Kay pulled her laptop out of her bag and set it on Heather's desk. "I've got extensive evidence…"

Heather pointed a long, pink fingernail at Kay's laptop. "Put that away. Who do you think you are, Jessica Fletcher?"

If the situation hadn't been so serious, Kay would have laughed. Heather certainly was aging herself. Jessica Fletcher was an amateur detective in the 1980's show *Murder, She Wrote*. She cleared her throat. "Heather, if you'd just take a look, you'd see—"

"If you know what's good for you, you'll stand up and walk out of this office right now," Heather replied with snarled lips, "and not utter another word about this nonsense, to *anyone*."

Kay looked blankly at Heather. She was in utter disbelief. She stuffed her laptop back in her bag and said, "You're making a big mistake. This is going to get out sooner or later."

Heather stood from behind her desk. "You don't know when to shut up, do you, Kay? I've always noticed that about you."

"And I've always thought you were honest and trustworthy," Kay retorted. "Obviously, I was wrong."

Heather walked out from behind her desk. "I'm going to pretend this little meeting never happened." She wagged a finger at Kay. "And I'd strongly encourage you to do the same."

Kay stood. She towered over Heather's and she tried to use that to her advantage. "You're going to regret this."

"I've warned you, Kay. There are certain people in this organization, people with a lot of power, who will make you pay dearly if you step out of line." The look on Heather's face softened ever so slightly. "You just need to put your head down and do your job."

Kay didn't respond. She grabbed her bag and marched out of Heather's office. She took the elevator to five. She needed to talk to Riley.

"Baby, are you okay?" Riley glanced at her watch. "I thought you were on your way to HR."

"I was."

"Did Heather refuse to see you?"

"No, she saw me."

Riley shook her head. "I don't understand."

Kay kicked the office door shut and flopped down in one of the chairs opposite Riley's desk. "Our meeting was brief. Very brief." She gave her a quick overview of what had happened.

"No fucking way."

"I told you this was a bad idea. Now I've got a target on my back and for what?" Kay set her elbow on the desk and rested her head on her hand. "I feel so powerless."

Riley leaned forward and looked Kay straight in the eye. "You are not powerless. We're going to figure out a plan B."

Kay held back tears. "I don't know, Rye."

"We're a team, you and I, and we are *not* going to back down now."

"I'm probably going to get fired. They're probably drawing up the paperwork as we speak."

Riley shook her head. "Heather isn't that stupid. She knows that would be the worst thing to do. Kicking you to the street would only add fuel to the fire. That, and you know too much for them to cut you loose."

Kay sat upright. "Fuck Rye. I *do* know too much—way too much—and now they know I pose a threat."

"Jesus, Kay. What the hell have we gotten ourselves into?"

"A massive snake pit." Kay banged her fist on the desk. "But you know what? You're right. I'm not going to let those fucking bastards scare me away."

Riley shot both hands into the air. "Now you're talking."

"How come you're so brave?"

"I'm not brave. I just refuse to be a coward."

Kay felt her eyes moisten, but this time it wasn't out of fear or anger, it was the wave of emotion she felt for the strong, beautiful woman sitting across from her.

Riley swiveled back and forth in her office chair. "You know what I don't get?"

"What?

"How did all these seemingly smart, accomplished people get caught up in this fucked-up shit and why do they continue to play a role in it?"

Kay yanked a tissue from the box on Riley's desk and dabbed her eyes. "It's simple. Good old fashion greed."

"Sure, maybe, but Greg, Gabe, although the jury's still out on whether he's directly involved, Heather and God knows who else, they're taking so much risk. I can't wrap my head around it."

"My guess is they all got sucked in slowly, sort of like me. Now their hands are dirty. At the same time, they're all directly benefiting from the corruption. Logan's share price is through the roof, which means Greg and everybody else involved are getting bigger bonuses, larger profit-sharing payouts…"

"One of them has got to crack soon," Riley said.

"Yeah, you'd think."

"In the meantime, we need to talk to a lawyer, ASAP."

Kay nodded. "That, and be careful, very careful."

# CHAPTER TWENTY-FOUR

"I need a drink," Kay said when they got home that night. "Preferably a stiff one." She'd been on pins and needles after her meeting with Heather Corn and the truth was, even though she'd talked a big game in front of Riley, she was petrified about the ramifications of having gone to HR. It was so messed up—going to HR had been the *right* thing to do—but she couldn't shake the feeling she might pay dearly for speaking out. Still, as long as Riley was at her side, she was determined to march forward.

"What a fucking day, huh?" Riley asked. "Why don't you call Ethan, and I'll make us each a dirty martini."

Kay gave Riley a peck on the cheek. "Sounds like a plan." Earlier that day, she'd suggested they ask Ethan for advice. Not only was he her best friend, but he was a lawyer, a very good one. "I'm going to run upstairs real quick," Kay waved a hand down her body, "and get out of this suit and then I'll call him." She looked over at Riley. "Did you bring a change of clothes?"

Riley held up an overstuffed tote. "Yep."

Once they were changed, Riley pulled the vodka out of the freezer and dug the martini shaker out of the liquor cabinet. Kay sat at her kitchen island and dialed Ethan. After a little small talk, she filled him on the events with Heather earlier that day. "Hold on a sec," she said, pausing while the shh-icka shh-icka sound of a martini shaker filled the room.

When it was quiet again, she continued. "You know that theory Riley and I had, the one about how the fraud at Logan might be more widespread?"

"Yeah," Ethan replied.

"Well, Riley did some digging into some of Logan's financial filings and turns out we were right."

"You're kidding?"

"You know me," Kay replied. "I wouldn't kid about something like this. Logan is using the increased revenue from fares to cover up problems elsewhere in the airline." Kay went on to tell him about the sagging bag fee and credit card revenue and how it appeared Logan was filing altered financial reports with the SEC.

"Wow," Ethan replied. "That means they are intentionally misleading investors. That's seriously fucked up. We're talking *massive* fraud."

"No shit, Ethan. That's why I'm calling you. We think it's time to talk to a lawyer."

"I think that would be wise. But you know Kay, if you continue to plow forward, things are only going to get more difficult. What you witnessed today when you confronted HR could be nothing compared to what you might face down the road. I just need to put that out there."

"Riley and I know we're walking down a perilous path. We're not backing down."

"Okay, if you're sure…you need to talk to someone who specializes in cases involving securities violations. Someone who's—"

"Hold on Eth. Riley's here too. I'm going to put you on speaker."

Ethan's voice filled the room. "Hi, Riley."

"Hi, Ethan. Nice to finally meet you."

"Nice to meet you too. Wish it was under better circumstances."

Riley handed Kay a very full martini glass and said into the phone, "So, you were saying we need to talk to…"

"An attorney who has experience with securities violations, someone who knows how to deal with the SEC."

"The SEC?" Kay asked. "But wouldn't the price fixing be considered an antitrust violation, like the Sherman Act, Federal Trade Commission kind of stuff?"

"Yes, Kay. You're right," Ethan replied. "Price fixing would fall under the FTC and they may very well get involved with this at some point, but if Logan *is* deceiving their investors, that's SEC territory. They deal with that kind of fraud and they have a very well-established whistleblower program. You know what a whistleblower is right?"

"Yes, of course," Kay replied. "It's someone who blows the whistle to alert people that something illegal is going down."

"Correct. Not to get all legal eagle on you, but if what you tell me is true, Logan is engaging in earnings management. The airline is adjusting, to put it judiciously, their financial filings to camouflage poor performance in bag fee and credit card revenue—and I think the SEC would be *very* interested to hear about this."

Riley piped in. "Not only that. Logan's creating the *illusion* of stellar revenue growth. They are artificially pumping up revenue by colluding with their competitors to fix prices."

"You're correct, Riley," Ethan said, "and the SEC is the government agency that's supposed to protect investors from fraud."

"So, do you happen to know anyone who specializes in this area of the law?" Kay asked.

"Not off the top of my head, but hang on a sec…"

Riley nodded toward Kay's martini glass. "Taste good?"

"God, yes. Just what the doctor ordered. Thank you."

Ethan came back on the line a few moments later. "I got a name. Fred Archie. He's based in Atlanta and he specializes in securities law. I'll text you his contact information."

"Fred Archie," Kay said. "That's a funny name."

Ethan laughed. "Yeah, I know. He's one of those people you always call by their first and last name, but according to my law school buddy, he's a brilliant attorney."

"Okay, thanks Eth," Kay said. "I'll give him a call. I hope he'll listen to us. I'm a little jaded after my interaction with HR earlier today."

"I won't sugarcoat it," Ethan replied. "Attorneys like Fred typically work on a contingency basis and they'll only take cases they think are rock solid. But, based on what you've told me, he'd be insane not to hear you out. You just need to clearly lay out the facts for him."

Kay put in a call to Fred Archie first thing the next morning, but given the impending Thanksgiving holiday, he was out of the office until the following week.

"Can I get on his calendar for a meeting early next week?" Kay asked his admin.

"I'm afraid not," the admin said. "Mr. Archie won't meet with anyone until he, or someone else at the firm, has had a chance to vet them on the phone first."

"Please," Kay pleaded. She tried to convey the urgency of the situation, but the admin was not swayed.

"As you can imagine, we get calls from a lot of crack balls," the admin said. "People who've read the news about big whistleblower payouts and think they can get in on the action by reporting this or that infraction about their employer."

Kay finally relented and scheduled a time to do a phone interview with Fred in early December, but the admin's comments had rattled her. A wave of nausea swept through her as soon as she got off the phone. She took a long pull from the water bottle on her desk and used a leftover napkin to dab the sweat beading on her brow. *What if Fred Archie wouldn't take their case? What if he didn't think they had enough evidence? There was only one choice, she had to go to the one place where there might be more.*

Kay grabbed her cell phone. "Do you have any plans the first Saturday in December?" she asked as soon as Riley picked up.

"Um, not that I can think of. Why?"

"Greg Brandywine is throwing his annual holiday party. He loves showing off his exquisite house in Buckhead and his wife lives to entertain. They always invite all the big wigs at Logan. I hadn't planned to go, but—"

"Now you're reconsidering."

"Yes."

"May I ask why?"

"Well," Kay said, "because if he's hiding the missing pricing data at his house, maybe we can find it."

"You can't be serious, Kay."

"I'm dead serious. We don't have a choice. We've got to get our hands on that data. It'll strengthen our case."

# CHAPTER TWENTY-FIVE

As they did every year, Riley and her family attended the annual holiday dinner dance at the country club the Saturday after Thanksgiving. The party was held early enough in the evening so that people with children of all ages could attend and the club hired a Santa to roam the party and hand out candy canes and Christmas ornaments. Even though it could be a little bit chaotic, Riley generally enjoyed the celebration. A lot of the kids she'd grown up with also attended with their families, and it gave her a chance to catch up with them.

Riley's friend Sally ambled over to her just before everyone sat for dinner. She had a toddler on her hip and her bulging belly signaled another baby was on the way. "When are you due?" Riley asked.

"Super Bowl weekend, if you can believe it. Johnny," she said, referring to her husband, "has already told me I better not go into labor during the game."

Riley chuckled. "Well, it's not like you have a lot of control over that. Certainly, he'll be understanding if it happens."

Sally rolled her eyes. "Yeah, fat chance." She shifted her toddler from one hip to the other. "How about you, Riley? Any wedding bells in your future?"

"No, I'm, um, seeing someone, but it's still pretty new."

"You should bring him by the club sometime. Maybe we can all have dinner or something."

Riley thought of Kay. She took a sip of her wine and smiled into her glass. "Um, yeah, maybe."

Sally's toddler started to wail. "I should probably bring him down to the nursery. Good to see you Riley."

Riley waved goodbye and scanned the room in search of her parents. She spotted her father talking to Philip, one of the boys she'd dated briefly in high school, and she wandered over to say hello.

"Hi pumpkin," her father said. He tipped his tumbler of bourbon toward Philip. "Phil here is joining my firm right after the first of the year."

Riley tried to hide her surprise. "Here in Atlanta?"

Philip looked down at his beer and then up at her. "Um, yeah."

"But, I… I'm sorry, it's none of my business." When Riley had seen Philip at the club the previous Thanksgiving, he and his wife had just finished building a house in Vermont and he was working for a small law firm in Burlington.

"It's okay," Philip said. "Kelly and I are getting divorced. It's for the best. I was like a fish out of water up there in the Green Mountain State."

"Oh, gosh. I'm sorry to hear that," Riley said sincerely. Philip was a good guy and even though she'd only met his wife a few times, she seemed pleasant enough.

Just then a bell rang to summon everyone to their tables for dinner.

"It was really nice to see you Riley," Philip said.

"You too," she replied. "Good luck with, um, everything."

She followed her father to the big round table reserved for the Bauer family. Her mother was already seated when they arrived, and she motioned for Riley to take the seat next to her.

She obliged. She took the white linen napkin off the table in front of her and set it in her lap.

"Are you having a nice time sweetie?" her mother asked.

"Yeah, I am." She looked up at her mother. "You did a great job with the decorations." Her mother served on the committee that organized the party every year.

"Thanks, honey." Her mother glanced around the room. "I must admit, we really outdid ourselves."

Riley took a sip of water and nodded.

"I saw you talking to Philip. You know, he and his wife have separated."

"So, I heard."

"You two made such an adorable couple…"

"Jeez mom, they aren't even divorced yet."

"I know, darling, but he's quite a catch. I'm sure he'll get snapped up the second he's back on the market."

She groaned in response. *Back on the market*. For God's sake, it was like she was talking about a front entrance colonial in a sizzling real estate market.

A waiter approached their table. "May I get anyone a drink?" He was quite effeminate and had a high-pitched voice.

Her father ordered two bottles of wine and the waiter ran off to get them.

Before he was even out of earshot, her mother leaned over and whispered, "We always get that fellow as a waiter. He's obviously, you know…queer."

Riley was mortified. She knew exactly what her mother was implying. The guy was obviously gay. "He's a very good waiter," she said flatly.

"Yes, yes, he is."

Riley stood. "If you'll excuse me for a moment."

She wandered back toward the kitchen in search of their waiter. She was certain he'd overheard her mother's crass comment.

"Is everything all right, Ms. Bauer?" he asked when she approached.

"Yeah, everything is fine. I just wanted to apologize for my mother's comments. They were terribly insensitive."

The waiter patted her on the shoulder. "You're sweet to come over, but that sort of thing comes with the territory, honey." He gave her a weak smile. "You've gotta have thick skin if you want to work at this place."

# CHAPTER TWENTY-SIX

When Greg's house came into view, Kay clutched the steering wheel of her Jeep. The massive Georgian was all lit up. Little white lights adorned every inch of its façade and a huge Christmas tree glowed from inside.

She inched up the large circular drive to the front door and a valet in an ill-fitting tuxedo greeted them. Riley grasped her arm as they made their way toward the house, her high heels no match for the cobblestone driveway.

They checked their coats at the door and went in search of the bar. Kay eyed the crowd as they made their way across the massive living room. The party had only started, but there had to be at least a hundred people, mostly employees of Logan and their spouses, milling around the house already. When they reached the bar, both she and Riley asked for a glass of Cabernet, which, knowing Greg, was probably some overpriced trophy wine. Kay fidgeted with the string of pearls around her neck while the bartender wrestled the cork off a fresh bottle.

When they stepped away from the bar, Mark Peters, the assistant general counsel, waved them down and he and his wife spent the next twenty minutes droning on about their recent trip to Cabo and the house they were building in Marietta. Even with his wife standing by his side, Mark was as grabby as ever, and Kay wished they would disappear into thin air. She collapsed against Riley when they finally excused themselves to go terrorize another couple.

While Riley went to the bar to get them each a sparkling water, Kay leaned against the fireplace mantel and took some calming breaths. She had to get her head in the game and keep her eye on the prize. They weren't here for the expensive wine and holiday cheer. They had a job to do.

Riley gave her an encouraging smile when she returned with their drinks. "It's time," she said.

Kay threw back half her glass of water. "I know."

"It's now or never."

Kay had been to Greg's house twice before—once for a coworker's retirement party and once when one of Greg's kids graduated from high school. There were two bathrooms on the main floor, a powder room off the kitchen/family room, and a full bath on the other side of the house, directly across the hall from Greg's study. The crowd in the living room had thinned a good bit as people had migrated to the mountains of food spread out in the dining room and family room. Kay took some comfort when she spotted Greg standing off to the side. He was deep in conversation with someone she'd never seen before—a hulk of a man with bright red hair. She set her water down on a nearby table and nodded toward Riley. "Okay, let's go."

They slipped into the hallway that led back toward Greg's study in the guise of searching for the bathroom. When they reached the study, Kay pulled the heavy wooden door open a crack and peered inside. "The coast is clear," she whispered.

Riley stood watch while she ducked inside. The room was two stories with a wraparound balcony on the second level. The walls were wood paneled, and an ornately decorated Christmas tree provided the only light in the room.

Kay didn't waste any time. She pulled a small flashlight from her pocket and got to work. She started with the desk, rifling through the contents of each drawer. Nothing. Next, she scanned the sparsely populated bookshelves—no surprise, a moron like Greg wouldn't own many books. It took a while, but she finally saw what she was looking for: a red, spiral notebook was tucked behind a slew of framed family photos.

Kay carefully extracted it and flipped through page after page of Greg's neatly handwritten notes about Concordia's activity for the last six months. She set the notebook on the desk and pulled out her phone, but before she had a chance to snap any pictures, the silence in the room was broken by commotion out in the hallway. She froze when she heard a glass break. That was Riley sending a warning shot. Kay snatched up the notebook, dove behind the Christmas tree and tried to cover the rest of her body with the heavy velvet, gold-edged drapes. She could see clearly through the branches of the tree and she hoped she wasn't visible from the other side.

The door to the study swung open and Greg and Riley's boss, Gabe Suarez walked into the room. Greg walked over to the desk and clicked on the lamp, sending a soft glow over the room. Kay held her breath when Gabe looked toward the tree. "What's with all the fucking Christmas trees, Greg?"

"Don't even get me started. My wife pays some highfalutin florist an arm and a leg to put them up every year, and I think they're ugly as shit. I mean, fuck, how many gold bows does a tree need?" Greg gestured toward a small butler's table in the corner of the room. "I need a drink. You want one?"

Gabe nodded. "Make mine a double. Howard Rome is driving me to drink."

Greg took the lid off the decanter, filled two glasses with a rich brown liquid and handed one to Gabe. "He's really been tightening the screws."

"Damn right he has." Gabe took a slug of bourbon. "The financials he wants Logan to report this quarter are downright ludicrous. When I pushed back, he basically told me to fuck off."

"All this Concordia crap is giving me a freakin' ulcer." Greg held up his glass. "And this shit isn't doing me any favors."

"We're going to get caught with our pants down. It's only a matter of time before—"

A small red ball fell off the Christmas tree and slowly rolled across the wood floor, coming to a stop near Greg's feet. "Fucking tree," he said and kicked the ornament across the room. He strolled over to the bookshelf. Kay pinched her eyes shut, praying he didn't go looking for the red notebook, the one she was currently clutching against her chest.

Greg picked up a picture of his four kids posing in the stern of a large powerboat. "I wish I could just walk away," he mumbled. "but I've got two in college and two in boarding school."

"Well," Gabe said, "at least Howard Rome is making us rich. My bonus this year was twice as big as last year."

"True. He certainly is making all this crap worth our while." Greg waved toward the door. "We should probably get back to the party. My wife will kill me if she realizes we're hiding out in here."

As soon as they were gone, Kay extricated herself from behind the tree. She set the notebook back down on the desk and began to snap photos of each page. After five minutes, she wasn't even halfway through. "Fuck it," she mumbled. In a quick movement, she slipped the notebook under her flowy designer coat, tucked it in the waistband of her pants and bolted for the door.

# CHAPTER TWENTY-SEVEN

When she got to work Monday morning, Kay couldn't help but chuckle when she spotted Greg in his fishbowl of an office. He was frantically tearing his desk apart, no doubt in search of a certain red notebook. *You're not even warm*, *Greg*.

The red notebook was safely tucked away in Kay's desk at home. As soon as she and Riley had gotten home from Greg's Christmas party, they'd worked well into the early morning hours, cataloging every note Greg had made about Concordia in the notebook. Every price change he referenced was logged into Kay's master Excel sheet. Finally, her data was up to date.

When Kay conveyed what she'd overheard in Greg's study, Riley had taken it pretty hard. It confirmed Gabe was a stinking rat, just like Greg. Both men were mega players in the scandal at Logan. Riley admitted, deep down, she'd known Gabe was involved; it was just tough to accept it was true. The fact that Logan's CEO, Howard Rome, was at the center of the scandal came as no surprise to either one of them. They'd had a hunch the rot started at the top, but now they knew for sure.

Kay was in the process of shrugging off her coat when Greg appeared at her office door. His hair was disheveled and his shirt was stained with big wet pit marks. "Have you seen a red notebook?" he asked, using his hands to give her its general dimensions. "It's one of the spiral ones. You've probably seen me carry it around."

"Good morning to you too, Greg," Kay replied. "And no, I haven't seen a red notebook. Maybe you left it at home." Kay tried not to smile when she said the last sentence. It was just so damn fun to mess with him.

"Goddamn it," he muttered and stormed out of her office.

"By the way," she called after him, "your holiday party was great. Thanks for inviting us."

Kay spent the rest of the morning trying to catch up on email and reviewing various monthly pricing reports. At exactly noon, she got up, put on her coat, walked out to her car and drove home. Riley was already there when she arrived. The preliminary call with Fred Archie was scheduled for one o'clock and Riley had insisted they take it together.

As much as she wanted to protect Riley, Kay had finally come around to the idea they needed to work as a team as they waded into the next chapter of the Logan saga. What had started as a sprawling price fixing scandal had morphed into something so much bigger and more complex, and together she and Riley made a formidable duo. There were no words to describe how important Riley had become to her, and for the millionth time, she wondered if she'd have survived the last few months without her.

Kay shook her head and tried to focus on the here and now. The clock on her stove read 12:58. She began to pace. "I'm pretty sure I'll lose it if he isn't at least willing to meet with us."

Riley pulled her into a hug. "He'd be nuts not to take this case. The fraud is massive, and we've got more than enough evidence to back up our claims."

"I hope you're right."

Riley stepped back and pulled out her phone. "You want me to do the honors?"

Kay nodded, grateful to have a copilot who was not only brilliant, but also beautiful.

The phone call with Fred Archie ended up being a total non-event. About fifteen minutes into the conversation, he agreed to meet with them in person later that week. He instructed them to back up all the evidence they'd collected and to guard it with their lives.

After the call, Riley headed back to the office, and Kay went upstairs to her study. She backed up all the Logan related files to an external hard drive, the cloud, Dropbox, and for good measure, to a thumb drive that she kept in her fireproof safe. Satisfied the files would survive no matter what tragedy might strike, be it a house fire or a hacked cloud, she went back downstairs and called Ethan.

"I'm not at all surprised he agreed to meet with you," Ethan said after Kay updated him about their conversation with Fred. "I mean, the guy would be an idiot if he'd turned you down. No doubt, Fred saw dollar signs as soon as he heard what you and Riley had to say. A whistleblower case like yours can be very complex, but it can also be *very* lucrative for the attorneys involved."

"He might change his mind once he sees the evidence we produce."

"He might, but I doubt it. You need to stay positive, Kay."

"I know. I'm usually a glass half-full kind of gal, but this whole thing has me in knots. Riley and I are taking a huge risk. We're skating on very thin ice."

"I can't say I blame you," Ethan replied. "You're about to go to bat in the big leagues. The stakes just got a whole lot bigger. You have to promise me you'll be careful. No more sneaking around people's houses. You have to assume you're being watched at all times because there's a damn good chance you are."

"Trust me, we're both on high alert."

"How's Riley handling all of this?"

"Better than me. She's been a complete rock. I don't know what I'd do without her."

"Things have gotten pretty hot and heavy with you two, huh?"

"Yeah, they have. We've gotten really close, really fast. I think all the crap at Logan has helped bring us together, but it's more than that. We just work. I've never met anyone like her. I'm in deep Eth, real deep."

"I know it's still early days for you two, but given how quickly things have progressed, are you planning on spending Christmas together?"

"Ha," Kay said. "I wish, but no. I suggested maybe spending Christmas Eve with our respective families and then doing Christmas dinner together, either with her family or mine…"

"And?"

"She's not out to her family."

"Oh."

"Yeah, it's weird to feel so close to her and to be going through this intense Logan ordeal with her, and her family doesn't even know I exist."

"You need to be patient Kay. Try and remember what it was like to come out to your family."

"I know and she has it a lot harder that I did. Her parents are *way* more conservative than mine. Still, it makes me sad."

"I bet it makes her sad too."

# CHAPTER TWENTY-EIGHT

The wall clock in Fred Archie's reception area was driving Kay insane. *Tick, tick, tick.* She and Riley had been waiting for almost thirty minutes and she was no less nervous now than when they'd first walked in. She desperately wanted to remove her suit coat, but her silk blouse was stuck to her moist skin. The pile of evidence they'd brought with them—a banker's box full of financial reports, a bag of flash drives, each full of data, a few of Kay's leather-bound notebooks, including the red one she'd swiped from Greg's home office during the Christmas party—was stacked on the chair next to her. Looking at it gave her confidence.

They were finally escorted back to a spacious wood-paneled conference room. Fred did not look at all like Kay had imagined. She expected bulldog and he looked more kind and grandfatherly. He had wire-rim glasses, a full head of well-trimmed gray hair that was held in place with pomade, and he was very tall. His finely tailored suit hung off his wiry frame. There were two other men in the room, one about Fred's age and one who barely looked old enough to shave. The young one was chubby, and he was hunched over his laptop. He typed furiously whenever someone in the room spoke.

After the usual pleasantries, Fred leaned back in his chair and crossed his arms. He nodded toward Kay and Riley. "Why don't you two walk us through what you've witnessed at Logan."

Kay cleared her throat. "A number of people at the airline are involved in an elaborate price fixing scheme." She went on to explain to Fred what Concordia was and what the group had been doing. She also mentioned she'd gone to HR and been completely rebuffed.

Fred interrupted with a question here and there but he mostly just listened and occasionally muttered, "interesting, very interesting." It was nearly impossible for Kay to tell if he was intrigued by her tale or bored out of his mind. *I'd hate to play poker with this guy.* When she was done talking, she gestured toward Riley. "I'll let her explain the second piece."

Riley began to explain the anomalies they'd uncovered in Logan's financial filings, but before she got too far he held up his hand like a traffic cop. "Hold on." He stood and walked over to a floor-to-ceiling whiteboard. "Okay, please carry on." Riley continued and as she spoke, Fred used various colored markers to sketch out the scenario she was describing. He wrote *inflating ancillary revenue* in big block letters and then scribbled *bag fees* and *Logan-branded credit card* in a different color marker.

"We've got reason to believe the CEO of Logan might have a hand in all of this," Riley explained.

He sat back down and said, "interesting, very interesting," again. He flipped open a manila folder. "I'd like to ask you both to sign this." He pulled two small packets of paper out of the folder and handed one to Riley and the other to Kay. "This is our boilerplate Contingency Fee Agreement," he said.

Kay and Riley carefully read the pages of the document as Fred walked them through it. Ethan had explained what a Contingency Fee Agreement was and had told them they'd likely be asked to sign something like it. Kay took it as a positive sign that Fred was presenting them with the document. Hopefully it meant he thought their case had merit.

"Do you think we should sign it?" Riley whispered.

"I don't see why not. If we want Fred to spend time reviewing the information we've gathered, we've got to show him we're committed. He needs to know we aren't going to run off and talk to another attorney."

Fred tucked their signed forms back into his folder and asked, "Do you two have any questions for me at this stage?"

"Do you think our case is compelling?" Riley asked.

He maintained his poker face. "Obviously, I haven't had a chance to look at the evidence you two have gathered, but based on what you've told me today, yes, I do." He took off his glasses and rubbed his eyes. "I've got to be honest with you, though, these cases aren't easy, far from it. Many whistleblowers enjoy the 'cloak and dagger' aspect of things, but if we move forward, it will be a grueling uphill battle. I need you to be aware of that."

"We understand," Kay replied.

"And, as I'm sure you know, some whistleblowers receive a financial award."

Riley and Kay both nodded.

"But the truth is, few whistleblower claims lead to an award."

"We understand," Kay said again. "We aren't in this for the money."

"Very well then, let's talk again right after the holidays, once I've had a chance to review all of the evidence you've provided." He pointed toward the banker's box and other items Riley and Kay had brought to his office. "I assume these are copies and that you've got the originals tucked away safely somewhere?"

"Yes," Kay said. "Except for the notebooks."

He looked at the chubby notetaker. "Chris, will you please run and get those scanned."

Chris grunted, closed his laptop and snatched up the notebooks.

"It should just take Chris a minute. I'll have him bring them back out to the lobby when he's done so you can take them home with you." Fred stood and shook hands with each of them. "It was a pleasure meeting both of you. I'll be in touch."

# CHAPTER TWENTY-NINE

Christmas was usually one of Riley's favorite times of year. She should have been singing along to the carols on the radio, but she just wasn't up to it. She felt more anxious than excited as she made the drive to her parents' house in Buckhead on Christmas Eve. It had only been a day since Kay had left for Asheville, but Riley already missed her like crazy, and she dreaded the love life interrogation she was certain to face from her mother over the holidays.

She chuckled when she spotted a huge blow-up Santa in her parents' front yard. Her brother Beau had to be behind it. He and his girlfriend Shelia had flown in from Singapore the day before, and they would be home for Christmas for the first time in years.

The front door to the house flew open before she was even out of the car and Beau beamed at her from the doorway. The gravel on the driveway crunched beneath his bulky six-foot-two frame. It had been almost a year since they'd seen each other, and she smiled at the sight of him. He gave her a big bear hug and asked, "Need a hand with your bags, little sis?"

She pressed a button on her key fob and the trunk of her car popped open. She waved toward the Santa towering nearby. "Where the hell did that come from?"

Beau's deep laugh echoed through the air. "I bought it as a joke," he said. "Mom made me promise I'd take it down tomorrow."

"Yeah, I bet she did," Riley said as she followed Beau into the house. Her mother was fussing over the tablecloth in the dining room and paused to give Riley a hug and kiss. "Hi, honey. How was the drive?"

"Not bad. I-75 was quieter than normal. I guess everyone left work early because of the holiday. What can I do to help?"

"The dinner napkins need to be ironed," her mother said before turning to her brother. "Beau, honey. Be a dear and go down and get the *good* wineglasses out of the basement."

"Sure thing, Mom."

Riley retrieved the massive pile of linen napkins from the laundry room and plunked them down on the side table in the dining room. Once she had the ironing board set up, she pulled the first napkin from the stack. Her mother puttered around, rearranging chairs and laying out the silver. "I have no idea how we're going to fit seventeen people around this table," she muttered.

"We always seem to manage," Riley said from her perch behind the ironing board.

Her mother nodded. "That we do."

"We're lucky," Riley said. "A lot of people spend the holidays alone. We should be thankful we need to squeeze around the table."

"I suppose. Oh, did I tell you cousin Charlie is bringing his fiancée?"

"No, no, you didn't, but that's great. I only met her that one time at the baby shower, but she seemed really sweet."

"Auntie Jo is beside herself. Charlie will be thirty next month. She was beginning to wonder if he'd ever settle down and—"

As if on cue, Riley's phone vibrated and nearly fell off the ironing board. When she saw Kay's name on the screen, a smile crept across her face. She set down the iron and snatched up her phone. "Hey, hi," she said and stepped into the kitchen.

"Hey, baby. I just wanted to make sure you made it to Buckhead okay."

Just hearing Kay's raspy voice made her warm all over. "Yeah, I got here about thirty minutes ago. My mom already has me busy ironing. How's Asheville?"

"Great. Of course, I've been talking about you nonstop. My family can't wait to meet you."

"Oh, gosh, that's nice. I can't wait to meet them." A feeling of sadness swept through Riley. She still hadn't told her parents about Kay, hadn't told them she was falling in love with this incredible woman. It made her feel hollow and she wished Kay was there next to her instead of on the phone. They'd talked a lot about it, and Kay had tried to be supportive, but Riley knew it made her sad too. Sad that Riley had to hide a big part of who she was from her parents and sad that they didn't know Kay existed. There was no doubt about it; the situation just plain sucked.

After they ended the call, Riley walked back into the dining room and her mother asked, "Who was that on the phone, dear?"

Riley slipped back behind the ironing board and looked at the floor. "Um, just a friend from work." As soon as the words were out of her mouth, she winced. Even though she'd dated her ex, Brianna for nearly a year, she'd never once mentioned her to her mother. But with Kay, it was different, and it made her heart ache to call her a "friend from work." She was way more than that.

The rest of the afternoon was a blur of activity. Once she finished the heap of napkins, she helped her mother polish the silver candlesticks and make last-minute preparations for Christmas Eve dinner. Bobby, Lynn and the baby showed up in the late afternoon and her aunt and uncle and cousins arrived not long after that. After saying her hellos, Riley retreated to her childhood bedroom to shower and get ready for dinner. She loved her family, she really did, but it felt good to have a few minutes to herself, and her bedroom had always been her sanctuary.

Cocktail hour was well underway when she got back downstairs. Beau was relegated to the role of bartender and Riley's mother quickly put her in charge of passing hors d'oeuvres. Once she'd made her rounds, she set the platters on the coffee table and struck up a conversation with her cousin Charlie and his fiancée. She listened to them talk about their wedding plans until they got called into dinner.

Right after they said the blessing, her youngest cousin declared she'd become a vegan and refused to eat anything on the table. Riley could tell her uncle was about to blow a gasket. "How about green beans, dear?" Riley's mother asked in an effort to defuse the situation.

"Um, duh, they're smothered in butter," her cousin replied.

"There's some hummus in the fridge," Riley said, hoping to avoid World War III, "Let me grab it."

Mercifully, the rest of dinner was a fairly mild affair, and as soon as it was over, she jumped up to help Shelia clear the table.

Beau wandered into the kitchen and helped them finish the dishes. "Scotch?" he asked when they were done.

Shelia set her dish rag on the counter and glanced at her watch. "I'm going to try my sister Kathy in Singapore. They should be getting up about now to open presents."

"God, yes," Riley replied and followed him into the study. Beau filled two glasses with ice, poured a healthy amount of Scotch into each and handed one to her.

"Where's Bobby?" she asked as she sank into one of the large leather armchairs flanking the gas fireplace.

Beau gave her a knowing look. "Lynn took him to bed."

"Have you talked to him at all?" she asked. "Is everything okay? This isn't the first time I've seen him pretty blasted."

Beau leaned back in his chair and crossed his long legs. "We chatted a little before dinner," he said. "Mostly about superficial shit like how awesome the Bulldogs' quarterback is and the team's prospects for next year, but I get the sense he's just a bit overwhelmed with adulting. He hates his job but obviously he can't just up and quit because of the baby and everything."

She tucked one of her legs underneath her and swirled the ice cubes in her glass. "Ah, life."

"Speaking of life, how are things with you?" Beau asked.

"I'm good...just in a little bit of a funk."

His kind eyes settled on her. "What's got you down?"

"You mean aside from Mom and Auntie Jo constantly riding my ass about not being married, not dating, biological clock ticking, blah, blah, blah."

"I know that's gotta suck, but, yeah, besides that."

She leaned forward in her chair and rested her elbows on her knees. He'd been supportive ever since she'd come out to him a few years back, and she knew he'd lend an understanding ear. "It's the same shit every holiday, but, well, it hurts especially bad right now because I'm seeing someone." She smiled up at him. "Someone really special."

Beau patted her on the knee. "Hey, that's great. What's her name?"

"Kay. She works at Logan. She's amazing, Beau, and things with us, well, they're starting to get serious."

"Have you thought about telling Mom and Dad?"

Her shoulders slumped. "Sure, I've thought about it, but I get sick to my stomach when I think about how they might react, especially Mom. God, we were at the club over Thanksgiving and we had this super effeminate waiter. Mom made some remark about him being, 'queer.' It was like she couldn't even bring herself to say the word gay."

"I'm sorry, sis," he said. "You want me to talk to her?"

"It's sweet of you to offer, but no, this is something I've got to figure out on my own. I'm mad at myself for letting it go this long. I'm just so goddamn terrified to come out and tell her the truth. Shit, I didn't even have the guts to call her out for whispering behind the waiter's back. She didn't even have the decency to make sure he was out of earshot, not that it would have excused her comments." Riley let out a long sigh. "I'm pathetic."

"Don't be so hard on yourself. Mom's not exactly approachable about this kind of stuff."

She tossed back a big swig of Scotch. "You are so fucking lucky you live 10,000 miles away. Sometimes I envy you. I mean, Mom doesn't ride you about the fact you and Shelia aren't married, does she?"

"No," he replied sheepishly. "And to be honest, I don't exactly broadcast that we live together... See I'm just as chickenshit as you are when it comes to Mom."

"Aren't we a pair. Do Shelia's parents give you guys grief about shacking up?"

Beau shook his head. "Not at all. Even though they live in Singapore now, they're from California and her parents are, how shall I say this, a little bit more progressive than Mom and Dad."

Riley groaned. "God, sometimes I just want to pull my hair out."

He held up his glass. "Want a splash more?"

"Nah, I should probably head to bed." She suddenly felt exhausted and she wanted to call Kay before she went to sleep. She just needed to hear her voice. "Merry Christmas, Beau."

# CHAPTER THIRTY

After the holidays, Riley and Kay met with Fred Archie again a half a dozen times. His team had spent countless hours poring over the data they'd provided and he felt confident they had enough to go to the SEC. "The information you've gathered clearly demonstrates a material violation of federal securities law," he told them one afternoon when they were all gathered at his office. "The SEC has limited resources and obviously they can't look into every tip they receive. However, what's going on at Logan... I have no doubt the SEC will consider it serious enough to warrant their attention."

Kay felt herself relax. After all these months of worrying about whether they had enough evidence, she felt a ray of hope. She looked over at Riley and they shared a smile. "When do you plan to officially submit the complaint?"

"In a couple of weeks. My team and I need some time to get our ducks in a row."

"I've got a question," Riley said. "Can Kay and I do this together. I mean, can more than one person be a whistleblower on the same complaint?"

"Yes, one or more people are allowed to act as a whistleblower."

"So, how does it work?" Kay asked. "Do we just send off all the information we've gathered?"

"There's a formal process for submitting a claim. It involves some paper work."

"Of course it does," Riley chimed.

"The key is," he continued, "the case we present has to be rock solid. The SEC will be looking for *specific* and *credible* information that indicates a material violation of the law." He turned his attention on Kay. "To answer your question, yes, we'll provide them with most of the information you two have gathered, but we've got to present it in a compelling way. We can't just send the SEC a pile of documents and expect them to figure it out. We need to provide them with a clear roadmap, spell it out for them."

"Okay," Riley said. "How do we do that?"

"Don't worry," he said and gave them a reassuring smile. "We've got years of experience working with the SEC. We know the drill. In the meantime, I'd like to answer any additional questions you two have. How familiar are you two with the SEC's Whistleblower Program?"

Kay and Riley both shrugged. "We know a little bit about it," Kay replied.

"Well, let me give you the highlights," he said. "It was created by Congress to give people an incentive to report possible violations of the federal securities laws to the SEC. And as I mentioned when we first met, if, and I stress the word *if*, the information you've provided leads them to open an investigation, you might be entitled to a financial award. There are a lot of factors that go into determining—"

"I'm not going to lie, a financial reward would be a serious bonus but that's not why we came forward," Kay reiterated, and Riley nodded in agreement.

"You made that clear when we first met. I just want you to understand how the program works."

"At this point, I'm most concerned about what submitting the complaint will mean for us," Riley said. "Will Logan know we've gone to the SEC?"

He shook his head. “No, none of this will be public.”

“Are you sure?” Kay asked.

“Yes, I’m sure,” Fred said. “We’ll submit the letter of complaint anonymously. As your attorney, I’ll submit it on your behalf. Nowhere in the letter, will you be identified as the whistleblowers.”

“When I was getting my MBA, we read some case studies that involved whistleblowers,” Riley said. “If I remember correctly, it’s pretty typical for whistleblowers to remain anonymous, is that right?”

He nodded. “In most cases, yes.”

“But someone might still find out it was us,” Kay said, “and I cannot imagine the higher-ups at Logan would be too happy with us.” She thought back to her conversation with Heather Corn. “I mean, it wouldn’t be a big stretch for someone at Logan to connect the dots if and when they find out they’re being investigated by the SEC.”

“There have been instances,” Fred said, “where whistleblowers were unmasked—their identities were exposed—and that’s always a possibility, even though it’s illegal to do so.”

Kay was under no delusion. She knew, even if their complaint was submitted anonymously, she and Riley were going way out on a limb. Still, they’d agreed it was the right thing to do, which was why they were sitting there in Fred’s office.

“As I’ve said before,” he said, “these cases are never easy for anyone involved, but the SEC Whistleblower Program strictly prohibits retaliation by employers against employees who report possible securities violations.”

“I don’t trust Greg or Howard Rome, for that matter, to give a shit about whether retaliation is prohibited or not,” Kay said. “If they knew we were sitting here with you right now, God, there’s no telling what they might do.” Considering the possibilities made her shudder.

Riley placed a hand on Kay’s arm. “They aren’t going to find out.” She turned back to him. “So, once we submit the complaint, what happens after that?”

“The SEC will review our submission and assess whether they think it warrants deeper scrutiny, and if they do, they’ll likely initiate an investigation.”

"If the SEC decides to open an investigation, will they notify Logan?" Kay asked.

He shook his head again. "No. It's very unlikely the airline will know they are under investigation, at least initially. Typically, the SEC conducts its investigations on a confidential basis. They do this to protect the integrity of the investigation and to protect the privacy of persons involved in an investigation."

"Will the SEC notify us if they decide to open an investigation?" Riley asked.

"No, the SEC is not in the habit of providing status updates on its investigations. They don't generally comment on whether they have opened an investigation in a particular matter." Fred leaned back in his chair. "I've got to be honest with you. Once we submit the letter of complaint, it is likely to be radio silence for a good long while. It can be extremely frustrating. We just need to be patient while the SEC does their thing."

"When you say 'a good long while,' are we talking weeks, months?" Kay asked.

"If I had to guess, once we hand over all the evidence, it could be six months or more before we hear anything."

The color drained from her face. "And during this time, we'll have virtually no insight into what, or even if, the SEC has decided to investigate Logan."

"I'm afraid not."

Kay sank down in her chair. Six months was a very long time in the scheme of things. During this time, they'd have to go to work day after day and keep up the charade. It was going to be a fucking nightmare.

# CHAPTER THIRTY-ONE

Final word came from Fred Archie in early February that everything had been submitted to the SEC. He advised them to keep their heads down and their mouths shut. Kay was both relieved and terrified. It felt good to have officially sounded the alarm on the fraud at Logan, but now she and Riley faced months of going to work and *acting normal* while things were anything but normal.

When Kay inquired about whether they could tell their families about the SEC complaint, Fred had been adamant that they not tell another soul. To date, Kay had only told Ethan about the fraud at Logan, but now that they'd gone to the SEC, the peril and severity of the whole situation had ratcheted up about fifty notches. It was like they were in a vice that was getting twisted tighter and tighter every day.

"A penny for your thoughts?" Riley asked her. They were sitting in Kay's sunroom, drinking coffee and reading the Sunday *New York Times*.

"Sorry," Kay said. "I was just thinking about my dad. It feels so strange that I haven't told him anything about what's going on at Logan."

"Fred was very clear."

"I know, I know. It's just… Logan is my dad's heart and soul. I feel like I'm deceiving him by not telling him, and now that the SEC is involved… I'm just sick about it."

Riley wrapped her arms around Kay and held her tightly. They sat there for a long time, just holding each other. When Riley pulled back, she looked Kay in the eye. "Our identities will be protected. There's no way your father or anyone else for that matter, will ever know it was us who went to the SEC, I mean, unless you tell them."

"Or unless someone at Logan gets wind of the investigation and hunts us down." Kay slumped back against the couch. "I just can't shake the feeling that someone's going to find out it was us who went to the feds. When I'm at work, I feel like I'm constantly looking over my shoulder. Fuck, I can't tell you how many times Greg has asked me about the missing red notebook. He always gives me this look like he's convinced I had something to do with its disappearance."

"If he knew you'd taken it, he would have come after you a long time ago. You can be sure of that."

"You're probably right." Kay paused for a moment before she continued. "That's not all that's bothering me. I'm constantly anxious about how all of this will impact the airline and all the people who work there."

"Whatever happens to Logan," Riley said, "that's on Greg Brandywine and Howard Rome. They're the ones who are at fault, not us. Like I keep saying, we're the good guys in all this. The ones with the courage to stick out our necks and expose the truth."

Kay ran a hand through her long dark hair. "Yeah, I know that in principle, but I don't know… My dad worked for Logan for almost thirty years and I've worked there for over a decade."

"The next few months are going to be really hard, but we've got each other, and we need to stay strong."

"I know, baby. There's no way I could've gotten this far without you. Not in a million years."

"I'm proud of us."

Kay smiled. "Yeah, I am too. None of this is for the faint of heart."

Riley stood to stretch her legs and glanced at her watch. "Oh, shit. I didn't realize it had gotten so late. I've got to be at my parents' house for dinner in less than two hours and I still need to go home and shower."

Kay rocked forward and pressed her face into her hands. She looked up at Riley and nibbled on her lower lip, trying to fight back tears. "You think you'll ever tell them about me?" she asked, and immediately regretted asking the question.

Riley stiffened and crossed her arms. "Please Kay, not now. Don't push me on this. We're both under enough stress as it is."

Kay stood and faced her. "Baby, I'm sorry. I shouldn't have—"

Riley stormed into the kitchen, yanked open one of the kitchen cabinets and pulled out a glass. "Don't you know it eats me alive." She held the glass under the faucet and filled it with water. "Especially after everything we've been through together. I want to tell them so badly. I just can't bring myself to do it. I get angry with myself, but I'm terrified of how they'll react. For all their faults, they're my family and I love them. I don't want them to push me away."

She gulped down her water and set the glass down in the sink. She leaned against the countertop, hung her head and began to sob.

Kay walked into the kitchen and rubbed her back. "Riley, baby, I'm sorry. I shouldn't have brought it up."

Riley lifted her head and sniffed back tears. "I know it bothers you too. I'll tell them soon, I promise. It just has to be on my terms."

"I know. God, I know and I don't envy the position you're in."

A faint smile crossed Riley's face. "Trust me, nothing would make me happier than to have you next to me at my parents' dining room table tonight."

Kay pulled her into a hug. "I know. Someday."

"Yeah, someday." Riley stepped back. "I should go."

"I know," Kay replied and slipped a finger under her chin. "We're going to get through all of this together."

Riley kissed her softly on the lips. "I know. I keep trying to remind myself of that." She walked toward the front door, picked her bag off the floor and stepped outside. She turned around and blew Kay a kiss before she closed the door behind her.

After she left, Kay dragged herself upstairs and changed into her running clothes. When she stepped outside, it had just started to rain. She took off toward the park running as fast as she could.

# CHAPTER THIRTY-TWO

The stress of being a "double agent" really began to wear on Kay. Now that the complaint had officially been filed with the SEC, she found it harder and harder to play along with the Concordia scheme and the paranoia that Greg was onto her intensified. Twice recently, she'd found out he'd convened a Concordia meeting without telling her, something he'd never done before.

And the other day she'd come back from a meeting to find a guy sitting behind her computer. He claimed to be from IT and mumbled something about a software upgrade, but he'd been really jumpy and had scampered out of her office almost immediately. When she mentioned the incident to Riley, she'd relayed a similar visit from IT. It made no sense. Most software upgrades these days were "pushed" to their computers; they didn't require an in-person visit.

Kay had also been having trouble sleeping, and as a result, her fuse was a lot shorter than normal. That morning she'd snapped at a junior employee for a minor infraction, and now she felt bad about it. Poor guy had just been in the wrong place at the wrong time. She made a mental note to apologize the next time she saw him and tried to focus on the report she had up on her computer, but it was a lost cause and a burst of commotion outside her office didn't help.

She stood up and stuck her head out the door to see what the fuss was all about. A giant vase of red and white roses sat on her admin's desk and it had drawn the attention of many of the women who sat nearby. "They're so beautiful," one young woman said. "You're so lucky. My husband never does anything romantic," another woman offered. Kay smiled at her admin. "Wow, Harry went all out this year, huh?" she asked. "They're gorgeous."

Her admin beamed. "Thanks, Kay."

Kay stepped back in her office. *Shit, it's Valentine's Day.* She'd totally forgotten or maybe it was she'd forgotten to remember. *Some girlfriend I am.* Kay had always sort of poo pooed the holiday, referred to it as VD Day and written it off as a "Hallmark Holiday"—something dreamed up by the famed greeting card producer as a way to sell more cards, stuffed bears and heart-shaped balloons.

This year, though, she didn't feel as grinchy about Valentine's Day as she normally did, and she got the sudden urge to do something special for Riley. She considered taking her out to dinner but quickly abandoned that idea. There was no chance in hell she'd get a reservation this late in the game, plus the lingering VD Day cynic in her believed restaurants used the holiday as an opportunity to gouge their patrons.

She tapped her fingers on her desk as she racked her brain for something incredibly romantic to do. It came to her in a flash. She'd whisk Riley off to Paris for the weekend—an idea that was made practical given her generous flight benefits. Most people would never dream of jetting off to Paris for the weekend, but airline employees did that sort of stuff all the time.

By the end of the day, the trip was all planned. They'd take the nonstop to Paris on Friday after work, two short days away. She'd tell Riley they were going away for the weekend but not reveal where. The only hint, a passport and a warm coat were required.

When they arrived outside the security checkpoint on Friday evening, Riley's eyes lit up when Kay presented their boarding passes. "Holy shit, Paris." She gave Kay a peck on the cheek. "You're such a romantic."

An hour later, they boarded a Logan Boeing 777 bound for the City of Lights and settled into their business class seats for the nearly nine-hour flight. Despite being in business class or maybe because of it—the food, wine and movies were too good to pass up, neither of them got much sleep during the flight and they were both zombies when they touched down in Paris early Saturday morning. The six-hour time change didn't help matters. It was seven a.m. in Paris but only one a.m. in Atlanta.

Kay squinted in the bright morning sunshine when they stepped outside the airport. A pair of sunglasses were somewhere in her bag, but she didn't have the energy to dig them out.

Riley stifled a yawn as they climbed into a taxi. "Tired?" Kay asked.

"Yeah, but I don't want to be. I'm so excited to be here with you."

"I'll let you in on a little trick," Kay replied. "For a quick weekend trip like this, it is better *not* to adjust to the time change."

Riley rubbed her eyes. "I'm not following you. Did you say *not*?"

"Yeah, we should keep our schedule here in Paris aligned with East Coast time. So, for example, we should go to the hotel and sleep until noon. By then, it will be morning in Atlanta. We can get up and enjoy the afternoon and evening in Paris. Think about it. If we stay out until two a.m., it will only be eight p.m. Atlanta time."

"I guess that sort of makes sense," Riley said through another yawn. "You think we'll be able to check in to the hotel this early in the morning?" She looked at the clock on the taxi's dashboard. "It's not even eight a.m."

Kay draped her arm over Riley's shoulder. "Don't worry. We're staying at this little hotel and I know the owner. My parents stay there all the time. Our room will be ready. I'm sure of it."

Kay was right. The owner led them to a bright and airy room as soon as they arrived at the hotel. It had a large bathroom, at least by European standards, and the queen bed was piled high with pillows and adorned with a puffy white comforter. One of the large windows was cracked open, causing the curtains to flutter. According to Kay's phone, it was only about ten degrees Celsius outside, but the room felt warm nonetheless.

Once they'd unpacked, they stripped off their clothes, showered and climbed between the bed's smooth cotton sheets. Kay was about to doze off when a warm naked body snuggled up against her. Soft fingers drew lazy circles over her breasts and sent shockwaves to her groin. In an instant, arousal supplanted exhaustion. Riley rolled her over on her back and teased one breast and then the other with her tongue. Her clit pulsed intensely, and she slid her hand between her folds to meet its need. She twitched when she touched herself, and after a few gentle strokes, she quickened the pace. Riley sucked hungrily on her firm nipples and Kay's muscles tensed. "Oh, God," she moaned as she came.

Riley kissed her softly on the lips and whispered, "Welcome to Paris." Sleep came easily after that.

# CHAPTER THIRTY-THREE

Riley's eyes fluttered open a few hours later. At first, she was confused. She had no idea where she was until her eyes fell upon the beautiful woman sleeping soundly beside her. A smile crept across her face. Kay was lying on her back and she'd kicked off the bedsheets, leaving her taut stomach and ample breasts exposed.

She placed a soft kiss on Kay's bare shoulder, causing her to stir.

"What time is it?" Kay asked, her eyes opening briefly before falling shut again.

"Time to go explore this wonderful city." Riley climbed out of bed. She brushed her teeth and washed her face and laughed when she peeked out into the bedroom. Kay had pulled the sheets and comforter over her head. Riley jumped on the bed and tickled Kay until she put her feet on the floor.

"You are so mean," Kay said as she padded to the bathroom.

"You'd never forgive me if I let you sleep the day away."

"I know," Kay said. "I was just so warm and happy in my cocoon."

After she'd pulled on some clothes, Riley peered out the window of their room. Clouds had moved in while they were asleep, and it looked like it might rain. "Brrr, it looks cold out there."

"We'd better bundle up." Kay opened the small closet and held up a sweater. "You can wear this if you want. I packed a few extra supplies since I didn't give you very many details about where we were going."

Since it was Riley's first visit to Paris, they started at the Louvre, making the requisite stroll by the Mona Lisa and trying to get a glimpse of the subject's captivating eyes through the throng of people crowded around the famous painting. "Oh well, at least I can say I've seen it," Riley said.

They made their way upstairs to the second floor to see the Dutch masters. "These are my favorite," Kay said as they lingered in front of a still life series.

Riley read the small plaque next to the painting. "Wow, this was painted almost 400 years ago."

Kay nodded without taking her eyes off the painting. "I know. It's hard to believe isn't it?"

The next painting depicted a bunch of aristocrats. "It's kind of amazing if you think about it," Riley said. "Back then, the only way to capture an image or a scene was to paint it. So different from the camera phone obsessed society of today." As if affirming her point, two women armed with selfie sticks walked into the room. "I fucking hate those things," she whispered into Kay's ear.

"God, I know, me too. I thought they'd been banned at the museum."

"If so," Riley said and gestured toward the two women, "they obviously didn't get the memo."

After a quick pass through the Egyptian and Greek antiquities, they stepped back out into the raw day. "Where next?" Kay asked.

"I know there are a million things to see in Paris, but given that we're here for such a short time, do you mind if we just wander around and soak it all in. I'm worried that if we run around and try to see everything, it will all just be a blur."

Kay took her hand and led her through the narrow streets of Paris. They taste tested croissants from multiple bakeries, peeked in shop windows, and enjoyed a much-needed double espresso. It was after dark by the time they get back to the hotel.

Riley kicked off her boots and rubbed her feet. "I bet we walked at least ten miles, and even though we ate all those croissants, I'm starving."

"Good, because I made reservations at La Tulipe. Thomas recommended it," Kay said, referring to the proprietor of their hotel.

"Do you think La Tulipe will have la wine?"

"Are we in France?"

Riley chuckled. "Okay, stupid question."

"And just for your reference, 'vin' is the word for wine in French."

"Ah, good to know."

La Tulipe only had a dozen or so tables, and even though it was only seven p.m.—early for dinner in France—most of them were occupied. Riley took that as a sign that the place must be good.

An elegantly dressed older woman greeted them near the door, and after exchanging a few words with Kay in French, she led them to a small table near the window.

Once they were seated, a waiter appeared with two carafes of water. "Gaz ou sans gaz?" he asked.

Riley looked at Kay, hoping she had a clue what he was asking. Kay gestured toward the bottle in his left hand and said, "Avec gaz."

He poured them some sparkling water, helped Kay select a bottle from their wine list and left them to look over the menu.

"Do you like escargot?" Kay asked.

"Is the Pope Catholic?"

Kay gave her a curious look. "Really, you like snails?"

"Uh-huh. Love them. Why is that so hard to believe? Just because I'm from the south, doesn't mean I lack culture."

"I wasn't suggesting—"

"I know, it's okay. I can get a little too defensive about my southern heritage."

When the waiter returned with their wine, Kay chatted with him in French while she tasted it.

"Bonne degustation," the waiter said after he'd poured them each a glass.

Once he was gone, Riley leaned toward Kay and whispered, "I love it when you speak French. It's so sexy."

"Is that a fact?" Kay winked at her. "Perhaps I should do it more often."

Riley picked up her glass and gave Kay a soft smile. "Whisking me off to Paris was incredibly *ro-man-teak*," she said with the best French accent she could muster. "And speaking of surprises, I've got one for you too." She reached into her shoulder bag, pulled a medium size package and handed it to Kay. "I got you a little Valentine's gift too."

Kay looked the package and then back up at Riley. "What's this?"

"Open it and you'll see. I think you're going to like it."

Kay peeled back the brown paper wrapping and a giant smile engulfed her face. "A copy of *Blue Highways*. Riley, I can't believe you remembered." Kay held the book against her heart. "What an incredibly thoughtful gift."

"It's a first edition. I found it online."

"Thank you." Kay teared up slightly. "This is, by far, the best Valentine's Day I've ever had."

"Me too," Riley whispered. She paused and slowly sipped her wine before seeking out Kay's eyes with her own. "You, Kay Corbett, are the most kind, wonderful, funny, smart, sexy woman I've ever met." A wave of butterflies swooped across her stomach and caused her to choke out her next words. "What we have… It's incredibly special."

That night, tears welled up in Kay's eyes as she and Riley made love. That had never happened to her before. She was a fairly passionate person and she'd had a few intense relationships, but nothing compared to how she felt now. It was terrifying and exhilarating all at once. She'd known her feelings for Riley were strong, but their intensity was nothing short of astonishing.

She spooned against Riley and they lay in silence for a long time. The room was dark except for the glow of a nearby streetlight. When Riley's breathing deepened, Kay wondered if she'd fallen asleep. She did it anyway. She jumped off a cliff and whispered, "I love you, Riley," into the darkness.

Riley slowly turned in her arms, and slid a hand into Kay's hair, drawing their lips together. They shared a few tender kisses, never breaking eye contact. "I love you too, Kay," Riley said when they broke apart. "So damn much."

Kay pulled Riley into her arms and hugged her with all her might. "I love you," she said again. Riley was only the second person she'd ever uttered those words to.

# CHAPTER THIRTY-FOUR

While Kay and Riley sat at Paris' Charles de Gaulle Airport waiting for their flight back to the US, Kay scanned the messages on her phone. "Hey, Rye?" she asked.

Riley looked up from the finance magazine she was reading. "Yeah?"

"Do you have any plans next weekend?"

Riley thought for a moment before shaking her head. "I don't think so. Why?"

"I just got a message from Doug," Kay replied, referring to her eldest brother. "He's throwing a surprise birthday party for my brother Connor next Saturday."

"In Asheville? They both live there, right?"

"Yep. So, anyway, wanna come with me?"

"Sure. I'd love to."

Kay reached for Riley's hand and gave it a squeeze. "Great. I can't wait for you to meet my brothers. We'll probably stay with Doug because he's got an in-law suite over his garage. It'll give us a tiny bit of privacy which, trust me, you'll appreciate with all the kids running around. Connor and his family live on the neighboring property and—why are you smiling?"

"You're so cute when you get all excited." Riley dog-eared the article she was reading and set her magazine aside.

"Ah, sorry…"

"Don't apologize. It's great that you get along so well with your brothers. I didn't know they were neighbors."

"They live on the land that once belonged to my grandparents—my mom's parents. It was divided between my brothers and me after my grandmother died. We each got about five acres. I'm hoping to build a house on my plot one day."

"Wow. You never told me you had property in Asheville. I love it there. There's so much to do and the town has such a cool vibe."

Kay nodded enthusiastically. "Yeah, I love it there too. I just wish I got there a little more often."

"What about Mikey, Russ and Scott?" Riley asked, referring to Kay's three other brothers. "Have any of them built places there?"

"No, not yet. I'm pretty sure Mikey wants to someday, but I'm guessing it won't be anytime soon."

"He's the one who's a pilot for American, right?"

"Uh-huh, and he's a bit of a ladies' man. At this point in his life, I think the pace of life in Asheville is way too slow for him. I have no idea what my brother Russ's plans are, but I know Scott—"

"We'd like to begin pre-boarding," a voice on the loudspeaker announced. "Any customers needing special assistance or additional time to board, including families with small children, may now board."

Kay looked toward the disorderly mass forming near the gate. "I guess we should go get in line, huh?"

"So, you were about to tell me about your brother Scott," Riley said once they were settled in their seats.

"Oh yeah," Kay replied. "So, Scott has *zero* interest in Asheville. He's way too caught up in his fancy New York City life, and last I heard, he had his sights set on a place in the Hamptons. And well, he's actually offered to sell me his land in Asheville. His parcel and mine are right next to each other."

"Are you thinking about buying it?"

"I'm seriously considering it," Kay replied. "If I did, it would give me a full ten acres, and as much as I love my brothers, a little space between us wouldn't hurt." She paused when a flight attendant approached their seats.

"Hello," the woman said and looked down at a sheet of paper, "Ms. Corbett and, um, Ms. Bauer." She peeked at them over her reading glasses. "I'm Monica, the purser on today's flight. May I get you anything to drink before we take off?"

"Just water for me," Kay replied.

"Same here," Riley answered.

Monica jotted down their drink orders and moved on to the passengers in the next row.

Kay briefly scanned the menu Monica had handed them before turning back to Riley. "If you want, we can check out my land when we're up in Asheville next weekend."

"Sure, that would be great."

"Both Scott's property and mine are fairly wooded and a bit overgrown but wait until you see the views. It's beautiful. Just make sure to pack some hiking boots." She gave Riley a smirk. "That is, assuming you own such things."

"Ha, aren't you the funny one. For your information, I happen to own an excellent pair of hiking boots." Riley waved a hand over her outfit. "Don't let these dresses fool you. I can tomboy with the best of them."

Kay picked up her phone. "I'm going to text Doug right now and let him know we'll both be there for Connor's party."

"Do you think he'll mind me tagging along?"

Kay didn't hesitate before answering. "No, not at all. In our family, the motto is, the more the merrier. Plus, I want you there. I want to introduce you to my family."

# CHAPTER THIRTY-FIVE

"Knock, knock. You ready to hit the road to Asheville?"

Riley looked up to see Kay standing at her office door. Instead of her usual power suit, she was wearing fitted jeans and a billowy white blouse. A denim coat was draped over one shoulder and her long dark hair was pulled back in a ponytail. *Damn she looked good.* "Um, yeah. Let me shut down my computer."

Kay eyed her as she stood to grab her coat. "What?"

"Ah, so you do in fact own pants," Kay said with a laugh.

"Spare me. You've seen me wear pants *many* times."

"Okay, fair enough. But I think I've seen you in jeans a grand total of once." Kay gave Riley a quick up and down. "They look new."

"They're not, smartass. I bought them when we were first courting."

"Courting? Is it the year 1834?"

They crossed the massive Logan parking lot and climbed into Kay's Jeep. It was five p.m. on Friday afternoon and traffic out of Atlanta was completely bumper to bumper. It didn't ease up until they were up near Lake Lanier.

"I'm sorry I couldn't leave the office earlier," Riley said waving her hand toward the sea of headlights.

"Don't worry. I would have been hard pressed to leave any earlier than we did. I was totally swamped all week, especially given that we were out Monday."

"Same here. Although, I am so glad we took Monday off." Riley smiled as she thought back to their trip to Paris. She meant it when she told Kay she loved her. Meant it from the bottom of her heart. Riley honestly didn't think she'd ever felt this way about another human being.

Kay glanced over at her. "Why the goofy grin?"

She reached out to touch Kay's arm. "I was just thinking about how much I love you…"

Kay got a goofy grin of her own. "Really?"

She nodded. "Yeah, really."

It was nearly ten o'clock by the time they turned off the paved road and started up Doug's long gravel driveway. The Jeep bumped along, its headlights cutting through the darkness. Big tall trees lined their way, and even though it was not quite spring, Riley could see small buds sprouting from their limbs. The driveway curved sharply, and a large well-lit contemporary house popped into view. It was like a massive spaceship had been dropped into the middle of the forest. The Jeep triggered a motion light as Kay maneuvered it around the circular driveway and parked in front of a hulking barn-like structure.

The door of the main house opened, and a tall dark-haired man stepped outside. "Hey Kay," he said with a wave.

Kay looked up toward the house. "Hey, Doug."

"Come on in. We've got lots of cold beer."

"Be right there," Kay hollered.

Riley pointed toward the back of the Jeep. "Should we grab our bags?"

"Nah, we can get them later when we head up to bed." She pointed to the upper level of the barn. "Our sleeping quarters are up there. It's a pretty good setup. We even have our own little kitchenette so we can make coffee in the morning."

Kay gave her brother a warm hug. "Good to see you, Dougie."

Seeing Kay and Doug together, Riley was struck by how much they looked alike. Doug was lean, but he was built like a rock, and he had Kay's twinkling brown eyes. He was handsome in a Ken doll kind of way.

Kay slid her arm over Riley's shoulder. "Doug, this is my girlfriend Riley. Riley, this is my big stud of a brother, Doug."

Doug extended a hand. She liked him immediately.

"Hi, Kay," a female voice said from inside the house. Moments later Doug's wife Miriam appeared at his side. She was about Kay's height and she was rocking a tomboy haircut.

"The kids in bed?" Kay asked as they made their way back to the kitchen.

Doug handed them both a beer and cracked one for himself. "Yeah. They wanted to stay up until you got here, but it was past their bedtime. Don't worry, the little monsters will be begging you to kick the soccer ball before the sun's barely up."

"We'll do our best to hold them at bay," Miriam said with a laugh. "But you might want to lock the door to your room."

Sure enough, there was soft knock on their door early the next morning. "Aunt Kay," a little voice called out. Riley picked up her phone. 7:23.

She nudged Kay. "You decent?" They most certainly were *not* decent when they'd fallen asleep the night before. She lifted the covers and got the answer to her question—a resounding no.

Kay swung her feet to the floor and gathered up her clothes. "Coming." They hastily dressed before Kay unlocked the door. Four big brown eyes stared in at them. Kay scooped the two little boys up in her arms and spun them around, soliciting squeals of joy from her nephews.

One of the boys spotted Riley. "Who's that, Aunt Kay?"

Kay set the boys down on the floor. "That's my girlfriend, Riley. Isn't she beautiful?"

The boys nodded in unison.

Kay looked toward the door. "Why don't you give me and Riley a minute to finish getting dressed and we'll be right down?"

Once the boys scattered, Kay said, "Sorry, I should have warned you that early mornings would be a given. And wait until you meet Doug's daughters. They're equally as cute, but believe it or not, they have more energy than their brothers. And they're also better soccer players but don't tell the boys that."

"Don't apologize. They're adorable. I'm happy I get to meet some of your family."

Kay pulled Riley into a one arm hug. "Me too. It means a lot to me."

Over the course of the day, Riley was struck by a couple of things. First, Kay was a total natural with kids. She played soccer with them for hours. It was obvious they all adored her. She kidded around with them, but when one of them fell and skinned his knee, she was compassionate, although she didn't baby him.

Riley was also struck by the interaction between Kay and her brothers. They joked with each other and shared frequent bouts of laughter. It was evident they shared a special bond. Kay was the butt of a lot of Connor and Doug's jokes, but Riley could tell they were both hyper protective of her. Family was vital to Riley and it was abundantly clear it was for Kay too.

The weekend made Riley eager to meet the rest of the Corbett family. From her perspective, neither Doug nor Connor seemed to have any issue whatsoever with the fact that Kay was gay. Even their kids appeared totally unfazed by it. They were still young but neither of her nephews even shrugged when she introduced Riley as her girlfriend. It was wonderful to see, but it also made Riley incredibly sad. Things were so different with her family.

Everyone gathered at Doug and Miriam's on Saturday night to celebrate Connor's birthday, and Riley smiled as she watched Kay bounce on the trampoline with a few of the kids, her wavy dark hair sailing above her head each time she launched into the air. It was hard to tell who was having more fun, Kay or the little leaping bodies beside her.

Just before they sat for dinner, Kay's cell phone rang. She glanced at the caller ID. "It's Mrs. Fairchild, my next-door neighbor. That's odd."

Riley had met Mrs. Fairchild once or twice. She was a very sweet elderly woman, although Kay said she could be a bit of a busybody. Nothing happened in Kay's neighborhood without Mrs. Fairchild knowing about it.

Kay stepped out of the porch and Riley could just barely hear her end of the conversation. "Hello Mrs. Fairchild.... Oh, I see... Um, okay, thanks for letting me know."

"What was that all about?" Riley asked when she came back inside.

"Mrs. Fairchild was up in her spare bedroom this evening after supper, and apparently she saw a large man lurking around my house. It was near dusk, and when her outside lights clicked on—evidently, they're on some sort of timer—the man scaled my back fence and ran away."

Riley and Kay exchanged a glance. "Did she get a good look at him?" Doug asked.

"All she said was he had bright red hair."

Riley pulled Kay aside after dinner. "I'm worried. The man your neighbor saw might have something to do with Concordia."

Kay waved her hand. "I'm sure it's nothing. Mrs. Fairchild's eyesight isn't so great, and you know how she is. She'd probably call the police on a pizza delivery man."

# CHAPTER THIRTY-SIX

Bright blue skies greeted Riley when she woke up Sunday morning. She stretched her arms over her head and nestled up next to Kay. "Wake up, sleepy head. It's a beautiful day."

Kay opened one eye. "What time is it?"

"Time for a hike," Riley chirped. They were planning to walk Kay's land before they had to get in the car to drive back to Atlanta.

They sipped coffee as they laced up their hiking boots. "My parcel of land borders Doug's," Kay said, "but in order to access it, we've got to drive back out to the main road and follow it around Doug's property."

Riley opened the mini-fridge tucked in the corner of the room and pulled out two yogurts. "Okay." She got two spoons out of the drawer and sat down on the bed next to Kay. They downed their breakfast and headed out the door.

Kay threw her Jeep into four-wheel drive and maneuvered it along what Riley thought may have once been a driveway.

"Like I said, my piece of land is pretty overgrown," Kay said. She pointed out the front windshield. "Pretty soon, this will become impassable. We'll have to continue the rest of the way on foot."

Moments later, they came upon a massive fallen tree that prevented them from going any further. Riley opened the passenger door and jumped out of the car. Her boots sank into the mud when they hit the ground.

Kay slung a backpack over her shoulder and pointed toward a barely discernable footpath. "This will bring us to the top of the ridge. There's a small clearing up there and you'll get a pretty good view of my property from there." Kay took a few steps forward and paused. "Oh, and just so you know, it'll probably be wet. I hope you don't mind getting a little muddy."

Riley shook her head. "I don't mind at all. Lead the way." She followed Kay into the woods. *Squish, squish, squish.* Turned out "pretty wet" had been a serious understatement. Within minutes, her pants were splattered with mud and her socks were soaked through. At times, it felt like they were walking in knee deep snow and every hundred yards or so, they had to scale a fallen tree or some other debris. Riley was in decent shape, but before long, she was sweating and gasping for breath. She peeled off her outer layer and tied it around her waist.

The path dried up considerably as they climbed out of the valley and up onto the ridge. When they finally reached a clearing, Riley shielded her eyes with her hand as she stepped out from under the shade of the trees. She loosened her Georgia Bulldogs baseball hat from where it hung on her pack, tugged it on her head and gazed out at the horizon. Rolling green hills swelled as far as the eye could see.

Kay came up beside her. "Beautiful, huh?"

"Uh, yeah. It's stunning up here." She turned back toward the clearing. "Is this where you want to build your house?"

Kay pulled a flower off a nearby bush and twirled it in her hand. "Yep, it's the perfect spot, don't you think?"

Riley nodded. "Where does your property begin and end?"

Kay pointed off to the left. "See that dead tree with the bird's nest?"

Riley squinted. "I think so."

"That's about where my property ends and Scott's begins." She pointed in the opposite direction. "And the line between my land and Doug's is way over by those two tall pine trees that are all by themselves."

"Wow, it seems like you have a lot more than five acres, but to be honest, I don't really have a reference point. I don't really know how big five acres is."

"Soon to be ten acres."

"Really?"

"Uh-huh. I talked to Scott about his land right after we got back from Paris and we finally agreed on a price. He's going to talk to his lawyer, but if all goes as planned, I should be the proud owner of his five acres pretty soon."

"That's awesome, but I think he's an idiot to sell. It's so gorgeous here. You can't even see another house."

"Like I told you, he's all caught up in his fancy New York life. Still, I'm eager to close on the deal before he comes to his senses."

"Smart, very smart," Riley said. "Any idea how soon you'll try to build?"

"Well, funny you should ask. Doug gave me the name of an architect last night and I may try to call him next week."

"Wow, how exciting, although, you might want to consider putting in a driveway first."

Kay laughed. "Ya, think?"

Riley waved her hand across the clearing. "Would you ever consider moving here full time?"

"I won't say the thought has never crossed my mind but probably not in the foreseeable future. It would mean giving up my job at Logan and I'm not quite ready to do that."

"What would you do if you moved here? For work, I mean."

Kay's face lit up. "Well, I've always had this dream of opening a small store. That's probably what I would do."

"What kind of store?"

"Nothing big. Sort of a gourmet version of the classic general store."

"What a cool idea. I think it would be so fun to have a place like that."

Kay plopped down on a nearby stump and pulled Riley down next to her. They held hands and sat in silence for a long time, staring out at the landscape. The trees rustled in the wind.

"Kay?" Riley said finally.

"Yeah?"

"Have you ever thought about having kids?"

Kay didn't answer right away. She gazed out at the horizon. "Yeah, I have."

Riley's heart skipped a beat.

Kay shifted slightly on the stump. "I mean, I guess I always assumed I would. I just haven't met the right person." She squeezed Riley's hand. "Until now."

Riley blinked back tears and turned to face Kay, wishing she wasn't wearing sunglasses so she could see her eyes.

As if reading her mind, Kay pushed her sunglass up onto her head and looked at Riley intently. "I mean it, Rye. I can see having kids with you."

Riley's heart swelled. "Really?"

Kay nodded.

"I can see having kids with you too," she said quietly.

# CHAPTER THIRTY-SEVEN

Kay whistled quietly as they drove back to Atlanta. There still wasn't a cloud in the sky, and the trees in the North Carolina mountains were just beginning to bloom. She glanced over at the passenger seat. Riley was sound asleep, the tiniest amount of drool trickling out of the corner of her mouth. She looked adorable.

Kay returned her focus to the winding mountain road and thanked her lucky stars that Riley had waltzed into her life. Even with all of the craziness at work, Kay was happier than she'd ever been in her life. Having Riley by her side over the last few months, dealing with the Concordia mess together… It had thrown them together and brought them so close, so quickly. Kay had always been fiercely independent, and suddenly, along came this incredible woman, who could go from tender to tough as nails in the blink of an eye, and now, Kay couldn't imagine life without her.

Riley's drowsy voice interrupted her thoughts. "Where are we?"

"Just crossed over the border into Georgia. We should hit the outskirts of Atlanta in a little over an hour assuming we don't run into bad traffic."

Riley rubbed her eyes and glanced at her watch. "Shit, I need to call my father. It's his birthday." She dug into her purse and pulled out her phone. "Do you mind if I call him real quick? He and my mom are in Bermuda, and I want to catch him before they go to dinner."

Kay shook her head. "Knock yourself out."

"Hi, Dad. Happy Birthday… How's the weather there? Oh, good…"

Kay could only hear Riley's side of the conversation, but it seemed a bit impersonal, stilted almost. "How's your dad?" she asked after Riley ended the call.

"Fine. He and my mom spent the day on the golf course, and it sounds like he beat her for once. Knowing her, she probably let him because she knew he'd pout all night if he lost."

"Speaking of birthdays, you've got one coming up pretty soon, right?"

"Yep, the big 3-0."

"I can't believe we haven't talked about it. Do you want do anything special?"

"Nah. You know I'm not big on birthdays."

"Come on," Kay said. "We've got to do something. This is a big one. Your birthday falls on a Saturday this year, right?"

Riley looked down at her lap. "I think so…"

"Maybe we could go to Key West or something that weekend."

"Really, we don't need to do anything."

She took one hand off the steering wheel and touched Riley lightly on the arm. "What's wrong, baby?"

"It's just, well…" Riley picked at a hangnail. "My mom's organizing this dinner thing at their country club." She peeked over at Kay and then focused back on the hangnail. "I didn't ask her to. She just sort of took it upon herself."

Kay put her hand back on the steering wheel and stared straight ahead. "Oh, I see." She tried to keep the anger out of her voice. "How come you haven't mentioned it?"

Riley gazed out the passenger side window. "Kay, please, we've been through this so many times. You know how my family is."

"I do, but I happen to be your girlfriend. *God, that word seemed so inadequate*. Ya think you might have mentioned your birthday party."

"It's not a party." Riley crossed her arms and sighed.

"Oh, really?"

"It'll just be a family dinner—me, my parents, my brother and his wife, my aunt and uncle and maybe a few of my cousins."

"Huh, that sounds a lot like a party to me."

Riley slapped a hand on her thigh. "Damn it Kay, can we please just drop it."

"No, we cannot *just drop it*," Kay said, her voice growing louder. "I think I've been pretty supportive of the fact that you're not out to your parents. I can't believe you lied to me about this."

Riley started to cry. "I didn't lie about anything. I'm sorry I didn't mention it." She wiped the sleeve of her shirt across her nose and dug around in her bag for a handkerchief. She glanced back over at Kay and gave her a weak smile. "Maybe I could ask my mom if it would be okay for me to invite a friend to the dinner. I mean it is my—"

The suggestion made Kay mad. She'd come out when she was twenty-four and she wasn't exactly keen on the idea of going back in the closet, even if it was just for Riley's family. "I don't think that's a good idea."

Riley huddled up against the passenger door. "Why not."

"Well, for one thing, won't it be a bit odd for you to invite a *new* friend to the party and not some of the friends, like Stephanie, who you've known for a long time?"

"I suppose you have a point."

Kay glanced over at Riley again. "I love you, you know that, right?"

"Yeah."

"I'm just not sure I can go to dinner with your parents and pretend to be your friend." Kay gave Riley a wry smile. "I'm sure I'd do something inappropriate. I have a hard enough time keeping my hands off you as it is. Haven't you noticed that I sit as far away from you as I can when we have meetings together."

This elicited a laugh from Riley. "Now that you mention it…"

"All kidding aside," Kay said. "It really hurts that you didn't tell me about the party. I like to think we can talk to each other about everything."

"We can. I'm sorry. I'm an idiot."

Kay believed Riley, but that didn't mean she wasn't upset. She most definitely was. It was funny how a minor thing like a birthday party could cause so much friction. She turned up the volume on the radio and focused on the road. Traffic grew heavier as they approached Atlanta. "Fucking traffic," she muttered as she tapped the brakes.

Riley pulled out her phone and opened her traffic app. "It's red for the next few miles."

"Fantastic."

They crawled along I-75 until they reached the exit for Kay's house and it was after dark by the time she pulled the Jeep into her driveway. Riley open the passenger door and nodded toward her car parked on the street in front of Kay's house. "I think I'm going to head home."

Kay walked around to the back of her Jeep and pulled out both their suitcases. "Are you sure?"

"Yeah, I'm sure," Riley said quietly. "I had a really nice weekend. I'm sorry I didn't tell you about my birthday party." She reached out for Kay's hand and gave it a squeeze but didn't say anything more. She picked up her suitcase and walked to the curb. Kay watched as she loaded her luggage into the trunk, climbed in the driver's seat and drove away.

As soon as she finished unpacking, Kay called Ethan. She needed a shoulder to lean on and he was usually up to the task. Her mood improved ever so slightly when she heard his voice on the other end.

"How was the weekend in Asheville?" he asked.

"God, Ethan, it was amazing."

"I'm happy to hear that, but there's something in your voice. Are you okay?"

"Yeah, I'm fine…It's just, Riley's mom is throwing her a birthday party and—"

"Let me guess, you're not invited."

"Not only that. Riley didn't even tell me about it."

"Oh."

"I know." Kay rehashed the conversation she and Riley'd had in the car on the way back to Atlanta.

"I'm sorry sweetie. That sort of sucks."

"To put it mildly."

"But you need to think about it from her perspective."

Kay groaned in frustration.

"I'm serious, Kay. You don't know what it's like to be in her shoes. I'm sure she wants to tell her parents about you just as badly as you want her to. If you love her, I think you need to be patient and—"

"I do love her, very much."

"And it sounds like she loves you too."

"Uh-huh."

"Well, the worst thing you can do is let her parents drive you apart. If that happens, then they, and their homophobia, win."

Kay let out a forced laugh. "You're right, but I feel like I've tried to be supportive. I'm starting to think she'll never come out to them and I'm not sure I can handle that."

"Just lay off her a little bit. You guys are going through a lot right now. There's no need to throw more fuel on the fire. I think you'll agree, it's hot enough already."

Once she got off the phone, Kay stood at the window in her sunroom and stared out into her backyard. One of her big clay flowerpots had tipped over. *Well, that's strange. It would take hurricane force winds to topple that thing.* She opened her back door and stepped onto the patio. It was a clear night and the temperature had dropped. She wrapped her arms around her torso as she walked over the flagstones. That's when she noticed it. The hairs on her arms stood up. A section of the bushes along the back side of her house was trampled. As if someone had marched through them. Maybe Mrs. Fairchild wasn't crazy after all.

# CHAPTER THIRTY-EIGHT

Riley went to her birthday dinner alone, and although it was nice to be with her family, she couldn't shake the sadness at not having Kay there.

They were seated in a private room at the club and a large cake and a pile of presents sat in the corner. She tried to remind herself she had a lot to be grateful for. She tried to be gracious and made her best effort to be cheerful, but for all her faults, her mother was extremely observant. "You're awfully quiet tonight, Riley. Is everything okay?"

She thought about telling her right then, telling her that she was sad because the love of her life wasn't at her side, but she held off. Now was not the time. "I'm fine Mom, just a little tired."

"She's just bummed about being thirty," Bobby bellowed. "Aren't you sis?"

She gave her brother a weak smile. "Yeah, that's it, Bobby." *God, he could be so thick.*

That night as she drove home, she made a promise to herself. She was going to come out to her mother, soon. Very soon. If her mother flipped, so be it. Kay was too important. She didn't want to keep her a secret anymore, no matter what the consequences.

A few days later, Riley was sitting at her desk when she got the sudden urge to do it. It was like a wave of courage came out of nowhere and washed over her. It was the middle of the workday, but without giving it another thought, she cleared her calendar, walked out to her car and drove out to Buckhead, praying her mother was home and not off playing golf at the club. As she barreled up I-75, she took lots of deep breaths and tried to get her heartrate under control. She considered aborting the mission about fifty times but gritted her teeth and kept her foot on the gas.

She inched up her parents' driveway, parked her car and peeked in the garage. She wasn't sure if she was relieved or petrified to see her mother's car parked in its spot. She crept up the front walk, and figuring she'd startle her mother if she just barged into the house, rang the doorbell. Moments later, she heard the door unlock. Her mother stood there and eyed her suspiciously. "Riley, what are you doing here?" She looked down at her watch. "It's three o'clock, on a Tuesday."

"I know Mom." She took a deep breath and slowly let it out. "There's something I need to tell you."

Her mother's eyes grew wide, sending her eyebrows far up her forehead. "Oh, my, God. You're pregnant!"

Riley burst out laughing. "No, Mom. I'm not pregnant." Her tension eased slightly. "Can I come in."

Her mother held the front door open wide. "Oh, yes, of course," she said. "I was just making a salad for tonight. One of your father's partners from the firm and his wife are coming for dinner."

"Oh, that's nice," Riley said as she followed her into the kitchen. She pointed to the small breakfast table. "Do you mind if we sit?"

Her mother gave her a questioning look. "No, of course not. Would you like some water or anything?"

"Um, no, thanks. I'm afraid I'll lose my nerve if I don't come right out and tell you what I need to say."

A worried look crossed her mother's face, and she slowly sat down at the table. "What is it, honey?"

Riley pulled out a chair and sat across from her mother. She looked down at her hands and then back up. "I'm gay."

Her mother's expression didn't change. She just stared back at her.

"Did you hear what I said, Mom?"

Her mother nodded. "Yes, I heard you."

"Well, aren't you going to say something?"

"Are you doing this to hurt me?"

"Jeez, Mom." Riley ran a hand through her hair. Anger bubbled up inside her, but she tried to keep her voice even. "I'm not *doing* anything. This is not about *you*. It's about *me*." She stood and stared at her mother. "I just thought you should know… I can show myself out," she said, biting back tears.

"Wait!" her mother yelled when she was halfway to the front door. "Why are you telling me this now?"

Riley walked back into the kitchen and leaned against the counter. A tear slid down her cheek. "Because I'm seeing someone…someone I think I could spend the rest of my life with."

"I see," her mother said and the expression on her face softened a bit, giving Riley a glimmer of hope. It was short-lived. "What about children?" her mother countered. "You've always talked about wanting a family."

"If Kay, that's her name by the way…if she and I end up together, I hope we'll have kids. There's no reason we can't have a family."

This comment seemed to push her mother over the edge. "I don't. I can't," she sputtered. "What am I supposed to tell my friends?"

"Tell them whatever the hell you want!" She softened her tone slightly and added, "Who knows, maybe they'll surprise you? I bet you some of them have gay children or relatives."

Her mother gave her a skeptical look but didn't respond. Riley almost felt bad for her. She rocked back and forth, unsure of what else to say. "Well, now you know, anyway. I need to get back to work."

After a long silence, her mother said, "I need some time to process this."

Riley nodded and left. As soon as she was safely in her car, she started to sob. She wasn't sure why exactly. She didn't know if it was because she was disappointed at her mother's reaction. *What did I expect?* Or whether it was relief at having finally come out to her. She rested her head against the steering wheel and cried until she had no more tears.

A quick glance in the rearview mirror told her she was in no shape to go back to the office. Her eyes were puffy and red, and mascara was streaked down her face. She wondered if her mother was fairing any better inside the house. For a brief second, she considered going in to check on her, but she felt emotionally raw and there was a good chance she'd say something she'd regret. She started her car and drove away.

Even though it was bordering on rush hour, traffic back into the city wasn't too bad. Most people were headed in the opposite direction—from work in the city to home in the suburbs—at that time of day. Typically both she and Kay stayed at the office until at least six, but Riley knew Kay had left the office early that day for a doctor's appointment and there was a good chance she'd be home by now. As the 14th Street exit came into view, she made a snap decision and maneuvered her car over into the right lane to get off the highway. Her mood improved dramatically as she made her way toward Virginia Highland, and she was feeling downright giddy when she spotted Kay's Jeep in the driveway.

"Anyone home," she said as she stepped into Kay's foyer.

"I'm back here."

Riley dropped her bag and made her way back toward the kitchen. A wave of emotion swept over her when she laid eyes on Kay. She had already changed out of her work clothes and she was wearing an apron. She looked up from the cookbook propped up on the counter in front of her and gave Riley a crooked grin. "This is a nice surprise. You left work early… Oh, have you been crying? Is everything okay?"

Riley didn't say a word. She walked around the counter and threw her arms around Kay's broad shoulders. "I love you so much," she said and immediately started to cry again. She felt Kay's arms circle her waist and pull them together. They stood that way for a long while until Kay pulled back slightly and looked her in the eyes. "What's the matter, baby? You look like hell."

Riley stepped back and dabbed her eyes with the sleeve of her blouse. "I went out to Buckhead this afternoon."

Kay gave her a curious look. "You went to see your parents?"

"My mother, specifically. My dad was at work."

"What made you…I don't—"

"I told her about you, about us," Riley said quickly. "I came out to her."

Kay set down the small whisk she was holding. "Oh, my God, really?" Kay pulled Riley into another tight hug but released her seconds later. A look of concern crossed her face. "How'd she take the news?"

Riley pulled one of the stools out from under the counter and sat down. "Hmm. I certainly wouldn't describe her reaction as happy, but she didn't pitch a fit or kick me out of the house."

"Well, that's good, I guess."

"I think she was more shocked than anything. Oh, and she's worried about how her friends will react."

"Oh, God, really?"

"Uh-huh. She said she needed time to process it, the fact that I'm gay."

"Well, I'm proud of you."

"I'm kinda proud of me too," Riley said. "I still can't believe I did it."

Kay rested her hands on the counter and her brow furrowed. "I hope I didn't push you too hard… I hope you told her because you were ready."

Riley reached across the counter, clasped Kay's hand and gazed into her dark eyes. "You're extremely important to me and I don't want to keep you a secret from my family anymore."

"You're incredibly important to me too," Kay said softly.

Riley settled back onto her stool and burst out laughing.

"What's so funny?"

Riley pointed toward the counter. It was littered with an array of spices and various other ingredients, multiple mixing bowls, a stack of measuring cups and a handful of other kitchen gadgets. "You, Kay Corbett, queen of takeout, are cooking? God, I can't believe I didn't notice all this when I first walked in."

Kay chuckled. "Yeah, I know, it's a miracle, huh? I stopped by the grocery store on the way home from the doctor, and I don't know, for some reason I got inspired."

"How did everything go with your appointment? It was just a routine exam, right?"

"Yeah, nothing out of the ordinary."

"Well, that's good news." Riley gestured to the mess on the countertop. "So what is it you're making exactly?"

"Scallops with an orange ginger sauce."

"Wow, that sounds pretty advanced. Need a hand?"

"Nah, I'm good. You could pour us each a glass of wine, and if you don't mind, maybe set the table."

Riley kicked off her heels and padded toward the wine fridge. "I'm on it."

The following day, Riley met Stephanie for lunch.

"So, what's new?" Riley asked once they'd placed their orders.

Stephanie shrugged. "Not much, same old, same old. I like my job in concept, but so much of what I do is repetitive brainless shit."

As she listened to Stephanie talk, Riley fidgeted with her silverware. As far as she knew, Stephanie knew nothing about the price fixing and tricky accounting taking place at Logan. Riley had told her nothing. Nothing about Fred Archie and nothing about the complaint they'd submitted to the SEC. She desperately wanted to but knew she couldn't or at least shouldn't say anything about it. It felt strange, dishonest almost, to keep something like that from her best friend, especially because it was constantly on her mind and had virtually consumed her life as of late.

"…But enough about me. How are things with you and Kay?"

Riley smiled and tried to push thoughts of Concordia and Fred Archie out of her head. "They're pretty fantastic. More than fantastic, actually."

"I'm so happy for you two." Stephanie reached over and squeezed Riley's hand. "You're downright glowing, Rye."

Riley blushed. "Thanks Steph. I'm pretty happy for us too. I've gone ahead and fallen head over heels in love with her."

Stephanie squealed with delight. "You think she's *the one*."

"I do."

"See, I told you that special someone was out there waiting for you."

"You did, my wise friend." Riley jolted upright. "Oh, and you are so not going to believe this…"

Stephanie scooted forward in her chair. "Believe what?"

Riley paused briefly for effect. "I told my mother. About Kay."

Stephanie's jaw dropped open. "I'm sorry, I must be at the wrong table. I'm supposed to be having lunch with my friend Riley, Southern belle extraordinaire."

"Ha ha. You are so *not* funny."

"I am in fact, hilarious," Stephanie protested. "But, in all seriousness, that's *huge*. I'm super proud of you. Did she totally flip?"

After giving Stephanie a quick play-by-play of the conversation with her mother, she said, "I may be delusional, but I'm hoping she'll come around and realize having a gay daughter is not the end of the world." As if on cue, Riley's phone rang. She pulled it out of her purse and gave Stephanie a mock look of terror. "It's my mother… Do you mind if I take it? Something's got to be up. She never calls me during the workday."

"Not at all."

Riley stood and hurried outside, answering the call with a tentative, "Hello."

"Hello, Riley. It's your mother."

"Yeah, I saw the caller—"

"I'm sorry to bother you at work. Do you have a moment?"

She paced on the sidewalk in front of the restaurant. "Yeah, sure, Mom. Is something wrong."

Her mother cleared her throat. "I had a talk with your father…"

*Oh, Lord.* "Okay."

"I told him about you and your *friend*, Kay."

*Girlfriend.* Riley fought off the urge to correct her mother. "And?"

Her mother's voice dropped to a whisper. "We both just want you to be happy, Riley, and if Kay makes you happy…"

"She does. Very happy."

"Anyway, I was calling to see if… Would you two, you and Kay, like to come to dinner next Sunday? I'd invite you this Sunday, but we've got the club championship all weekend and—"

"Next Sunday would be great Mom." Riley smiled into the phone.

"Okay honey, we'll see you then and I…I look forward to meeting Kay."

Riley was too stunned to speak. That last statement, coming from her mother. Maybe she'd underestimated her. She croaked a goodbye, ended the call and scurried back inside the restaurant.

"Well?" Stephanie said when she sat down.

"Did you see that pig fly by the restaurant?" Riley asked with a laugh. "My mother just invited me and Kay to Sunday dinner."

# CHAPTER THIRTY-NINE

"Well, here we are," Riley said as they approached a big white mailbox, the name BAUER stamped on the side in big block letters. She crept up the long circular drive and came to a stop in front of the house. She peered over at Kay in the passenger seat. "Ready?"

"As I'll ever be."

"All right. Here goes. God, I'm a nervous wreck. I mean, I know they'll love you but I'm just..."

Kay squeezed her hand. "I know, baby. It'll be fine."

Perfectly manicured boxwoods lined the path to the heavy oak front door. Riley took a deep breath, reached for the handle and stepped inside. Fresh flowers adorned the table in the foyer and the scent of Pledge assaulted her nostrils. She could hear a baseball game on in the family room. "Hello, anybody home?" Her voice echoed in the large, two-story foyer.

An instant later, her mother came bustling out of the kitchen, tugging off her apron. Riley glanced at her watch. They were a few minutes early.

After giving Kay a not so subtle up and down, her mother stuck out her hand. "You must be Kay."

Kay smiled broadly and shook the outstretched hand. "It's nice to meet you, Mrs. Bauer."

Her mother craned her neck toward the family room. "William," she hollered. "The girls are here. Come say hello."

She heard her father get up off the couch and shuffle toward the foyer. "Well, hello there, gals," he bellowed. He embraced Riley warmly and turned toward Kay. "Welcome." Riley smiled to herself. Her father had always been a man of few words.

After her father retreated back to the family room, Riley and Kay followed her mother into the kitchen. "What can we do to help?" Riley asked.

Her mother slipped the apron back on. "Nothing at all. I'm in good shape. You girls just sit and relax," she said pointing toward the kitchen stools. "We'll sit for cocktails as soon as your brother gets here. You know, ever since the baby, they're always running late."

"Bobby's coming?"

"Oh, yes, didn't I tell you?"

Riley bit her lip. This was so typical. She forced a smile. "No, you didn't mention it." Bobby and Lynn's appearance at Sunday dinner had become less and less frequent lately, and she couldn't help but wonder if they were coming because they were curious to meet Kay or whether her mother had called them in for moral support.

While they waited for Bobby, they carried on pleasant but forced small talk. Riley's tension eased somewhat as she watched her mother flutter around the kitchen, occasionally dropping a mixing spoon here or a measuring cup there. Her mother, normally Mrs. Confidence, was also a bundle of nerves.

When Bobby and Lynn showed up, Carly, their baby girl, took to Kay immediately, and during cocktails, she fussed if anyone else tried to hold her.

While she passed hors d'oeuvres, Riley leaned over and whispered in Kay's ear. "Are you okay?"

"I'm fine. She's adorable," Kay replied as she bounced the baby on her knee.

She sat back down and watched Carly and Kay while she sipped her wine. The baby obviously wasn't aware of it, but she was doing a splendid job of breaking the ice between her family and Kay.

During dinner Kay had her dad and Bobby in stitches with some story she was telling. If someone were to peek in the dining room window, they might assume the group gathered around the table had been having Sunday dinner together for years, a thought that made Riley tear up.

Once they were done eating, her mom stood and began clearing the table. She gestured toward Riley. "Sweetheart, will you give me a hand?"

Kay moved to help but her mother gently touched her arm. "No, dear. You're the guest. We've got this."

For the umpteenth time, Riley mused that it wouldn't kill her brother to lend a hand, but she bit her tongue. The last thing she wanted to do was ruffle feathers during Kay's inaugural Bauer family dinner.

Riley stacked the last of the dishes in the sink and went in search of the dessert plates while her mother started the coffeepot. When she walked back into the kitchen, her mother was pulling a large tray out of the extra fridge in the pantry. It was covered with small glass dessert dishes full of fruit. Using her head, her mother gestured toward the freezer in the kitchen. "Grab the ice cream, would you, honey."

While Riley added a scoop of vanilla to each mound of fruit, her mother busied herself arranging coffee cups on a platter. They worked in silence until her mother said, "Kay seems very nice…not at all what I expected."

Riley didn't even want to hazard a guess to what her mother *expected*. God knows what ill-informed notion she had of what a lesbian should or could look like. Still, she appreciated the fact that her mother was trying. "I'm glad you like her. Thanks for having us over."

Dessert was a relatively uneventful affair except for the few borderline inappropriate questions her brother asked Kay about lesbians. Riley rolled her eyes and tried to brush them off. As usual, he'd had a few too many.

After dinner, Riley led Kay upstairs to her childhood bedroom. As controlling as she could be, Riley's mother had pretty much let her decorate it the way she'd wanted, and it still looked almost like it did the day she left for college, although the pink and green flowered wallpaper was slightly more faded than it had been back then. A large poster of Mia Hamm, the soccer icon, hung over the neatly organized desk, and the shelves next to her bed overflowed with books, photos and trophies.

A look of surprise crossed Kay's face as she scanned the shelves. "You were a cheerleader? You never told me that."

Riley looked at her sheepishly. "Yep, but only for one year. I didn't like it as much as other sports, if you can even call cheerleading a sport."

"I think you can. I mean it involves coordination and they do all those pyramids and stuff."

"I guess."

Kay eyed the trophies. "Ah, and based on all of these, I'd guess you were a pretty good tennis player."

"Yeah, I did okay. I don't play much anymore though."

"That's one game I've never really mastered."

"Sweet. Maybe there's at least one sport I can beat you at."

"You know better than to challenge me," Kay said with a smile.

"Good point." Riley pulled Kay into her arms and kissed her softly on the lips. "Thanks for having dinner with my family."

"They're actually kind of nice," Kay said.

"Sorry about my brother. He can be sort of an ass sometimes."

Kay waved it off. "It's okay. I'm just happy to be here."

# CHAPTER FORTY

When Kay's thirty-fifth birthday rolled around in mid-May, Riley surprised her with a trip to a golf resort in South Carolina. She'd rented a small condo and if they squinted, they could just make out the ocean from its balcony. Unfortunately, or maybe fortunately, it rained practically nonstop the entire time they were there. They managed to get in nine holes of golf before the worst of the rain blew in, but otherwise, they spent most of the weekend in bed.

"Sorry about this weather," Riley said. "I thought it was supposed to be 'April showers, bring May flowers.'"

Kay snuggled up next to her. "I've got no complaints."

"Yeah, at least we've gotten a lot of, um exercise." Riley said with a laugh. They were lying naked together in bed after having made love for the third time that day.

"Mmm-hmm. I couldn't have asked for a better birthday." Kay rolled over on her back. "But, shit, I'm starving. How about you?"

Riley tickled Kay's stomach. "No surprise you've worked up quite an appetite. Want me to warm up some of the leftover chicken parm from last night's dinner?"

"Yum. Yes, please."

Riley rolled out of bed, pulled on a robe and padded into the kitchen. When the food was ready, she carried it back to the bedroom and called out, "Room service." She set both plates full of steaming food down on the night table next to Kay and handed her a set of silverware and a napkin.

Kay sat up in bed. "Rye?"

"Yeah?"

"I was just thinking... When's your lease up?"

Riley sat down on the bed next to her. "End of July. Why?"

"Well, I was wondering if maybe you wanted to move in with me."

Riley's eyes about popped out of her head. "You mean live together?"

Kay nodded. "Yeah, unless you think it's too soon."

Riley shook her head. "No. No, I don't think it's too soon... I'm...it's just... We've never talked about it."

Kay tugged at a loose thread on the bed. "Well, what do you think about it?"

Riley gripped Kay's face with both hands and gave her a slow deep kiss before she replied. "Nothing would make me happier."

"Really?"

"Uh-huh."

"Okay, great. How about tomorrow?"

"Ha ha, very funny."

"Okay, then, how about the day after tomorrow?"

"I pretty much live at your house anyway," Riley replied. It was true. She spent five or six nights a week at Kay's. "But it would be wonderful to make it official and actually live there with you, hang my clothes next to yours in the closet, stack my books on the night table..." A wicked grin crossed Riley's face. "Fill your bathroom drawers with my makeup, scatter my shoes across your bedroom floor..."

Kay punched her arm softly. "Hmm, maybe this isn't such a good idea."

"Well, if it makes you feel any better. I have almost zero furniture. Most of the stuff at my house belongs to my landlord. I'll ask him if I can get out of my lease a little early, but even if he says no, I don't see any reason to wait until my lease is up. I could move in sooner if you want."

Kay nuzzled her head in Riley's neck, uttering a muffled, "Yes, I want."

Riley draped an arm over Kay's shoulder and kissed the top of her head. "Maybe we can start bringing some of my stuff over next weekend?"

Kay lifted her head. "Perfect. In the meantime, I'll work on making some room in the dresser and closet so my beautiful girlfriend can move in with me." She paused. "I love you. This feels right."

Riley smiled. "It feels more than right."

* * *

When they got back to Atlanta, Riley went back to her house like she did almost every Sunday night. It was her one night to do all the stuff she didn't get done during the week when she was at Kay's—things like cleaning the house, doing laundry, paying bills, calling her mother and other exciting stuff.

However, Sunday evenings had always been one of her favorite nights of the week and she always hated having to leave Kay to head home, especially after they'd spent a relaxing weekend together. She whistled while she ran a vacuum around her house. Pretty soon, she and Kay would be able to spend every Sunday evening together.

There was no doubt that moving in with Kay was a big decision. Riley had never lived with anyone before. Sure, she'd had roommates in college and when she'd lived in a decrepit farmhouse with some friends after graduation, but she'd never *lived* lived with someone else. It represented a significant step forward in their relationship, one Riley was more than ready to take.

She shut off the vacuum, coiled its long cord and stuck it back in her kitchen closet. After she tossed a load of darks in the washer, she grabbed her phone and shot Stephanie a text. *Guess what? Kay asked me to move in with her!*

Stephanie's reply came back with lots of smiling emojis.

*Let's hope my mother is half as excited.* Riley was tempted to call her parents and break the news, but she was on cloud nine and she wanted to stay there for a little while longer. Part of her was convinced her mother still harbored at least some fantasies that being a lesbian was just a phase for Riley. When Riley announced she was moving in with Kay, it would probably chip away at those illusions, which wasn't necessarily a bad thing, but there was no telling how her mother might react.

# CHAPTER FORTY-ONE

For a few weeks, Kay basked in the joy of living with Riley, waking up next to her every morning in what she now considered *their* bed and having dinner with her every night. As she had promised, Riley's makeup and curling irons had taken up a lot of real estate in the bathroom, but Kay didn't care. In fact, it made her happy just to have Riley's stuff occupy her space.

Once Riley moved in, the house felt like *home* in a way it never had before. Kay got that tingly warm feeling when Riley walked in the door after work at night. From an emotional perspective, their relationship was intense, but at the same time effortless. Kay had never felt this connected to another human being.

For a brief snapshot in time, she almost forgot about the saga at Logan—almost. Just as Fred Archie had predicted, it had been complete radio silence since they'd filed their complaint with the SEC. They'd received confirmation from the SEC that the complaint had been received, but otherwise, total crickets.

However, the spell of tranquility was short-lived. After they filed the complaint with the SEC, things at work continued to be fairly normal, at least under the circumstances, until one day they weren't. Greg called Kay and her team into an impromptu meeting first thing one Wednesday morning. It looked like he'd slept in his clothes and stubble dotted on his normally cleanly shaven face. He started the meeting by announcing a massive sale in the European markets Logan served, a move that made absolutely no sense. They were in the midst of one of their busiest seasons and their planes were flying with few empty seats. Kay put her hand up and began to protest but Greg cut her off.

"No one asked your opinion, Kay."

"But these markets are my responsibility and what you're proposing doesn't—"

"Did you hear what I said? Shut the fuck up."

Kay was stunned, and from the looks on their faces, her colleagues were too. Greg had never been a saint, but he'd always treated her in a reasonably professional manner. The most curious thing though was that it, the sale Greg was suggesting, would knock them out of sync with Concordia. Greg had never strayed from the Concordia game plan—ever. Being in sync with the group had been a cornerstone of the scheme from the very beginning.

The environment at work only got worse from there. The following afternoon, Greg called her an "overrated bitch" during an executive committee meeting. Many of the people in the room were senior to Greg and she was sure one of them would call him out, but no one did. The last straw came when he made her the fall guy for an abysmal revenue report that had just been released, a report that was the result of a fare structure he'd demanded she implement. This time when Kay protested, Greg charged at her. She jumped out of her chair, afraid if she didn't, he'd tackle her.

She escaped to the ladies' room and broke down in tears. After years of climbing the corporate ladder in a heavily male dominated industry, it took a lot to rattle Kay, but with all the SEC-related shit hanging over her head, her nerves were frayed. She stared at her reflection in the bathroom mirror. *Something was going on, goddamn it.* Why else would Greg be behaving the way he was?

Kay's colleague Rita walked in the ladies' room and stood next to her at the sink. "Kay, are you okay? Greg is out of control. I can't believe he—"

"Yeah, I'm all right." Kay let out a long sigh.

"You better come back into the conference room," Rita said. "Greg keeps throwing you under the bus. I think you should be there to defend yourself."

Kay dabbed her face with a paper towel and followed Rita back to the meeting. All eyes fell on her when she reclaimed her seat at the table, but no one uttered a word.

Greg smirked at her and gestured toward one of the executives. "Brad was just asking me about the updated Asia market analysis, Kay. Why don't you give us an overview of what it revealed?"

Kay glared at Greg. He knew damn well the market analysis wasn't done. Not even close. They took weeks to prepare and he'd only just asked her to update it.

"Well, Kay. We're all waiting."

She desperately wanted to tell him to go fuck himself. Instead she said, "Greg, as I know you are well aware, we've just started working on it."

"So, are you saying it isn't done?"

"Yes, that's what I'm saying."

"Well, that's very disappointing, Kay."

The dreadful meeting dragged on for another hour and it was nearly six p.m. when Greg called it to a close. As soon as it was over, Kay bolted from the conference room and took the stairs down to the seventh floor. A shiver ran down her spine as soon as she stepped into her office. Someone had left a large gray rubber rat on top of her keyboard.

Her heart started to race, and her mind immediately went to Riley. She'd be home from work by now. Her mind flashed back to the call from Mrs. Fairchild about the red-headed trespasser. She yanked her phone out of her suit pocket and shot Riley a text. *Turn on the alarm. I'm on my way home.*

It had been an oppressively hot summer day in Atlanta, and even at that time of the evening, the short walk across the Logan parking lot made Kay sweat. She jumped in her Jeep and threw the car in gear. Taillights greeted her as soon as she turned onto the ramp for I-85. "Fuck!" She glanced around for her phone. It had slipped between the seats and she couldn't reach it. "Goddamn it."

As she crawled along the interstate, she glanced in her rearview mirror. A matte black BMW coupe was two cars back. It looked remarkably similar to the car that had pulled out of the Logan parking lot right behind her. The coupe kept its distance but followed her off the exit.

Even though the A/C was on full blast, a bead of sweat had formed on Kay's forehead. When she stopped at a light, she wriggled out of her suit jacket and rolled up the sleeves of her blouse. It didn't help much. She needed fresh air. She lowered all the windows in the Jeep and once she hit the gas, the wind blew her hair up off her neck. It felt wonderful.

Unless she was stopping at the grocery store, she always took the exact same route home from work. Not today. She was anxious to get home to check on Riley, but she made a small loop around her neighborhood. It wasn't until she reached her street, that the BMW stopped tailing her. She turned right and it continued straight.

Her house alarm blared as soon as she opened the front door.

"Kay?" Riley called out.

"Yeah, it's me," Kay replied as she scrambled to enter her security code on the wall panel.

Riley ran into the foyer and pulled her into a hug. "Is everything okay."

Kay stepped back and looked her in the eye. "I honestly don't know. Greg was even more of an ass to me today. He actually lurched at me during a meeting. Scared the crap out of me."

"What the fuck is going on with him?"

"Hell if I know, but get this. Someone left a big rubber rat on my desk this afternoon."

"Jesus."

"I know, baby. And that's not all. On my way home, there was this black BMW. It was totally fucking following me."

"Shit, Kay. I'm scared."

"Me too, baby."

"This all has to be related to the—"

"The SEC," Kay whispered. "It would explain what's going on at the office."

"You think they've gotten wind that someone went to the feds?"

"I don't know, but if I had to guess, I'd say yes. I can't put my finger on it. There are no blaring sirens or flashing red lights, but I don't know, people at work seem really on edge. It's like a big dark cloud has moved over Logan headquarters. There's this tension that wasn't there before."

"Do you think this whole thing is about to blow?" Riley asked.

Kay nodded. "I'm certain of it."

# CHAPTER FORTY-TWO

After a week of constantly looking over her shoulder and getting even less sleep than normal, Kay was nearing a breaking point. Greg continued to treat her like utter shit and she desperately wanted to quit. There was no doubt in her mind that he was acting the way he was in an effort to wear her down. She couldn't cave now. She couldn't give him that satisfaction.

She was dutifully plugging away at the Asia market analysis when her office phone rang. She knocked over her water bottle, promptly soaking her keyboard, and cursed under her breath when she saw the name on her caller ID: Cynthia Abbott. *What on earth*? Cynthia was the personal assistant for Logan's CEO, Howard Rome. Kay grabbed some napkins from her desk drawer and dabbed up the spilled water as she snatched up the receiver. "Hello, this is Kay Corbett."

"Kay, this is Cynthia Abbott from Mr. Rome's office."

"Oh, um, hi."

"Mr. Rome would like to see you. Would you please come up to ten?" Her voice was devoid of emotion.

"Now?"

"Yes, right now."

"Of course. I'll be right up," Kay replied.

She popped a mint into her mouth, pulled her suit coat off the back of her chair and grabbed her cell phone. As she trudged up the three flights to the tenth floor, a pit formed in her stomach. Being summoned to Howard Rome's palatial office did not spell good news.

"Hello Cynthia," Kay said when she stepped into the executive suite.

Cynthia looked up from her computer and grunted hello. She bore a striking resemblance to *Grumpy Cat*. "Please have a seat. I'll let Mr. Rome know you're here."

Before Kay had a chance to sit down, the door to Howard Rome's office flew open and Greg Brandywine strolled out. "Hello Kay," he said without making eye contact.

"Hello, Greg." *You fucking slime ball.*

Greg waved toward the CEO's office. "He's all yours."

Kay marched into Howard Rome's office with as much confidence as she could muster.

Howard gave her the most insincere smile she'd ever seen. "Please close the door behind you."

Kay lowered herself into one of the sturdy chairs flanking his heavy wood desk.

Howard crossed his arms over his chest and scowled, causing his bushy eyebrows to touch. "I've done some digging…"

She tried not to twitch under the glare of his beady eyes. She knew what was coming.

"It seems," he spat, "you're responsible for the *goddamn* subpoena the SEC just threw in our face." He loosened his tie and tugged at the collar cinched around his neck, his face red with anger. "Who the hell do you think you are?"

"I wasn't aware the SEC had issued a subpoena," Kay stammered. It was true; the SEC had given her no warning. She had no idea where they stood in their investigation.

"Bullshit!" He leaned across his desk. "I've got it on good authority that you're the one who went to the feds."

Kay's hands began to tremble. *How the fuck did he find out it was me?*

As he rattled on, Kay's fear morphed into anger. She wanted to lash out, but she bit her tongue. She wanted to watch Howard dig himself deeper into shit. If he was going to fire her, and she was pretty sure he was, his problems were about to get a whole lot bigger. He'd just pegged her as a whistleblower—the person who'd reported Logan to the SEC. Was he really that stupid. Surely, he knew retaliating against a whistleblower was a big giant no-no. The law was *very* clear on that.

She fought off the urge to bolt from the room and drive straight to her attorney's office.

"What? Don't have anything to say for yourself?" he spat. "Not that anything you could say would help the *goddamn* situation."

Kay pursed her lips and glared back at him, but she remained silent and this seemed to further enrage him.

He foamed at the mouth like a rabid dog. "I'm sure you're wondering why I called you up here?"

Kay nodded and tried to keep a smile from creeping across her face. Her fear and anger turned to amusement. He really was stupid enough to fire her.

Howard pounded his fist down on the desk. "Your employment at Logan is hereby terminated, effective immediately." He pointed toward the door with his chubby finger. "Now, get the hell out of my office. Security will escort you out of the building."

Kay desperately wanted to punch the bastard in the face, but in an act of great restraint, she managed to maintain her composure. She sauntered toward the door of Howard's office. As soon as she crossed the threshold, the first thought that crossed her mind was Riley. If Howard Rome knew Kay had gone to the SEC, there was a damn good chance he knew about Riley's involvement too. She needed to…

"If you'll come with us, Ms. Corbett."

Kay's head snapped up. Two hulking security guards dressed in blue military-looking outfits were stationed next to Cynthia's desk. Kay's legs started to shake. She was in shock and she had to reach Riley. The security guards didn't touch her, they didn't need to. One flanked her right, the other her left, as they escorted her to her office to grab her purse, and then through the sea of cubicles toward the elevators, past the inquiring eyes of all of her coworkers. The hulks walked her all the way to her Jeep, confiscated her Logan ID badge, and watched as she drove out of the parking lot.

As soon as she was outside the imposing metal gates, she pulled over, tugged her phone out of her pocket and called Riley. It went straight to voice mail. "Shiiiiit!" The clock on her phone read 2:03 p.m. Riley was probably still in the air on her way back from Seattle. Kay tossed her phone on the passenger seat, threw the Jeep in gear and hit the gas. Twenty minutes later, she was sitting in a conference room at Fred Archie's law firm in downtown Atlanta. She pounced the second her attorney entered the room. "You promised us our identities would be protected!"

Fred settled into the seat next to her. "Take a deep breath, Kay." His voice was deep and carried a heavy southern drawl. "Tell me what happened."

"I got fired! That's what happened." Kay proceeded to give him a quick synopsis of her not-so-pleasant encounter with Howard Rome.

Fred leaned back in his chair and interlaced his hands behind his head. "Interesting," he said. "Very interesting." He started to say something more but paused and asked, "Where's Riley? Was she fired too?"

Kay shook her head. "I haven't been able to reach her. She's in the air on her way back from Seattle."

Fred tapped his finger on the table. "Okay, well, nothing we can do about that right now. Going back to Howard Rome… If what he told you is true, that Logan has been subpoenaed by the SEC, then the SEC's investigation into the airline has moved very quickly, very quickly indeed."

Kay felt like she was going to burst. She knew Fred was brilliant, but he talked irritatingly slow, and right now, she wanted to strangle him. "How do you mean?"

"Well, the SEC would only issue a subpoena after they'd thoroughly reviewed all the evidence we handed over."

"Issuing a subpoena is a good sign, right?"

"A very good sign indeed. They must feel there's a *very* strong indication of wrongdoing on the part of the airline."

Kay briefly wondered if Fred had been tipped off about the subpoena, knew one had been issued, but as usual, his poker-faced expression gave away nothing. She crossed her legs and sat back in her chair. "We freakin' handed the SEC this case on a silver platter. I mean, the evidence we gave them was pretty damning."

He nodded. "It certainly was."

"And now I've been fired..."

"Yes, and now you've been fired. Which means," Fred boomed, "Howard Rome just made a very serious mistake. The SEC investigation may end up being the least of his problems. As a whistleblower, your identity is protected by the law, not even the SEC knows—"

"I know," Kay said. "The question is, how the hell did Howard Rome find out I was the one who went to the SEC? And does he know about Riley's involvement in all of this?"

Fred stared out of the window of the conference room for a few moments before responding. "Well, let's see. If I had my guess, Howard Rome panicked when he learned about the subpoena, and he probably assumed someone from *inside* Logan had gone to the feds."

"That seems reasonable, but it doesn't explain why—"

Fred held up his hand. "Let me think about this for a second."

Kay bit her lip and waited. This whole thing had Heather Corn written all over it. *That bitch.*

"Howard Rome told you he *knew* it was *you* who had gone to the feds, correct?"

"I believe his exact words were 'I've got it on good authority that you're the one who went to the feds,' or something like that."

"Well it stands to reason, when he learned about the subpoena, and I'm just speculating here, he asked someone to dig around and find out who was behind it."

"Isn't that illegal?"

"It *most* definitely is illegal. It's what the government calls 'unmasking', revealing the identity of an anonymous whistleblower."

"Yeah, I remember the term. You mentioned it in one of our early meetings. I just didn't think..." Kay blew out a long breath. "I don't know why I'm surprised. Howard Rome obviously thinks he's above the law."

Fred stood and paced. "Well he most certainly is not, and not only did he unmask you, he went a step further. He retaliated against you—he fired you—for blowing the whistle, for going to the SEC." Fred turned to face her. "The law is extremely clear on this matter, Kay. Retaliating against a whistleblower is in grave violation of the law. An employer may not fire, demote, suspend, harass or discriminate against you for cooperating with the SEC." The tiniest smile crept across his face. "This case just got *a great deal* more interesting."

Kay threw her head back. "Ha, well, I'm glad you think so. If you want my two cents, this case just got a whole lot more fucked up."

"That it did. That it did."

"I'm going to sue that little shit for wrongful termination."

"Based on what you've told me, you'd have a pretty strong case, but let's not get ahead of ourselves."

"Fine, okay. Where do we go from here?" she asked.

"Let me make some calls. Why don't you and I regroup tomorrow."

Kay stood to leave.

"And Kay," Fred said.

"Yeah?"

"If it's any consolation... If all of this is true, you'll most certainly bring down Logan's CEO in all of this."

# CHAPTER FORTY-THREE

As soon as her flight from Seattle touched down in Atlanta, Riley switched her phone out of airplane mode and within seconds, the device began to vibrate like it was having a seizure. Text message after text message fought to populate her screen. One was from Kay but most of them were from Stephanie, and a knot formed in Riley's stomach as she scrolled through them.

*2:19 p.m. Did you hear about Kay?????*

*2:21 p.m. Where are you???*

*2:27 p.m. I think you're in the air. Call me the second you land!*

The clock on her phone read 3:57 p.m. As soon as they pulled into the gate and the captain turned off the seatbelt sign, Riley sprung from her seat. Unfortunately, the passengers ahead of her didn't seem to be in any hurry. They leisurely tugged their bags from the overhead bins and filed off the plane. While she waited her turn to disembark, she tried Kay. No answer. She let out a low groan, eliciting looks from her fellow passengers. When the coast was finally clear, Riley slid her overnight bag over her shoulder and dashed off the plane. The second she stepped into the terminal, she tried Kay again. It went straight to voice mail. She dialed Stephanie.

Before she even had a chance to say hello, Stephanie asked, "Oh, my God. Did you hear about Kay?"

"No, I just landed. "Is she all right? I just tried to call her, but she didn't pick up."

"She got fired!"

"What?"

"Yeah. Security escorted her out of the building, right in front of everyone. People at the office are going nuts. No one knows what's going on. And Kay's like a rock star around here…"

"Fuck, fuck fuck."

"I know, seriously. It's crazy."

Riley began to weed through the massive airport. She pushed by a man and a woman in matching leisure suits. "I need to call—"

"Watch where you're going, lady," leisure suit man yelled when Riley bumped him with her shoulder bag.

She waved him an apology. "Steph, I gotta go. I'll call you later."

She ended the call and tried Kay's cell again. Still no answer. *Kay, where are you?* She threw her phone into her purse and picked up her pace, her shoulder bag banging rhythmically against her hip as she trotted through the corridor and down the escalator to the train that ran between terminals. As luck would have it, her plane had parked at Terminal E, the terminal they dubbed E for End of the World because it was furthest from the exit.

She was sweating by the time she reached the daily parking garage, and for the life of her, she couldn't remember where the hell she'd parked her car the day before. "Fuuuuck," she yelled as she repeatedly stabbed the unlock button on her key fob. When she finally heard the familiar chirp of her car, she lurched in its direction, tossed her bag in the backseat and peeled out of the garage.

Riley had planned to swing by the office when she got back from Seattle, but immediately aborted that plan and sped north on I-85 toward Virginia Highland.

Before she was up the front steps, Kay opened the door. She was still in her suit, but her shirt was untucked, and her feet were bare. Kay clutched onto her and they stood holding each other on her front stoop for a long time.

"I'm so glad you're here, baby," Kay finally uttered. "I assume you've heard the news?"

Riley stepped back and nodded. "What the hell happened?"

Kay gave her a sad smile. "Come on in and I'll give you the highlights."

Riley dropped her bag on the floor and followed Kay into the kitchen.

"Want some water?" Kay asked. "I was just getting myself some, although I may switch to something a bit harder in the very near future."

"Water would be good, thanks."

Kay pulled two glasses from the cupboard, filled them from the tap and handed one to Riley.

Riley climbed up on one of the kitchen stools. "So, tell me what happened."

Kay drained her glass and set it on the counter. "I got fired."

"I don't understand, why?"

"You know how Fred Archie *assured* us our identities would be protected?"

"Yeah, of course."

"Well, he was wrong. Fucking Howard Rome evidently put two and two together and figured out I went to the SEC. The question is, does he know about you too?"

"Wait, hold on, back up," Riley said. "How did Howard Rome find out Logan was even under investigation?"

"Well, apparently, and I say apparently because I don't know for sure, the SEC recently issued a subpoena—"

"So we were right. That's why people at Logan have been acting so weird lately, but how'd you hear about it? Fred Archie?"

"No. Howard Rome told me. He took the pleasure of personally firing me, and in the process, he referenced a subpoena from the SEC."

"I've heard he's a vindictive little shit," Riley replied.

"You can say that again."

"Did Howard say *when* the subpoena was issued?"

Kay shook her head. "My conversation with him was pretty brief, but if I had to guess, I'd say it was a few weeks ago, not long before you and I started sensing something at the office was amiss."

"Do you know what the subpoena is for?"

"I don't know for sure. Howard didn't offer a lot of details. But, based on what we've learned through this whole process, it was probably for some of Logan's internal documents—memos, emails, financial documents, stuff like that."

"I can't believe we got zero heads up from the SEC about this."

"I know, me neither. It's funny, we formally filed the initial complaint, but yet we're in the dark about everything."

"Fred warned us about that," Riley said. "He said we'd likely be out of the loop, at least from the SEC side of things."

Kay leaned up against the counter. "I know, but it still seems odd that we had no clue about the subpoena, if in fact one was actually issued."

"It sure sounds like it was, but wait, you still haven't explained how Howard Rome knew you went to the SEC. Our identities are a secret, or at least they're supposed to be."

"I met with Fred this afternoon—I'll get to that in a minute—but his theory is that when Howard Rome learned about the subpoena, he asked someone to snoop around and determine who the internal leak was. That's another reason why I think the subpoena was issued a few weeks ago. Howard's goons needed time to carry out their fishing expedition."

"Is that even legal?" Riley asked

"No, not even close. This is where things get even more fucked up. As I mentioned, I went to see Fred Archie this afternoon and told him what had happened. According to him, Howard Rome really stepped in it when he unmasked me."

"I remember Fred using that term. That's what they call it when the identity of a whistleblower is revealed, right?"

"Right, but then, Howard went a step further. He fired me. He retaliated against me for being a whistleblower, which by the way, is also seriously illegal."

"Stupid fucker. I'd love to see him go down."

"You and me both."

"Fuck this is so nuts. You couldn't make this shit up." Riley ran both hands through her hair. "And there's no way for us to know whether my name surfaced during Howard's little investigation."

"I've been going back and forth about that. Part of me thinks it's possible he doesn't know you're involved. His goons may have just zeroed in on me because of my direct involvement with Concordia and because I went singing to Heather Corn. On the other hand, it's no secret around the office that you and I are a couple and you do work in Finance…"

"I guess we'll find out tomorrow. If they suspect I played a role, one's got to assume they'll fire me too."

"I can't believe how calm you are," Kay said.

"What choice do I have?" Riley asked. "Flipping out isn't going to do any good." She was quiet for a second and then she asked, "Who else at Logan do you think knows about the subpoena and everything?"

Kay shrugged. "I don't know for sure, but given that we had no clue a subpoena had been issued, I've got to imagine only a handful of people at the airline are aware of it and the underlying investigation. Probably the general counsel plus maybe a core group of top-level executives."

"Ha, them, and a small team of underlings who've been tasked with actually gathering the documents referenced in the subpoena. I mean, some poor soul actually has to get the SEC all the stuff they've requested."

"True," Kay replied, "but I think we're still talking a pretty small group of people."

Riley scratched her head. "But wait, Stephanie told me the whole office knew you'd been fired."

"That wouldn't surprise me," Kay said. "It was pretty public. They marched me out of the building like a damn prisoner." She massaged the base of her neck. "But I doubt very many people know *why* I was fired."

"I can't believe none of this has leaked to the press."

"Good point, especially given the fact that the subpoena was probably issued a few weeks ago."

Riley let out a deep laugh. “I bet no one has spilled the beans because Howard Rome threatened to kill them if they uttered a single word about it.”

“Ha, I wouldn’t put it past him.”

“So, what do we do now? Is Fred Archie going to go after their asses?”

“I don’t really know. He and I are meeting again tomorrow, hopefully I’ll find out more then.”

“It looks like you could use a glass of wine,” Riley said.

“More like a bottle. It’s not like I have to go to work tomorrow.”

# CHAPTER FORTY-FOUR

Riley reluctantly dragged herself out of their warm bed at six thirty the next morning to get ready for work. She'd really wanted to call in sick, but Kay had talked her out of it the night before, believing it would only serve to make a bad situation worse.

At this point, they didn't know if Riley had been caught in Howard Rome's dragnet, and Kay was anxious about Riley doing anything that would draw attention to herself. The night before she'd urged Riley to fly beneath the radar. Riley didn't think that was even remotely possible. There was no doubt news of Kay's firing had spread like wildfire and the gossip mill at the office would be in full swing. If she and Kay hadn't already been one of the most notorious couples at Logan headquarters, they certainly would be now. She might as well have a neon sign on her back.

Although not a certainty, Riley was fairly confident that the vast majority of people at Logan hadn't the slightest clue why Kay was fired—even though a few dozen people at Logan likely knew about the subpoena, it stood to reason that only Howard

Rome, plus one or two of his goons, knew Kay's firing was directly related to her suspected role in the SEC's investigation. This meant there would be no shortage of inquiring minds eager to find out why "superstar Kay" was shown the door.

She and Kay had stayed up half the night trying to figure out what Riley should say when she was asked this question. They didn't want to lie, but they also couldn't tell the truth. Even though the CEO of Logan didn't care much about protecting the whistleblower's identity, she and Kay sure did and even if Howard Rome decided to leak the identity of the whistleblower, they planned to stay mum on the topic.

After splitting a bottle of wine the night before, they'd finally come up with what they thought was a suitable explanation for Kay being fired: she refused to do something she thought was unethical. She stood up for what was right. This answer was not the whole truth, but it wasn't a lie either.

Riley slugged through her morning routine of showering and getting dressed. It was going to be a seriously long day at the office. When she wasn't fielding questions about Kay, she'd be constantly looking over her shoulder, wondering if she was next on Howard Rome's chopping block. On top of that, she somehow had to go about her day acting like she knew nothing about the SEC investigation. *No problemo.*

When she wandered down into the kitchen, Kay handed her a cup of coffee and asked, "You okay, baby?"

Riley cupped the coffee mug in her hands and took a sip. "Yeah, just dreading what promises to be a day from hell."

"I know, baby." Kay gently rubbed her back. "I'm sorry I'm sending you off to the front lines alone."

"It's not your fault," Riley reminded her. "It's not like you asked to get fired. Speaking of which, what time are you meeting with Fred Archie?"

"At two this afternoon."

"Let me know the second you hear anything."

"I will, I promise." Kay pulled Riley into her arms. "Be strong today. I'll be with you in spirit."

Riley was barely out of her car when Wayne, her asshole coworker, cornered her in the parking lot. "So, what's the deal with Kay?" he asked with absolutely no preamble.

"Oh, hello, Wayne." Riley paused to get her thoughts together. She stood tall and looked him in the eye, "Kay stood by her convictions and got fired for it. It's called ethics. You should google it."

Wayne grunted something and walked away.

She locked her car and walked across the parking lot. *That was probably a little harsh. Be strong. Try to smile.*

It turned out the encounter with Wayne was just a precursor to what Riley would face the rest of the day. Not surprisingly, a lot of people assumed Kay had done something wrong. Riley understood that people weren't generally fired for doing something good and Kay *was* marched out of the office by security. It just made her so damn mad she couldn't tell them the truth.

Mostly, though, people at the office were worried about Kay. They just wanted to know how she was faring. They seemed less interested in the juicy details surrounding her dismissal, or at least they had the decency not to ask. Not only was Kay exceptionally good at her job, she was universally well liked and well respected.

Early afternoon, while Riley was attempting to get some work done, her office phone rang, something that rarely happened in the days of email and instant messaging. As soon as she heard it, her heart began to race. This was it. She jolted upright so fast she almost fell off her chair. She reached for the receiver without looking at the caller ID and clenched it in her sweaty palm. "Riley Bauer," she squeaked. There was no reply on the other end. "Hello," she said. "Is anyone there?"

"Oh, hey Rye, it's Stephanie."

Riley slumped back in her chair. "Why are you calling me on this phone?"

"I sent you like twelve texts and tried calling your cell. When you didn't respond, I thought I'd go old school."

"Oh," Riley said as she searched around for her cell phone. "Fuck."

"What's the matter?"

"I must have left my phone in the car."

"Anyway, I was calling to see how you were holding up."

"Um, okay, I guess, under the circumstances, but hey, do you mind if I call you back in a bit. I'm anxious to get my cell phone. Kay might be trying to reach me."

Riley hung up, dug around her purse for her car keys and sped out of her office. Just before the doors to the elevator closed, a man with shocking red hair stepped on and stood next to her. His thighs were the size of steel drums. Riley knew she'd seen him before, but she couldn't recall where. She gave him a timid smile, but he didn't smile back. As soon as the elevator began to move, he grabbed her arm.

She stared into his ice blue eyes. "What the fuck." She struggled to pull away, but his massive hands pinched tighter. "Ow, you're hurting me?" She kicked him in the shin, but he didn't even flinch. No one else was on the elevator and she figured that was by design.

When the elevator reached the ground floor, he growled, "Don't move."

The door opened and two men tried to step on. "This elevator is out of service," the red-haired giant said.

The men didn't argue with him. They stepped aside and the doors slid shut. Riley's captor stabbed the button for "B" – the basement, which also housed the executive parking garage.

Riley tried not to panic. "Where are we going?"

"Someone wants to talk to you," he said as he dragged her off the elevator. Riley had never been to this level of the building. She'd never had a reason to go down there. Her high heels clattered on the bare concrete floor. The man paused when they reached a door labeled Executive Locker Room. He pushed open the door and shoved her inside.

She stumbled across the plush red carpet. Seconds later, Gabe emerged from behind a row of lockers. His hair was ruffled, and his tie hung loose around his neck. He looked at the giant with glazed eyes and said, "I'll take it from here." The hulk nodded and left them alone.

Riley instinctively felt for her phone, but then she remembered, it was in her car. She could feel the blood pulse through the veins in her neck. "Gabe, what the—"

His wild eyes bore into her. "Is it true?"

"Is what true?"

"Don't play games with me, Riley. Did you play a role in this fucking mess?"

Riley didn't know what to say. Given that she'd just been dragged down to the basement, she had to assume Gabe at least had a hunch she had something to do with the SEC investigation, but she didn't want to come right out and tell him she'd blown the whistle. When she didn't respond right away, he grew even more agitated.

"Tell me the truth," he screamed. "You went to the feds."

"I don't know what you're talking about, Gabe."

"Bullshit!" He pounded the wall with his fist. "McFadden's been following you."

Riley didn't know who McFadden was, but she guessed it was the red-haired muscle man who'd *escorted* her to the locker room.

Gabe lunged toward her. "Do you have any clue what you and Kay have done. One iota?"

She backed away and rammed against the cold metal lockers.

He got in her face and hissed, "This will ruin me."

She inched sideways along the lockers, and thankfully, he let her have some space. "Don't do anything rash, Gabe. It'll only make things worse."

Gabe stared at her. His eyes were bloodshot, like he'd been crying, and his bottom lip trembled. "I've got a family, three kids."

Riley tried to keep her voice even. "I know, Gabe."

"You were always my favorite, you know? So smart." His hand slid inside his suit coat.

She charged at him, but he was too quick. He jumped out of the way and she went face first into the carpet.

When she flipped herself around, she saw the barrel of a gun waving in the air. She rolled behind a nearby laundry cart and looked for somewhere to hide. *Could she make it to one of the shower stalls?* She got into a crouch and heaved herself behind one of the metal stall doors. That's when she heard it. Crying. She peered around of the edge of the door. Gabe had turned the gun on himself. "Don't Gabe!" she screamed.

He pressed the gun against his temple.

"I know Howard Rome coerced you. It was all him. He was the mastermind."

"I don't want to go to jail."

"You didn't have a choice. You had to go along. I'm sure they'll understand that."

His hand shook and she was sure he was going to pull the trigger.

"Think of your family, Gabe. They need you."

He looked at her. The fury in his eyes was no longer there. Instead there was sadness and hopelessness. Gabe lowered the gun to his side and slid down the wall.

Riley stayed behind the metal door until he set the gun on the floor. As she approached, his shoulders slumped, and his head sank into his hands.

She kicked the gun away and leapt for the phone on the wall near the door. She picked up the receiver and called for help.

# CHAPTER FORTY-FIVE

Kay arrived at Fred Archie's office a little before two, and this time she was led straight back to his office. It was the first time they'd met outside of a conference room.

He gestured toward the two antique chairs in front of his desk. "Have a seat."

"Have you learned any more?"

"I have." He glanced at the yellow legal pad in front of him. "I spoke to Kenneth Hoover this morning," he said, referring to one of the members of Logan's Board of Directors. "And I brought him up to speed on the situation. I explained that my client had been fired for *purportedly* blowing the whistle and reporting Logan to the SEC."

"Did Kenneth indicate he knew who your client was?"

"No. He did not." Fred set down the pen he had in his hand. "Kay, I'll continue to do everything in my power to keep your identity anonymous, but Kenneth, and the rest of the board, may learn your identity from other sources."

"Yeah, like maybe the fucking CEO." Another thought occurred to Kay. Her firing had been pretty high profile. It wouldn't be all that hard for Kenneth, or any of the other board members for that matter, to put two and two together.

Fred cleared his throat. "Let me assure you, after talking to Kenneth, I'm confident he understands the gravity of the situation."

"Did he confirm Logan had in fact been subpoenaed by the SEC?"

"No, he did not and he's under no obligation to do so. As you can imagine, he chose his words very carefully."

Kay snorted out a laugh. "Yeah, I bet he did."

Fred picked up his pen again and tapped it on his legal pad. "If in fact Logan was subpoenaed by the SEC, then there's no question, he, along with the rest of the board of directors, are aware the airline is under SEC investigation. The board is likely doing their damnedest to contain knowledge of the investigation to the executive level. That would be standard operating procedure in a case like this. News of the investigation probably won't be made public until a later date."

Kay gnawed on her lower lip. "Do you think we can trust him? I've met him a few times and he seemed like a nice enough guy, but, at this point, I don't know who to believe at Logan."

Fred looked her right in the eye. "Yes, I think we can trust him. He's very highly regarded. As you probably know, he was Secretary of State for a spell and he's known for being a straight shooter. Right now, I think he's our best bet."

She nodded. "Yeah, I remember when he was Secretary. I was only in college, but my recollection is he was trustworthy, and he helped get the country through a few tricky situations."

"Anyhow," Fred said, "I reached out to Kenneth on this matter because of his reputation and because he's the non-executive director of Logan's board. As you're probably aware, many large corporate boards have a non-executive director—someone who's a member of the board but who's neither currently employed by the company nor receives any compensation from the company, outside of their compensation for being on the board. In his position, Kenneth's role is to provide independent oversight of the board, at least in theory."

Kay nodded. She was familiar with his role.

Fred flipped the page on his yellow legal pad and made a note. "Based on my discussion with Kenneth," he said when he looked back up, "the board was not aware Howard Rome had terminated a suspected whistleblower, and he made it abundantly clear that the board played absolutely no role in the decision to fire you."

"You and Kenneth must have had an interesting conversation," she said with a laugh. "Without admitting to the SEC investigation, he had to defend the board from conspiring to fire the person responsible for reporting Logan to the SEC. Sounds like Kenny-boy did a bang-up job of dancing around the issues."

"Yes, he did a masterful job," Fred replied. "The guy isn't an idiot. He knows these are serious allegations."

Kay drummed her thumb on the armrest of her chair. After all these months of waiting and hearing nothing, things were suddenly moving incredibly fast. "So, if we believe what Kenneth told you, we assume Howard Rome acted on his own?"

"Yes," Fred replied. "It appears that way, at least based on the limited information we have so far."

"So, what do we do now?"

"Kenneth will report back to the board. He may recommend they conduct their own internal probe of Howard Rome's conduct. If that happens, the board will likely form a committee—made up of a handful of board members and led by Kenneth—to oversee it."

"Who will conduct the actual investigation?"

"Typically, an internal investigation of this sort would be conducted by a third party—outside counsel or a security firm—who is completely independent from Logan."

A mix of anxiety and excitement was causing Kay to overheat. She wriggled out of her suit coat and threw it over the neighboring chair. "But isn't Howard Rome on the board? What if he tries to prevent the internal probe from taking place?"

"Yes, Howard is on the board, but he only has so much clout. If Kenneth Hoover recommends an internal investigation and petitions the board to form an oversight committee, my guess is, most of the board members will go along with him, especially because Kenneth is so well regarded. Once the committee is actually formed, only those board members who are *on* the committee will be privy to all the details of the internal investigation."

"Okay, so say they decide to conduct an internal investigation, how long are we talking? Like how long until we know what the board's probe uncovers?"

"It'll take some time...maybe a month or two if I had to guess. And remember, all of this is completely independent from the SEC's ongoing investigation."

"What are Riley and I supposed to do in the meantime? I've been fired and for all we know, she might be next."

"That's another thing. Kenneth is going to request a temporary freeze on terminations. They don't want this thing to get any bigger before they have a chance to sort things out."

"Well, that's a relief. But it doesn't mean I'll sleep easy at night. People at Logan now have us in their sights. There's no telling what they might do."

"Look, Kay, I know this is difficult, but we have to let it play out. These things take time."

She slumped back in her chair and rested her chin on her hand. "I know. I know. It's just so damn infuriating. It's like things are moving too fast and too slow at the same time."

"Well, look on the bright side. From what we can deduce, it appears the SEC is moving forward in their investigation."

She sat back up in her chair. "Yeah, I know. You mentioned that yesterday. It's just... This last year has taken a serious toll on both me and Riley, and after everything we've been through, it sure would be nice to see justice prevail."

He changed his tone slightly. "Are you two okay financially, given that you're out of a job, at least for the immediate future?"

She tried to shrug off her irritation and gave him as much of a smile as she could muster. Rationally, she knew he was trying to help her and she shouldn't take out her frustration on him. "Yeah. We're good. I've got a decent amount of savings and for the moment, Riley's still gainfully employed, but thanks for asking."

Kay's cell phone rang as soon as she stepped outside Fred's office building.

"Kay," Riley sobbed into the phone.

"What is it, baby? Are you okay?"

After a few heaving breaths, Riley said, "It's Gabe. He tried to kill himself."

"Oh, my God. What happened?"

After Riley summarized what had taken place, she said, "They just took him away in an ambulance."

"Are you still at the office?" Kay asked.

"Yes."

"I'm coming to get you. I'll be there in fifteen minutes."

# CHAPTER FORTY-SIX

Riley lay on the couch in the sunroom. She hadn't moved since Kay had brought her home. An untouched plate of food sat on the coffee table nearby.

Kay walked in from the kitchen and handed her a glass of wine. She sat up and Kay scooted next to her on the couch. "Do you want to talk more about it?" Kay asked.

Riley shook her head. "No." They'd spent the better part of the evening talking about Gabe and what had happened at the office that afternoon. "I just hope I never see that red-headed beast again."

"Thank God he was arrested."

Riley winced. "Shit, I know. I still can't believe he tackled the first cop who tried to enter the locker room after I called 911. If nothing else, the guy's loyal."

"Ha, yeah, to a fault. I'll sleep a little easier tonight knowing he's not roaming around my backyard."

"Ditto," Riley said. She shifted on the couch. "I haven't even asked, how was your meeting with Fred Archie?"

Kay recapped her meeting with Fred while Riley sipped her wine.

"Did Fred have any idea how long the Logan internal investigation might take?" Riley asked when she was done.

"He thought probably a month or two."

Riley set her wineglass down and hugged one of the throw pillows on the couch. "It's good to hear Logan's board is going to investigate, and I hope it brings the truth to light, but honestly, I don't know how much more I can handle. I'm not sure I have it in me to keep working there, especially after what happened today."

"I can't say I blame you."

Riley rested her head on Kay's shoulder. "Do I really want to work for a company that's basically thrown ethics out the window?"

Kay gently rubbed her back. "I hear you, baby, but remember one thing, most of the people who work for Logan are good, honest, hardworking people. We know there are some rotten eggs, but we have to hang in there for all the good eggs, not to mention Logan's customers."

Riley smiled up at Kay. "That's a good point. I hadn't really thought about it that way."

"As you think about whether you want to keep working there, just remember why we blew the whistle in the first place. But no matter what you decide, the next few months are going to be brutal."

"I know."

"We can't let them beat us down."

Riley smiled weakly. "You're right."

Kay laughed. "I knew we were taking a big risk when we went to Fred Archie. It's just, I never imagined, not in a million years, it would all play out like this."

"Yeah, me either."

"It's all so surreal."

Kay patted her on the knee. "Come on, let's see if we can get a little of this dinner in you." She picked the plate up off the table and fed Riley a few bites of food.

Riley held up her hand. "I can't eat anymore. I need to go to sleep."

"Okay, baby." Kay helped her upstairs and got her into bed.

Riley leaned up against the pillow and slid a hand over Kay's shoulder. "I love you so much," she said and kissed her on the temple. "We're going to get through this together."

Kay nodded. "I know." She nestled closer to Riley. "I can't imagine going through this with anyone else." She slipped a hand under Riley's chin and kissed her lightly on the lips. "You get me, Rye. It amazes me sometimes how in tune you are with how I'm feeling or what I'm thinking. No one's ever gotten me the way you do." Kay closed her eyes and whispered, "I love you too, so damn much."

After she put Riley to bed, Kay called her brother Doug. In the circus that was the last day and a half, she hadn't yet told anyone in her family she'd been fired from Logan and she wanted to make sure they heard it from her first. Her father was still pretty dialed in to the goings on at Logan because he'd spent a lot of time at the headquarters before he retired, serving on a bunch of different advisory and regulatory committees, and he'd become close with some of the senior executives.

While she waited for her brother to pick up, Kay stared out her family room window that overlooked her backyard. It was dark, but the spotlight on the corner of her house lit up the large birch tree at the edge of her lawn. She envied the carefree life of the birds fluttering in and out of its branches.

"Wow, sis, I'm really sorry to hear that," Doug said when she told him the news. "What the fuck happened?"

No one in her family knew about the complaint she and Riley had filed with the SEC. They'd steadfastly followed Fred Archie's advice and not told anyone. "It's kind of a long story. Let's just say I didn't deserve to be fired. A few heads may roll as a result."

"Geez Kay, could you be any vaguer?"

"I'm sorry. Just trust me on this, okay. Someday, the truth may come to light."

"Okay, but you've certainly got me curious." Doug said. "Have you told Dad yet?"

"No, I plan to call him and Mom tomorrow."

"He's probably going to flip."

"Yeah, I know."

If and when he learned the whole wretched tale, Kay was confident Doug would respect her. Her father, on the other hand, was more of a wild card. It would sting if he found out his own daughter had ratted out the airline that had been his heart and soul for the last thirty years. Hopefully, if the truth came out, he'd be proud of her for doing the right thing.

"So, what are you going to do with yourself now that you no longer have a job?" Doug asked.

"I'm not really sure. It's only been twenty-four hours since I got canned. It hasn't really sunk in yet and there's been so much going on."

"Maybe you should give Sean Ionescu a call, that architect in Asheville I recommended."

"Yeah, maybe."

# CHAPTER FORTY-SEVEN

Riley eventually returned to work and each morning Kay hugged her goodbye as she dutifully trudged off to the office. Kay was so proud of her. The strength she'd shown through everything was nothing short of remarkable. They'd likely never know for sure, but they both assumed the *firing* freeze Kenneth Hoover implemented after Kay's termination saved Riley's job.

During the day, Kay tried to keep herself busy. She puttered around the house, knocked off a few small home improvement projects and even played a round or two of golf, but it did nothing to shake her frustration with the situation. She felt useless and she began to crawl the walls.

"What are you going to do today?" Riley asked one morning over breakfast.

"Pull my hair out. Watch paint dry. Maybe catch a soap opera or two. I haven't seen an episode of *General Hospital* since college."

"Is that show even still on?"

"It wouldn't surprise me."

"Maybe you should go up to Asheville for a little while," Riley suggested, "especially now that you and Scott have signed all the papers."

Kay shrugged. "Yeah, maybe." Somewhere in the turmoil of the last few weeks, the deal to purchase her brother Scott's parcel had closed, bringing her property to a full ten acres. "But that would mean being away from you and I don't know if I could stand that, not right now."

"You are going to drive yourself crazy if you keep sitting around here all day."

Kay used her fork to push the scrambled eggs around on her plate. "I know. I guess I could call that architect Doug recommended, maybe try to set up a time to meet him."

"That sounds like a great idea. Might as well while you have the time on your hands."

After Riley left for the office, Kay relented and called the architect. They set up a time to get together in Asheville the following week.

When the weekend rolled around, she and Riley drove up to Asheville in separate cars. The leaves on the trees were just starting to turn, but the weather was still fairly mild and being away from the city did wonders to ease Kay's tension. She and Riley spent hours surveying her property, her original five acres plus the land she'd recently acquired from her brother Scott.

As they walked, Kay pointed toward the ridge. "Like we talked about before, I want to build the house up there, I just don't know exactly where." She looked at Riley. "What do you think?"

Riley set her small daypack down on a nearby stump and pulled out her water. "I'm not sure. I need to look at the views again once we get up there." She took a swig of water and held it out for Kay. "Want some."

"Nah, I'm good."

Riley stowed her water and slung her pack over her shoulder. "Onward and upward."

When they reached the clearing on the ridge, Riley turned in place to take in the view. "Gosh, it's even more beautiful than I remember. I can't believe you own all this."

Kay stood beside her. "I know, me neither."

"You hungry?"

"Starving."

Riley pulled a large blanket out of her pack and pointed to a sunny flat spot a few yards away. "How about over there?"

"Perfect."

There was a light wind and the blanket floated to the ground. Riley sat down and rummaged around in her pack. "Turkey or ham?"

"Turkey."

As they ate their lunch, Riley scanned the surrounding area and the horizon. When she was done eating, she crinkled up her deli paper, tucked it in her pack and pulled out a notebook.

Kay watched as Riley furiously scribbled notes. A few strands of blond hair had escaped her ponytail and she kept brushing them off her face. Her brow was crinkled, and her eyes never left the page in front of her. "How do you manage to look so serious and so beautiful at the same time?" Kay asked.

Riley looked up and gave her the sweetest, softest smile she'd ever seen. Kay smiled back and pointed at the notebook. "Whatcha writing about in there?"

"Observations about the property, thoughts about the house, stuff like that." Riley closed her notebook and tucked the pencil behind her ear. "Mind if we walk the perimeter of the ridge again?"

"Not at all," Kay said and popped the last bit of her turkey sandwich into her mouth.

Riley brushed the crumbs off her lap and hopped to her feet. She reached for Kay's hand and pulled her up off the blanket.

They strolled along the ridge hand in hand, stopping occasionally to discuss the view from this vantage point or that. "How big a house do you think you'd like to build?" Riley asked. "We should probably start there."

Kay stopped walking. She looked down at the ground and kicked a small stone like a soccer ball. "I, um."

"It's okay if you don't know for sure. I was just thinking it might help to—"

"It's not that, Rye." Kay felt a lump form in her throat. She looked up and stared into Riley's bright blue eyes. "It's just, this house we're talking about, I hope it'll be *our* house. I want to make decisions about it together."

"Really?"

"Yeah, really."

Riley didn't say another word. She linked her arm through Kay's, and they finished walking the perimeter arm in arm. Kay's step felt lighter than it had in weeks.

When they got back to the spot where they'd left the blanket, Kay broke the silence. "To answer your question—"

"What question?"

"About how big a house I want."

"Oh, yeah. What are you thinking?"

"Honestly, I don't want anything too big."

Riley draped her arm over Kay's shoulders. "I'm 100% with you on that. None of that McMansion stuff you see everywhere. We just need to make sure there's enough—"

"Room for kids," Kay said quietly.

Riley smiled and kissed her softly on the lips. "Yeah, that."

# CHAPTER FORTY-EIGHT

Over the next few weeks, Kay spent much of her time up in Asheville and Riley joined her there on the weekends. Waiting for the Logan board to finish their investigation was agonizing but they did their best to stay positive and focused their energy on the new house.

After a handful of meetings with Sean Ionescu, the Asheville architect, the house in Asheville started to take shape. As they'd discussed, it was going to be on the small side—about 1,800 square feet with three bedrooms plus an office—plenty of room to accommodate future little ones who might come along. The architect's preliminary plans included a cozy bookshelf-filled loft overlooking a wide-open kitchen/living area with a wall of windows offering sweeping views of mountains. At Kay's insistence, the drawings included two fireplaces, one in the living area and another in the master bedroom. Growing up in the North, she had fond memories of gathering around the fire with her family in the winter.

Sean also came up with the idea to build a small two-story barn-like outbuilding—a lower level garage area and an upper level studio apartment—where Kay and Riley could live while the main house was being built. This would enable them to move out of the studio in Doug's barn sooner than they expected.

Kay was delighted with the way things were coming together with the house, and she sang along to the song on the radio as she drove toward downtown Asheville after a morning hike off the Blue Ridge Parkway. Her karaoke was interrupted by an incoming phone call. It was Fred Archie. She crossed two lanes, pulled over to the side of the road and answered the call.

Fred skipped the usual pleasantries and got straight to the point. "I just got off the phone with Kenneth Hoover, our contact from Logan's board."

"And?" Kay asked, gripping the steering wheel as she waited for his answer.

"The Logan's Board of Directors has completed its internal probe. A press release is imminent."

Kay sucked in a big breath of air and leaned back against the headrest. "Any idea what it's going to say?"

"Nope. Kenneth didn't share any details, but he did say he'd like to meet with us tomorrow afternoon."

"Us, as in you and me? So, he's connected the dots and knows I'm the whistleblower."

"Yes, you and me. And no, it's not probable Kenneth has any *concrete* evidence you're the whistleblower. More likely, your name came up in the board's probe as the person Howard Rome fired because the CEO *suspected* you were the whistleblower. The board isn't fixated on whether you're actually the whistleblower. All that matters to them is that Howard Rome fired you because he *thought* you were the whistleblower. It's all about the CEO's intent when he fired you."

"Gotcha. Okay. I'm in Asheville but I can head back to Atlanta later this afternoon."

"Great, I'll let Kenneth know."

"Fred."

"Yes, Kay."

"Would it be all right if Riley came to the meeting too?"

"I don't think that would be a good idea. The board's probe centered around your firing. Let's not muddy the waters."

"I understand. I get your point."

"Keep your eyes out for the press release. I'll circle back with you later today."

Kay ended the call with Fred and dialed Riley.

Riley picked up on the first ring. "Hey, baby."

"Logan's Board of Directors has finished their probe," Kay said quickly. "They're expected to issue a press release any minute."

"Holy shit! Any idea what it's going to say?"

"No idea. Fred just called to give me the heads up."

"Stephanie and I just finished lunch." Riley quickened her pace. "We're on our way back to the office."

"Okay. Call me as soon as you get in front of a computer. I'm going to drive back to Atlanta this afternoon. I'm meeting with Fred tomorrow afternoon."

"Drive carefully. I'll call you as soon as I get back to my office."

"What is it?" Stephanie asked as soon as Riley ended the call.

"Logan's about to issue a major press release. Come on, we gotta hurry. I want to be in front of my computer when it comes out."

As soon as they stepped off the elevator on the fifth floor, it was obvious the press release had already dropped. Everyone was huddled around the smattering of television monitors that silently piped CNN into the office. As she and Stephanie made their way toward her office, a few people glanced in their direction, but Riley didn't break stride until they were safely inside her office with the door closed behind them. Seconds after she pulled the press release up on her computer, her cell phone rang. It was Kay. Riley put her on speaker phone.

"Have you read it yet?" Kay asked.

"No, I just pulled it up. I'm scanning it now."

*... Logan Airlines today announced that it has named Andrew Lanier as president and chief executive officer... The company also announced that Howard Rome has stepped down from his roles as chairman, president and chief executive officer, and as a director. These changes are effective immediately.*

"Holy fucking shit, Kay. This is incredible."

"I know, I know. Go to CNN.com," Kay urged.

Riley quickly navigated to the news site and began to read out loud. "*Logan Airlines announced today that CEO Howard Rome, along with one of his top lieutenants, is stepping down… The airline has also admitted in a disclosure filed hours ago that it is being investigated by the Securities and Exchange Commission. Regulators are investigating potential earnings management by the airline...*"

"Can you believe it?" Kay asked.

"No, this is so awesome. Good riddance Howard Rome, you fucking cockroach! And the news about the SEC… I mean we were pretty sure, but this confirms the feds are investigating Logan for sure."

"Yeah, looks like it," Kay answered. "And I love how they say Howard Rome is *stepping down*. Stepping down, my ass. I'm sure *a lot* of pressure was placed on the bastard to leave."

Stephanie peered over Riley's shoulder to get a better look at her screen. "What's going on? Why is Logan being investigated by the SEC?"

Riley looked up at her. "Have a seat, I'll fill you in."

"Hey, Stephanie," Kay's voice chirped over the speaker.

"Hey, Kay."

"I'll leave Riley to give you the scoop."

As soon as Riley ended the call, Stephanie peppered her with questions.

Riley held up her hand. "Hold your horses. I'll tell you what I can." She paused for a moment to consider exactly what she should say. In the coming weeks, a lot of people, including Stephanie, would probably deduce Kay's firing was somehow connected to the SEC investigation, but Riley would never confirm it, not even if someone asked her directly. She looked Stephanie straight in the eye and said, "I don't know any more about the SEC investigation than what is being reported in the news." The statement was borderline truthful. Neither she nor Kay were privy to the details of the SEC's investigation.

Stephanie stared back at her. "I don't believe you," she said. "I think you know more than you're admitting."

Riley had zero acting skills and she hated to lie. "Okay, I know a tiny bit more, but I can't elaborate. Trust me Steph, I would if I could."

Stephanie started to protest but then sank back in her chair.

Riley leaned forward and rested her elbows on her desk. "I can tell you this. Howard Rome is probably not stepping down voluntarily. He was likely forced to do so for a whole host of reasons, but if I had to bet on it, one of them was improper conduct surrounding Kay's termination."

"Wow, really?"

"Yep."

"I know you said Kay had been treated unfairly, but shit, whatever happened must have been a pretty big deal. I mean it brought down the fucking CEO."

"A lot more is likely to surface in the coming days, some true, some not true. Take everything you hear with a grain of salt and trust me, Kay's the good guy in all this. Don't believe anyone who tells you otherwise."

# CHAPTER FORTY-NINE

When Kay got home from Fred's office the following evening, she was exhausted, and a sense of relief washed over her when she spotted Riley's car in the driveway. Riley had been anxious about the meeting with Kenneth Hoover and she'd wanted to come along but had finally agreed Fred was right. It was better if she stayed out of Kenneth Hoover's orbit.

Riley bounded out and escorted her into the house. Kay kicked off her heels and plopped into one of the leather armchairs in the living room.

Riley sat on the ottoman across from her and rubbed her feet. "So, what did good old Kenneth Hoover have to say?"

"Remarkably, quite a lot. He gave Fred and I a detailed account of what the board's internal investigation had uncovered."

"And?"

"Well, apparently, and this will come as no surprise to you, Howard Rome completely flew off the handle when he first learned about the subpoena from the SEC. He demanded to know if someone at Logan had tipped off the feds. According to Kenneth, Howard Rome was told, in no uncertain terms, that an effort to identify an internal tipster would be *highly* inappropriate and possibly illegal."

"But let me guess, Howard Rome was not deterred. He went ahead and did it anyway."

"Uh-huh. Howard… Did you ever see that show *The Good Wife*? The drama about that law firm."

Riley gave her a curious look. "Yeah, I loved that show, but what does that have to do with anything?"

"Do you remember that character on the show named Kalinda?"

"Of course. She was the totally hot bisexual investigator for the law firm."

Kay tugged her long dark hair out of its bun, letting it fall loosely over her shoulders. "Yeah, well, I guess the airline has their own Kalinda type person, although their investigator isn't a hot bisexual woman, it was that red-haired guy, Connor McFadden, and it sounds like Howard Rome asked him to dig around to see if he could identify the person who went to the SEC."

"No shit."

"Yep."

"So," Riley said, "when the board discovered all of this, they asked Howard Rome to step down?"

"Yes, and it sounds like he put up quite a fight. It was only when the board threatened to fire him, that he finally gave in."

"Fucking narcissistic prick."

"That's putting it mildly."

Riley stood up. "I need a glass of wine. You want one?"

Kay nodded. "Please."

When Riley returned with the wine she asked, "Are you surprised Logan decided to go public with the fact that the airline is under investigation by the SEC? I mean, up to this point, you and I didn't even know for sure that the investigation was active."

Kay took a sip of her wine and set it on the table. "I asked Fred Archie about that. He said under normal circumstances they probably wouldn't have disclosed this information publicly, but Logan likely opted to go public about the investigation because it, in legal speak, suited their purposes. Once the board completed its internal probe, they didn't want to hold off firing the CEO and they needed to offer their shareholders an explanation for the firing. It *suited their purposes* to be transparent."

"I guess that sort of makes sense."

"Oh, and get this," Kay said. "Kenneth offered me my job back, including back pay."

Riley sat up in her seat. "Wow, Kay, that's fantastic. What did you tell him?"

"I told him I needed to think about it. Of course, I want my name cleared but I'm honestly not sure what to do."

"Why don't you go change out of your suit and we can talk about it after we eat? I picked up dinner from the Vietnamese place down near the park. It's in the warming drawer."

The more they discussed Kenneth's offer to reinstate her employment at Logan, the more it became evident to Kay, her heart just wasn't in it. "You remember me talking about my dream to open a store in Asheville?" she asked Riley after dinner.

"Yeah, of course."

"Well, it certainly wasn't something I'd planned to do this soon, but now, given everything that's happened…"

"You're thinking that's what you want to do?"

"Yeah. I am," Kay said. She reached out and took Riley's hands in hers. "But I want to be with you. Right now, that's all I care about."

Riley snuggled up next to her on the couch. "That's all I care about too. Us being together." She kissed Kay softly on the lips. "How about this. How about I stay at Logan for a little bit longer, give you some time to make the store a reality, and then, once you've got it off the ground, I'll come join you in Asheville."

"Like move to Asheville with me? You'd do that?"

"In a heartbeat," Riley said. She looked Kay straight in the eye. "I don't imagine a future that you're not part of."

"I don't imagine a future without you either. I wouldn't even consider a move to Asheville unless you were totally onboard."

"I'm totally onboard, but, and I don't mean to throw a wet towel on things, how will we swing it? Like financially?"

Kay smiled. "My sweet Riley, always so pragmatic."

"I'm sorry. It's not terribly romantic, but I can't help it."

"It's okay. I think it's cute, and smart. We can't just traipse off to Asheville without some sort of plan." Kay swept her hand across the room. "I'd definitely sell this place if we moved up there. I bought it eight years ago and it's appreciated a lot in that time. I've also got a fair amount of savings, and well, I don't want to jinx it, but there's a chance we'll get at least some kind of financial reward when this whole debacle with the SEC finally ends."

"True, but that could be a long way off and there are no guarantees the SEC investigation will go anywhere."

"I know, but if it does and if the SEC and Logan settle or the SEC prevails in filing suit against Logan, we stand to get somewhere between ten and thirty percent of whatever fine Logan has to pay. That could add up to some serious cash."

"It could, and don't get me wrong, a whistleblower reward would be a sweet bonus, but we need to make sure we can pull off the move to Asheville financially no matter what, especially if Logan isn't willing to settle with the SEC. The airline could get tangled in a long, drawn-out suit with the government."

Kay kissed the tip of Riley's nose. "I know, we can't count our chickens before they hatch."

Riley wrapped her arms around Kay and held her tight. "How'd I get so lucky as to have you in my life?"

"I think I'm the lucky one."

Riley pulled back slightly and got a serious look on her face. "I give thanks every damn day. I truly had no idea it was possible to love someone as much as I love you. Sometimes, I'm so overwhelmed by the strength of my feelings for you. I know this sounds cliché, but it actually takes my breath away."

Kay's eyes got teary at Riley's words. "Oh, baby," she said softly.

"It's crazy," Riley whispered. "We haven't been together that long, what, a little over a year, but I feel closer to you than I ever felt to another human being."

Kay rested her head on Riley's shoulder. "Yeah, it's crazy. Being with you just feels so right, so easy."

Riley nodded. "And we've had to deal with some pretty big bumps in the road. I mean, with all the shit that's been going on with Logan. I think we've weathered the storm pretty well together. That's a testament to the strength of our relationship."

# CHAPTER FIFTY

After spending the early part of the week in Asheville to meet with the architect and builder, Kay jumped in her Jeep and put the petal to the medal. Her goal was to get to Atlanta by late afternoon, giving her enough time to swing by the grocery store and whip together one of Riley's all-time favorite meals—fried chicken, sticky rice, and lima beans—before she got home from work. Kay had never made fried chicken before, but how hard could it be?

When she got home, she pulled out her grandmother's old recipe book and got to work. Pretty soon, flour was flying everywhere. It was all over her clothes and there was even some in her hair. She was so focused on dipping the chicken in the egg and coating it with flour, she didn't even hear Riley come in the front door.

"Oh, my, God, Julia Child is back from the dead," Riley panned when she walked into the kitchen.

Kay dropped the piece of chicken she was holding, causing the egg mixture to splatter everywhere. She laughed. "Surprise."

Riley gave her a peck on the cheek. "I'm no expert, but I think the flour it supposed to go on the chicken," she said as she brushed some of the white powder off Kay's cheek. "But I shouldn't laugh. My dear, sweet, beautiful girlfriend is making me one of my super most favorite dinners ever. Want some help?"

"Yes, please."

Riley opened the pantry door and pulled out an apron. She nodded toward Kay. "Apron, this is Kay, Kay, apron."

"Bite me. I didn't know this would be so hard. The chicken is so slippery. It's been playing hard to get."

Riley slipped the apron over her work clothes and salvaged the meal.

"Yum, this is delicious," Kay said when they finally sat down to dinner. "Thanks to you."

"You deserve some credit too." Riley gave her a sideways glance. "I mean, you did do the grocery shopping."

Kay snapped her napkin at Riley. "Thanks, Bauer. All kidding aside though, now I get why you love this meal. It's comfort food at its best." She took a few more bites and set down her fork. "I know the last few months have been hectic—"

"To put it mildly."

"But, I don't know, I feel like I've turned a corner. All the shit with Logan, it doesn't haunt me as much anymore. That, and I'm excited and optimistic about the future, *our* future. In fact, I'd say I'm feeling downright buoyant."

"Buoyant, huh?" Riley reached across the table and gave Kay's hand a gentle squeeze. "That's good to hear. I have to say, I'm feeling pretty rosy about the future myself."

Kay picked up her wineglass and said, "To us."

Riley followed suit and then asked, "Speaking of the future, how'd the meeting with the architect and the builder go this morning? Did they say when we'd be able to break ground?"

"The meeting went well. If everything goes according to plan, the goal is to break ground before the end of January."

"Does it matter that it'll be in the middle of winter?" Riley asked. "Asheville's a little bit colder than Atlanta in the winter, right?"

"I actually asked them that same question, but the builder doesn't foresee any issues getting the foundation in during the wintertime. In fact, starting the house that time of year may actually speed up the timeline because it's the low season for most of the subcontractors."

Riley picked up her wineglass to give another toast. "Wow, this is so freakin' exciting. I can't believe building the house is coming to fruition."

Kay smiled. "I know."

"When are you planning to head back to Asheville?"

"I'd hoped to wait and drive up with you on Friday afternoon, but I'm scheduled to meet with the realtor in Asheville Friday morning. I've given her a general sense of the kind of space we want to rent for the store, and she's got a place near downtown she wants to show me."

Riley nibbled on her lip before responding. "Oh, wow, that's great."

Kay could tell by her body language that Riley wasn't completely thrilled with the news. "You don't seem as excited as I thought you'd be."

Riley fiddled with the small airplane shaped salt and pepper shakers on the table. "I am excited. I think it's good to start looking at spaces to see what's out there and get a sense for how high the rents are. It's just…our plate is pretty full right now with the new house."

Kay was slightly taken back. "But I thought the plan was for me to get the store off the ground. The sooner I do that, the sooner you can leave Logan and live in Asheville full time."

"I know, but I'm just anxious about signing a lease. That's a big financial commitment." She waved her hand across the dining area. "And we haven't made a decision about what to do with the bungalow here."

Kay tried to appreciate where Riley was coming from. They did have a lot of balls in the air and they were confronting some pretty big decisions. She took a sip of her wine while she considered how to respond. She was eager to plow forward, but she had to accept she wasn't making decisions just for herself anymore. "I guess we need to sit down and figure out how we're going to manage everything."

"We do."

"The first order of business should probably be getting this place on the market."

"If you're sure you're ready to sell it," Riley said.

"I won't lie. It'll be a little bittersweet. I put a lot of time and money into this house and I love it dearly, but at the same time, selling it will mark a significant milestone in the path toward our new life together in Asheville."

"Okay, if you're sure then yeah, let's list it. Although, one catch. I need to keep working at Logan until we feel like we're on stable, or at least somewhat stable, ground financially with the store. So, if this house sells quickly, and I'm sure it will, I need to find a temporary apartment here in Atlanta. Someplace for me to live during the week."

"You sure you're ready to jump into this adventure with me?"

Riley reached up and brushed her fingers over Kay's cheek. "I've never been more sure about anything in my entire life."

Kay turned her head and kissed Riley's hand. "Here's to the next chapter of our lives."

"You make me the happiest woman in the world, Kay."

"I feel the same way," she replied, biting her bottom lip to hold back the tears that were creeping around the edge of her eyes.

"Oh, now you're going to make me cry," Riley said.

Kay sniffled. "It's ironic isn't it, I got fired from my job, yet, the future seems brighter than I could ever have imagined."

"Life sure has a funny way of working out doesn't it?"

"It sure does." Kay didn't say it out loud, but, to her, it felt like their relationship had moved to a whole other level. It was not quite marriage, but it felt like a giant step in that direction. That thought sent a shock wave of warmth through her body.

Riley stood up and pulled Kay to her feet. "I love you, Kay Corbett."

Kay snaked her arms around Riley's waist and kissed her softly on the lips. "And I love you, Riley Bauer."

Riley reached for Kay's hand. "Come here," she said and tugged her back toward the family room. They stood in the

# CHAPTER FIFTY-ONE

Not long after Riley got settled in the temporary apartment, Atlanta received a rare snow storm. Admittedly, "storm" was a big word to describe the two inches that fell on the region, but in a city unaccustomed to any snow at all, it wreaked havoc on he roads. The combination of people having no clue how to rive on slick roads and the city's measly snowplow fleet meant affic was an utter horror. On top of that, she had her annual am at the gynecologist first thing that morning. Obviously, en she'd scheduled the appointment twelve months earlier, e had no idea what the day would hold.

By the time she finally got to work it was almost ten and was surprised to find almost everyone in her department gregated around one of many TVs mounted around the n. Riley stopped at the TV closest to her office. Normally s on mute, but not today. The volume was on full blast he news anchors' voices bounced off the office walls. Riley on her tippy toes and craned her neck to get a glimpse screen. The small banner under the announcer read *KING NEWS: Logan Airlines settles with the SEC.*

moonlight and shared lingering kisses while they slowly undressed one another.

A shudder ran through Kay as Riley ran her hands over her breasts, circling each one with a delicate finger. Riley grabbed hold of one breast and sucked it gently while her other hand tickled down Kay's body toward the mound between her legs.

"You're like silk," Riley whispered as her fingers danced across Kay's wetness.

Kay guided Riley inside her and they fell down onto the couch, never breaking contact. Kay straddled Riley, her back arched into the air while she thrust herself hard against Riley's hand, crying out loudly when she came.

Without pausing to catch her breath, Kay slid her thigh between Riley's legs. "Hmm, someone's pretty wet," she said. She increased the rhythm of her leg while she teased Riley's nipples with her tongue.

"Kay, I need your mouth on me," Riley cried. "Please. Now."

Kay slithered down the couch and pulled one of Riley's le
over her shoulder, giving her perfect access to her target.

Riley let out a low hiss when Kay's tongue found her clit.
head fell back on the couch until the orgasm jerked through

Logan related images—pictures of its headquarters, some of its planes and one if its gates at the Atlanta airport—circulated on the screen behind the gangly male news anchor. He stared straight at the camera and his lips barely moved when he spoke. "It was announced today that Logan Airlines has agreed to pay a $50 million penalty to settle SEC charges of securities fraud. According to the SEC, the charges are in connection with improper earnings management beginning as early as 2010."

Wayne let out a whistle. "Fifty million smackers. Geez Louise that's a lot of money. And what the fuck is earnings management."

"Shhh, I want to hear this," someone snapped.

Wayne glared at no one in particular but shut his trap.

The announcer looked down and read a statement from the SEC on the matter. "For years, Logan deceived the market into believing it was exceeding its financial projections and market expectations, when, in fact, the company was propping up its finances primarily through the use of price fixing and manipulative accounting devices."

Riley slipped away from the crowd, stepped into her office and shot Kay a quick text. *Turn on to MSNBC.*

She sat down at her desk, logged onto her computer and navigated to the *Wall Street Journal* website. Not surprisingly, an article about Logan was front and center on their homepage. Before she had a chance to read it, a reply came back from Kay. *Holy shit. Calling Fred Archie now.*

Riley whipped off a quick response and turned her attention back to the *WSJ* article on her computer.

> *NEW YORK—The Securities and Exchange Commission today announced that Logan Airlines has agreed to pay $50 million to settle charges that it deceived investors about its true performance, profitability, and growth trends in regard to ticket revenue and ancillary fees. The SEC considers these acts "earnings management" when companies employ them in an effort to fraudulently prop up their stock price. Furthermore, Logan's senior management exerted consistent pressure to have the company report smooth and dependable earnings growth in order to present investors with the image*

*of a company that would continue to generate predictable and diversified earnings.*

*The WSJ has learned that the Federal Trade Commission (FTC) is also investigating Logan for matters that are related to the SEC probe. A source, who was not at liberty to discuss the case, indicated the FTC is looking into allegations of price fixing. These allegations, according to the source, suggest Logan colluded with other airlines to artificially inflate fares. No word on whether other airlines are also under investigation….*

*Logan Airlines agreed to pay the $50 million penalty without admitting or denying the SEC's findings. The charges announced today conclude the SEC's investigation with respect to the company…Logan did not have an immediate comment on the settlement.*

Riley clicked through a few more of her favorite business news sites and they were all reporting about the same thing.

*REUTERS—It keeps getting worse for Logan Airlines…*

*BLOOMBERG—Logan's stock soared after the company reported third quarter results in mid-October, then the airline's bombshell about a government accounting probe triggered a sharp pullback. Today the SEC announced they had reached a settlement with Logan, sending the stock slipping further….*

"Knock, knock."

Riley looked up from her computer. Her colleague Jill was standing at her door. "Do you have a second?"

"Sure, Jill, come on in."

"Crazy news about the SEC, huh?" Jill asked as she took a seat across from Riley.

"You can say that again," Riley replied. "I mean, it was no secret that Logan was under investigation, but the settlement implies the airline knew they were up shit's creek without a paddle."

"Yeah, $50 million is a pretty steep fine. No way the airline would pay that much if they were innocent."

"And that may not even be the end of it," Riley said.

"What do you mean?"

"I read in the *Wall Street Journal* that the FTC might be investigating the airline too." Riley clicked the back button on her internet browser a few times to return to the article. "Look." She turned her computer monitor so Jill could see it.

Jill scanned the article. "Yikes." She turned and waved out toward the group of their coworkers still gathered around the TV. "People are already going ape shit. I hope it doesn't get worse."

Riley turned her monitor back around. "Yeah, me too."

"Do you mind if I ask you a question?"

"No, what's on your mind?"

Jill hesitated before answering. "Was Kay caught up in this? Is that why she got fired?"

Jill was not the first person to pose this question to Riley. When news of the SEC investigation first broke back in late October, a lot of people had wanted to know if Kay was somehow involved. It irked Riley to no end, but at the same time, she couldn't really blame them, given the timing and circumstances that surrounded Kay's firing. It was not at all unreasonable that people would assume the firing was connected to the SEC investigation. Riley paused before she responded, wanting to choose her words carefully. "No, Kay was not fired for wrongdoing related to the SEC investigation."

"Why was she fired then?" Jill asked. "She was… I'm sorry, that's really none of my business."

"It's okay. Kay didn't deserve to be fired. Howard Rome tried to use her as a scapegoat which by the way, was ludicrous because she didn't have a hand in whatever got Logan in this mess."

"Poor Kay. To have her reputation tarnished for something she didn't even do. Is she doing okay?"

Riley rested her elbows on her desk and leaned forward. "She's doing better than okay. She's moved on to the next phase in her life."

"Good for her. I always liked Kay. She just seems like a good person and she's so crazy smart."

Riley couldn't help but smile. "Yeah, she's pretty awesome."

"You know what else I don't get?"

"What?"

"It seems like this 'earnings management' or whatever they call it, all happened right under our noses." Jill gestured between her and Riley. "I can't believe none of us had any idea what was going on."

*Well, some of us did...* Riley thought back to what Kay had told her when they first uncovered the falsified SEC financial filings, back when Riley had asked a question very similar to the one Jill had just posed. "People above us, senior executives, did a masterful job of covering it all up. They fooled us, deceived our investors, and screwed our passengers."

"I hear what you're saying, but I still find it so hard to believe this went on for as long as it did, and that so many people were willing to go along with it."

"Howard Rome was a snake. He built and cultivated a corporate culture at Logan that was based on fear and intimidation. My guess is that most people were too afraid to speak out about what was going on."

"Well, based on the news about the SEC investigation and the settlement, it sounds like someone was finally brave enough to speak out. I wonder if we'll ever find out who that courageous person was?"

Riley bit back a smile. "Yeah, I wonder."

# CHAPTER FIFTY-TWO

Right after she saw the press release about Logan's settlement with the SEC, Kay called Fred Archie. He said he didn't know much more about the settlement than what was being reported in the news, but Kay's conversation with him had been enlightening nonetheless, and she couldn't wait to tell Riley what he'd had to say.

Kay had planned to drive back to Asheville that afternoon, but given the snowstorm and the bombshell news about Logan's settlement, she decided to stay in Atlanta with Riley for at least one more night. She puttered around the tiny apartment while she waited for Riley to get home from work. She had so much pent-up energy, a mix of anxiety and excitement, and she was crawling the walls by the time Riley walked in the front door.

"How'd it go with Fred?" Riley asked while she wriggled out of her winter coat. "What did he have to say about the settlement?"

"You're going to think I'm nuts," Kay said as she peeked out the window. The sun had come out mid-afternoon and melted most of the snow that had fallen that morning. It was starting to get dark and the lights around the neighboring park wer flickering to life. "But how about I fill you in while we run i the park?"

"I suppose I could rally although a glass of wine sounds a lc more appealing."

"Come on. I'm going to go crazy if I don't get out of th apartment. A run will feel good and I promise, the wine will sti be here when we get back."

Twenty minutes later they were out trotting around th park.

"So, tell me about Fred," Riley urged.

"Well…he had some interesting things to say."

"Really, like what?"

"He said he'd be reaching out to the SEC very soon."

"What do you mean, why? I thought the thing with Loga was a done deal now that they've agreed to settle?"

"It is a done deal *except* for one thing. Now that the airlin has agreed to pay a $50 million penalty…" She paused for effec "He's going to apply to the SEC for our whistleblower awar Apparently, there's some form we need—"

Riley stopped in her tracks. "Holy shit! Does he think we'r eligible for a reward? I know he said there was no guarantee."

"Sounds like it," Kay said, pausing alongside Riley. "H seemed very confident and he's got a lot of experience wit these types of cases."

Riley smacked her hand on her forehead. "If I recall correctl Fred said the whistleblower rewards were typically between te and thirty percent of—"

"Of whatever amount Logan ends of paying to the SEC."

Riley's eyes grew wide. "Even if we only get ten percen that's a boatload of cash."

Kay brushed the hair out of her face and gave Riley a broa smile. "Guess paying for the house in Asheville won't be such big deal after all, huh?"

"Ha, guess not." She pointed toward a nearby bench. "I nee to sit down for a minute. I feel like I might pass out."

Kay jogged in place. "Fred Archie said it could take week or months before Logan actually pays the settlement."

Riley sat down and put her head between her legs. She let out a muffled, "But they're definitely going to pay it, right?"

"Yes, of course. Logan has to pay, that's part of the settlement agreement, but still, these things don't happen overnight. Fred thinks the SEC will push to get the deal done before summer. Soon after the SEC receives the settlement from Logan, they'll pay out our reward, assuming they determine we're eligible for one."

Riley lifted her head and slowly stood up. "So, we might get a seriously awesome housewarming gift, compliments of Howard Rome and his cronies," she quipped.

"Fingers crossed. You feel any better?"

Riley nodded and took off running again.

Kay sprinted to catch up with her.

They ran in silence for a while before Riley asked, "How will the SEC determine the size of the reward we should get?"

"I don't know for sure how they decide what percentage a whistleblower gets, but according to Fred, they'll weigh a whole bunch of factors. Ultimately it will come down to the *value* they place on the evidence we provided."

"Sounds like it's sort of objective. Kind of a wildcard."

"Sort of. Fred said, if he had to guess, he thinks we'll get twenty percent, and remember, he'll keep a pretty good chunk of the reward. It will be his fee for representing us in all of this."

"Makes sense," Riley says, "but God, I still can't get my head around the size of the reward. In the back of my mind, I always knew there was a possibility we'd get something for putting our necks on the line, but I never ever thought we might see a payout in the millions."

"Yeah, I'm with you on that," Kay replied. "I certainly didn't expect it to be this big either." They were nearing the end of their fourth lap around the park. "Up for going a little further today?" Kay asked. "I'm still feeling kind of wound up."

"Sure. I've probably got one more lap in me." She paused briefly to take a pull from her water bottle. "Did Fred say anything about our identities? Like, will they be made public now that a settlement has been reached and the investigation is basically over?"

"Well, if you believe what Fred Archie says, and I guess I do, our identities will *not* be made public." Kay blew out a long breath. "Unless, of course, some asshole at Logan thinks it would be fun to expose the identity of the whistleblower."

"But no one at Logan can *prove* you or I blew the whistle," Riley protested.

"Well, we don't know that for sure. The SEC would never reveal our identities, but we have no idea what kind of evidence Howard Rome's covert investigation turned up."

Riley let out a low growl of frustration. "I guess I hadn't thought about that. By the way, mind if we walk for a bit. I feel a cramp coming on."

Kay slowed to a walk and glanced down at her running watch. "Wow, we've gone almost six miles."

"No wonder I'm cramping up."

"Anyway," Kay said as they approached their temporary apartment, "even if neither of our identities is actually revealed, there's likely to be a lot of speculation about who the whistleblower was. Fred warned me that if the SEC pays out a whistleblower award, they'll issue a press release. It'll probably only identify our counsel—Fred Archie—plus the dollar amount of the reward. It won't mention our names but—"

"It wouldn't be a huge stretch for people at Logan to connect the dots, at least where you're concerned."

Kay nodded. "Exactly. And well, I'm worried—"

"You're worried about me?"

"Yes, sweetheart, I am." Kay paused before continuing. "I think it's time for you to resign from Logan. I'd feel a lot better if you were out of there before the shit hits the fan."

Riley took a moment to consider it. "Okay," she said simply. "I knew this day was coming, I just didn't expect it this soon. And if we get the award, money will no longer be an issue."

"Are you sure?"

"Yeah, I'm sure. Truthfully, I'm more than ready to resign. Working at Logan has really started to wear me down. I used to love working there, but with you gone, and with all the shit that's gone on, the passion I once had for my job has evaporated."

Kay draped her arm over Riley's shoulders. "Good. I want you out of there before the SEC issues their press release about the whistleblower payout. If you quit right after that reward is announced, it will only stoke people's suspicions."

Riley dug into the pocket of her running tights for the key to their apartment. "As soon as we get confirmation from Fred that we're eligible for an award, I'll submit my resignation."

# CHAPTER FIFTY-THREE

Kay mindlessly flipped through a three-month-old copy of *The Economist* while she and Riley waited to see Fred Archie. They'd been waiting for almost fifteen minutes and her patience was wearing thin. It didn't help that she'd skipped breakfast. The sludge-like coffee she'd poured from the coffeepot in the corner of the room was burning a hole in her stomach.

She fidgeted in her seat and was about to get up and pitch a fit when Fred's receptionist called out, "Mr. Archie can see you now, Ms. Corbett and Ms. Bauer." Her singsongy voice grated on Kay's nerves. Kay gave her a forced smile and they followed her back to a conference room. Moments later, Fred rushed in, a laptop under one arm and an overstuffed manila folder under the other. "Good news gals," he bellowed. "The SEC has received the settlement payment from Logan, and," he gave them a toothy grin, "they've determined you are eligible for a whistleblower award in the amount of twenty percent."

Kay practically slid off her chair. She looked over at Riley and she looked as stunned as Kay felt. After all they'd been through, after all the risks they'd taken… It had all paid off.

They'd prevailed over Howard Rome and all his cronies and now this. A major financial windfall. A windfall that would allow them to literally and financially pursue their dreams. "It's nice when the good guy wins," she said with a smile.

Riley reached for her hand and squeezed it. "I'll second that."

"I'm proud of you both," Fred said. "You earned this reward, no doubt about that." He flipped open the manila folder and Kay tried to pay attention to what he was saying. "There are a bunch of forms I need you both to sign. I'll walk you through each one. Once we're done, I'll send everything off to the SEC. If everything goes smoothly, and there is no reason to think it won't, the money should come through in a matter of weeks."

He handed them each a pen and slid a stack of papers in front of them. "Okay," Kay croaked. Her palms began to sweat as she glanced over the first form. It and most of the subsequent forms were pages of legal gobbledygook but Fred patiently explained them in layman's terms before asking them to sign each one.

"The award will be split evenly between the two of you."

"Will the SEC just deposit the funds right into our bank accounts?" Riley asked.

"No," he replied. "The money will get funneled through our law firm. That way, your identity remains protected and," he paused briefly, "it will allow us to deduct our legal fees and some of the required taxes before we transfer the remaining balance to you."

"Ah, got it," Kay replied.

He leaned forward and cleared his throat. "I should warn you both," he said. "News of the whistleblower reward will be made public. That's just SEC procedure. Your identity will not be revealed. I just want you to ready yourself for the public announcement."

"Thanks, Fred," Riley said. "After what we've been through, this should be a walk in the park."

"Hold on," Kay said as they drove home from Fred's office that afternoon. "Pull in here."

Riley cranked the wheel and pulled into the gravel parking lot. Kay jumped out of the car before it was even stopped and trotted into the store. She emerged triumphantly a few minutes later, a brown paper bag in her hand.

"What you got there?" Riley asked.

Kay pulled a bottle from the bag and held it up.

"Shit. Pappy Van Winkle," Riley said when she eyed the bottle of rare bourbon in Kay's hand.

"Sure is. We've got some celebratin' to do!"

Riley peeled out of the parking lot and made a beeline for their temporary apartment.

Kay kicked off her high heel shoes and wandered into the apartment's galley kitchen. "I don't imagine this place came stocked with any crystal tumblers, did it?"

Riley chuckled. "Yeah, right, good one, babe. I know it's a crime, but I'm afraid we'll have to drink the Pappy Van Winkle from plain old water glasses."

"My brother Doug would be horrified. It's like drinking fine wine from a sippy cup."

"I gather he's a Pappy Van Winkle fan?"

"Totally. He's obsessed with the stuff."

"Maybe we should buy him a bottle to thank him for letting us camp out in his barn all these months."

"That's a great idea," Kay said as she pulled two glasses out of the cupboard. She wrestled the cap off the bottle of bourbon and poured two fingers of the rich brown liquid into each one.

Riley raised her glass and clinked it against Kay's. "Here's to our future."

Kay sipped her bourbon and purred in delight. "Ooh, that's good stuff."

"I feel like I need to pinch myself to make sure this isn't all a dream," Riley said. "All this time, I've been so worried about how we're going to make ends meet with the house and the store and now…"

"We are going to be very wealthy women." Kay let out a laugh.

"What's so funny?"

"I can tell you are doing math in your head."

"Busted. I'm just trying to calculate how much we're actually going to get."

"Well, twenty percent of $50 million is..."

"$10 million," Riley interjected. "And Fred's cut is thirty percent so, let's see, that leaves $7 million, split evenly between the two of us, before taxes."

"Lucky Fred. Although, in all fairness, we would never have gotten this reward if it hadn't been for him." Kay leaned back in her chair and tucked her hands behind her head. "And we're still walking away with a pretty nice chunk of change."

"To put it mildly."

"So, what should we do with it?" Kay asked.

"Well, once we pay for the house and everything in Asheville," Riley smiled up at Kay, "we could open a 529 plan, you know to help put our kids through college one day."

"Our kids, I like the ring of that...although, believe it or not," Kay said with a laugh, "a 529 plan was not the first thing to enter my mind."

"Ha, ha, I'm shocked."

"I was thinking of more exciting things."

"Yeah, like what?" Riley asked.

"Like maybe a new Jeep and I know we had to skimp on a few things when we originally drew up the plans for the house. Now that cash is no longer an issue, maybe we can make a few upgrades. Get nicer appliances, stuff like that."

"I don't see why not. Oh, and I know we've been looking for a space to rent for our store but maybe now we can look at space to buy, a small building or something. That'll give us a lot more flexibility to remodel the space just the way we want."

Kay jumped to her feet. "Oh, my God. I'm so freakin' excited. I have so many ideas. I'm going to make our store the coolest space ever."

Riley took a small sip of her bourbon and smiled at Kay over the top of her glass. "You're so damn cute when you get excited."

Kay reached over and pulled Riley to her feet. She swallowed hard to fight back tears. "You know Rye, we've weathered a lot together. You were so strong through it all. I don't know if I could have gotten through it without you. I mean it. You've been my rock and I cannot wait to start building a new life with you."

A tear slipped down Riley's cheek. "I love you."

Kay wiped away her own tears and snaked her arm around Riley's waist. "I love you too, baby."

Riley pulled back slightly, a serious look on her face. "There is only one problem."

"What?"

"If we start buying stuff and spending more money, it may raise a few eyebrows. People, like my father, are going to seriously wonder how we happened upon a bundle of cash."

"Good point. I hadn't even considered that." Kays replied. "Same will probably go for my father. He's pretty bright. He'll probably put two and two together and realize I'm the whistleblower."

"You think so?"

Kay sat back down. "Yeah. He knows I used to work in pricing, he knows I was fired and I'm sure he's heard lots of rumors from his buddies who still work for Logan."

"This is something you and I should probably talk about."

"Yeah, it is, but not right now. I want to finish my bourbon and take my beautiful girlfriend to bed."

# CHAPTER FIFTY-FOUR

Two weeks later, Kay and Riley were in Asheville having their morning coffee up in Doug's barn when Kay's phone rang. She tossed aside the paper she was reading and reached for her phone. It was Fred Archie.

Kay answered the phone and put him on speaker. "Hi, Fred."

"Hey Kay. Is Riley with you?"

"Yep, she's right here. What's up?"

"I'm calling to give you a heads up. The SEC just put out a press release, the details of which are being reported by most of the major business news outlets. It pertains to the whistleblower award…"

Riley grabbed her laptop off the counter and popped it open.

"Okay, thanks Fred. Riley's bringing up the *Wall Street Journal* website right now." Kay ended the call and peered over Riley's shoulder. The story about the whistleblower award in the Logan case was right on the main page.

*The Securities and Exchange Commission today announced an award of $10 million to a pair of whistleblowers* *who alerted the agency to widespread securities violations at Logan Airlines.*

*As was previously reported by this paper, the regulator recently reached a $50 million settlement with Logan. The airline agreed to pay the penalty without admitting or denying the SEC's findings.*

*The SEC, in keeping with its usual practice, didn't identify the names of the whistleblowers. By law, the SEC protects the confidentiality of whistleblowers and does not disclose information that might directly or indirectly reveal a whistleblower's identity.*

*Fred Archie, a partner at Archie-Row LLP who advises corporate whistleblowers, said he represented the award recipients cited anonymously in the SEC announcement. Mr. Archie confirmed that the whistleblowers provided original information to the SEC that helped the regulator in its investigation of Logan Airlines.*

*"These awards demonstrate that whistleblowers can provide the SEC with significant information that enables us to pursue and remedy serious violations that might otherwise go unnoticed," said Jane Bergdorf, spokesperson for the SEC's Office of the Whistleblower.*

*Whistleblowers may be eligible for an award when they voluntarily provide the SEC with original, timely, and credible information that leads to a successful enforcement action. Whistleblower awards can range from 10 percent to 30 percent of the money collected when the monetary sanctions exceed $1 million.*

*All whistleblower payments are made out of an investor protection fund established by Congress that is financed entirely through monetary sanctions paid to the SEC by securities law violators. No money has been taken or withheld from harmed investors to pay whistleblower awards.*

*An SEC spokesman declined to comment, as did Logan Airlines.*

Kay rested her hands on Riley's hips and kissed the top of her head. "Wow. That's a little surreal isn't it. To see an article in the *WSJ* that's about us."

Riley reached for Kay's hands and pulled them snug around her torso. "Yeah, it's surreal all right."

Kay held her tight and swayed from side to side. "What a wild ride it's been, huh?"

Riley laughed. "You can say that again." She craned her neck to give Kay a kiss on the cheek. "When I fell into bed with you in Tokyo, I had no idea what I was signing up for."

"Any regrets?"

"None. You?"

"Nope. I'm crazy proud of us and I couldn't have asked for a better partner in crime."

"Ditto," Riley said and then added, "I know it's cruel, but I hope to hell Howard Rome sees that article in the *WSJ*. I want him to know we got rewarded for being honest."

"That's not cruel. The guy's a snake and he got exactly what he deserved."

"I wonder what he's been up to since he was asked to *step down*?"

"I don't really care," Kay said. "I just hope we never see the guy again."

"Do you think he'll face any criminal charges for his role in everything?"

Kay reached for her coffee mug. "He might. I remember Fred Archie mumbling something about the Department of Justice going after some of the Logan executives. He said there might also be a civil class action suit brewing."

"A class action suit?"

"Yeah. Remember all Logan's customers paid a price in all this too."

"Ah," Riley said. "Makes sense. The airline's customers faced steeper airfares because Logan was colluding with other airlines to fix prices."

"Yep. Unfortunately for Logan, this debacle is far from over."

Riley closed her laptop and faced Kay. "What about you? Are you still thinking you want to sue Howard Rome and Logan for being wrongfully terminated or something along those lines? That, and for dragging your name through the mud."

Kay thought about Riley's comment for a moment. "I could, and a few months ago I was dead set on it, but now, I don't know." She stretched her arms over her head. "Between you and me, we've got a few million bucks in the bank. I certainly don't need any more. I just want to put this whole thing behind me and focus on the future. *Our future.*"

# EIGHT MONTHS LATER

"This place is absolutely a-maz-ing Rye," Stephanie said.

Riley scanned the horizon. "It is, isn't it? Heaven on earth." It was mid-October and they were sitting out on the deck of her and Kay's newly built house.

"Seriously dude, you and Kay have outdone yourselves. I'm sure you're going to get a call from *Dwell* or *Architecture Digest* any day now."

Riley couldn't contain a smile. "Thanks, I'm pretty damn happy with the way the house turned out. It's like Goldilocks, not too big, not too small. It just feels like home." She waved her hand across the horizon. "And you can't beat these views. Trees as far as the eye can see." It was a sparkling fall day. The leaves were just starting to show kisses of orange, yellow and red.

"You better watch out," Stephanie said with a wink. "I may never leave. The weather here is heaven compared to Atlanta and the sun feels so good on my skin." Stephanie stretched out on the chaise lounge like a cat and closed her eyes.

"Don't get too comfortable," Riley said with a chuckle. "We've got to leave in about ten minutes to drive downtown to pick up Kay."

Stephanie perked up. "Oh, I'm so excited to see your store."

"Wait until you see what Kay's done with the place," Riley said proudly. "It's like she pulled out a magic wand. She transformed the dingy warehouse we bought into an oasis, practically overnight."

Stephanie shifted slightly on her chair and shielded her eyes from the sun. "How's business been so far?"

"Well, we've only been open for a few months, but so far, so good," Riley said. "We already have two full-time employees and we're looking to hire another one soon."

"Wow, that's great, Rye."

"Yeah, like I said, Kay's done a wonderful job with the place. She carefully curated everything we stock, and she's got it all displayed so beautifully—she gets grumpy when even one label isn't perfectly straight, it's adorable."

"What sorts of stuff do you sell?"

"Well, you'll see when we go down there, but we call ourselves a gourmet market. Lots of tasty sauces, dips, olive oils, cheeses, breads, pastas, spices…and chocolate."

"So, how does it work? Kay manages the front of the store and you handle the back of the house?"

"Yeah, pretty much," Riley said. "She's a lot better with the customers than I am, and she's really good at managing our employees. Me, I'm the numbers queen."

"Well there's a real shocker."

"I really love that end of the business. I'm like a pig in shit or whatever that saying is. I track every item we sell. I've created all these spreadsheets to help me monitor what sells quickly and what doesn't, and I analyze the margins on everything. Oh, and we're trying out this new retail analytics software and I'm super excited about that. Why are you laughing?"

"Because you are so passionate when you get going about your spreadsheets."

"Some things never change, huh?"

Stephanie got a serious look on her face. "How are your parents dealing with everything? The move and stuff?"

"Better than I expected. My mom blew a gasket when I first told them we were moving to Asheville. She couldn't believe I was going to leave the city where I'd lived nearly my entire life, but then they came for a visit and I think she understood why I love it here. And it's not like I moved to Timbuktu."

"How about your dad?"

"The tricky part with him was the financial elements of the move. I'd never made a single financial decision, big or small, without first consulting him and he kinda went into a tailspin when I first told him I was quitting my job to open a store. He's not exactly the entrepreneurial type." She laughed. "He's worked for the same law firm for almost forty years."

"But he's come around?"

"Uh-huh. When they were here, he spent an afternoon down at the store with Kay and he was impressed. He hasn't given me an ounce of shit since then."

Stephanie reached over and squeezed Riley's hand. "You seem crazy happy, Rye."

Riley smiled broadly. "I am. Happier than I've ever been in my life. And it's not just the store. It's Kay, it's everything."

"So, I take it things are good with you two?"

Riley nodded. "Better than good. Speaking of which, we've got a little news. I was going to wait to tell you when Kay was here but…"

Stephanie leaned forward in her chair. "Spill it, girl."

Riley felt herself blush. "We're trying to get pregnant."

Stephanie let out a squeal. "Oh my God, that's wonderful! Who's going to carry the baby?"

"Me, assuming it works, of course."

"You know you're beaming right now," Stephanie said, grinning at her friend. "It's wonderful to see. You are going to get that family you always dreamed of after all."

Riley cocked her head and grinned. "Yeah, I guess it all did work out pretty well in the end, didn't it?"